10/11

W9-BBE-218

CROSS MY HEART

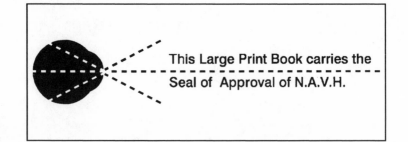

This Large Print Book carries the
Seal of Approval of N.A.V.H.

CROSS MY HEART

CARLY PHILLIPS

WHEELER PUBLISHING

An imprint of Thomson Gale, a part of The Thomson Corporation

Detroit • New York • San Francisco • New Haven, Conn. • Waterville, Maine • London

LIBRARY OF CONGRESS CATALOGING-IN-PUBLICATION DATA

Phillips, Carly.
    Cross my heart / by Carly Phillips.
        p. cm.
    ISBN-13: 978-1-59722-406-2 (alk. paper)
    ISBN-10: 1-59722-406-5 (alk. paper)
    1. Children of the rich — Fiction. 2. Orphans — Fiction. 3. Uncles — Fiction. 4. Abused teenagers — Fiction. 5. Runaway teenagers — Fiction. 6. Absence and presumption of death — Fiction. 7. Trusts and trustees — Fiction. 8. Large type books. I. Title.
    PS3616.H454C76 2007
    813'.6—dc22   2006030542

Published in 2007 by arrangement with Harlequin Books S.A.

Printed in the United States of America on permanent paper
10 9 8 7 6 5 4 3 2 1

To the Plotmonkeys, Janelle, Julie and Les —
you aren't just colleagues, you are my friends, and my sisters.
To Robert Gottlieb, thank you for taking this journey with me
and for believing in me every step of the way.
An extra-special thank-you to my editor, Brenda Chin,
for pushing me to the limit on this one. Don't ever let up!
As always, this book is dedicated to my family.
To my husband, Phil, my daughters, Jackie and Jen,
and my doggies, Buddy and Dylan; and to Mom and Dad.
You make every day worthwhile. I love you all.

ACKNOWLEDGMENTS

Writing this story was a stretch for me, a huge leap of faith in myself and my writing. Thanks to those who helped me along the way: the Plotmonkeys — Janelle Denison, Julie Leto and Leslie Kelly, the best writers and friends a girl could have. Susan Kearney, whose plotting mind works in ways that astound me, thank you for sharing your insight and for putting up with my questions no matter how silly they might have been. Any factual inaccuracies, such as the New York State statute of limitations on declaring a missing person legally dead, are for story line purposes. It is what writers call the willing suspension of disbelief, and thank goodness for it!

PROLOGUE

The sky was jet-black. No stars. No moon. No light to give them away. Tyler Benson led the way to the top of the cliffs with Lilly by his side. Daniel Hunter, their best friend, lagged behind. Lilly held on to Ty's hand, every once in a while giving it a squeeze, showing her fear. Otherwise Ty would think this was just another of their adventures. He knew better.

Soon, he would start the car, slam it into Drive and then jump out before it toppled off the cliff into the murky quarry waters below. Afterward, Lilly Dumont would be reported missing. Her uncle's car would be found at the bottom of the lake. Or it wouldn't be found at all. No body would ever be recovered. Lilly would head for New York, take the new name the three of them had chosen for her and Ty would never see her again.

All so Lilly wouldn't have to leave the

safety of Ty's mother's foster home and return to her bastard uncle for more abuse. She was only seventeen. She wouldn't survive a month let alone a year if she returned to her uncle. The man didn't love her, he loved her trust fund, Ty thought.

"Hurry up, Daniel!" Lilly called back to Hunter, breaking the silence. She was probably afraid he'd lose them in the dark.

"It's Hunter," their friend and foster brother muttered, loud enough for them to hear.

Ty grinned. Once Ty had told him to go by his last name, the kids at school stopped calling him "Danny Boy" and Hunter quit trying to beat the crap out of anyone who got in his face. Hunter and Ty were like real brothers and Ty looked out for his own. Hunter did the same, which was why Hunter stayed back now, so Ty could have these last few minutes alone with Lilly.

The girl they both loved.

Hunter had never said as much, but Ty knew. He wasn't sure Lilly did, though. She was so damn innocent despite her attitude and that was what made Ty care about her so much. They weren't boyfriend and girlfriend but they were *something.*

Too bad they'd never have time to figure out just what that was.

The locket he'd bought her burned a hole in his pocket. He'd got it so she wouldn't forget him. Ever. His stomach cramped and he halted suddenly.

Lilly bumped into him. "What's wrong? Why are you stopping? We aren't there yet."

Ty swallowed hard. "I just wanted to give you something." He whispered, even though he knew nobody was around to hear.

Hunter, who understood what Ty had planned, waited somewhere behind them.

Ty shoved his hand into his pocket and pulled out the small gold heart. A hot flush washed over him as he held out his palm. Good thing it was dark and she couldn't see his burning cheeks.

"Here," he muttered. It wasn't much and that embarrassed him as much as giving the gift.

Lilly accepted the tiny locket. Though it was hard to see, she turned it over in her hand, studying it for so long Ty shifted uncomfortably on his feet while waiting for her reaction.

"It's beautiful," she finally said, a catch in her voice.

He exhaled his relief. "I . . ." Ty wasn't a guy of many words and he didn't know what to say now.

"I know." As always, she stepped in, reading and easing his mind. She clasped the heart in one hand and threw her arms around his neck, holding him tight.

He smelled the sweet scent of shampoo in her hair and he hugged her back, pulling her soft body against his. Too many feelings and sensations rushed through him at the same time.

All the things they'd never do or get to say to each other passed between them in this one final touch.

Ty couldn't think or even speak past the lump in his throat.

Lilly pulled back suddenly and looked down. She messed with the necklace and somehow she managed to hook the heart around her neck despite the lack of light.

"Thank you," she said softly, meeting his gaze.

He nodded stiffly. "You're welcome."

Seconds of silence passed, neither one of them wanting to say the words but someone had to. They couldn't risk getting caught.

"We need to get moving," Hunter said, joining them. "The longer we spend here, the more we risk being seen."

Ty nodded. "He's right. We have to go," he finally said.

"Okay then, let's do this," Lilly said and the three friends started forward.

A few minutes later, they walked through the underbrush and came out near the cliff. A car was waiting for them just like Ty's friend, the one who worked with him at the gas station, had promised. So was the reality of what they were about to do. He was feeling nauseous and struggled against getting sick.

"Is it really Uncle Mark's?" Lilly asked, rubbing her hand over the dark-blue Lincoln.

Ty nodded. "A buddy of mine knows how to hot-wire cars. He owes me a favor for not turning him in to the cops, so this was no biggie." Ty had friends in different groups, different places. Pulling this off had been too easy.

"I can't believe we're doing this," Lilly said.

She stared at him, wide-eyed and afraid. But behind the fear, Ty saw her determination. She was strong and gutsy and he was really proud of her.

"It's not like we have a choice," Hunter reminded her.

"I know." She nodded, her dark hair falling over her face before she tucked it behind her ear. "You guys are the best, helping me like this."

"One for all, all for one," Hunter said.

13

Ty shook his head, trying not to laugh and embarrass his friend. Hunter always said the dumbest things, but Ty didn't mind. Besides, he figured Hunter wasn't thinking any clearer than he or Lilly was at the moment.

"We're the three musketeers," Lilly said, grinning. Just like always, she stepped in to agree with her friend and prevent him from being mortified.

Besides, she was right. So was Hunter. The three of them were alone in this and it would bind them forever. Ty stuffed his hands into his front jeans pockets.

"So tonight Lilly Dumont dies and Lacey Kinkaid is born." Her voice quivered.

He didn't blame her for being afraid. She was leaving Hawken's Cove, their small upstate New York town. She'd take off for New York City alone with just the summer money Ty made working at the gas station and the petty cash Hunter picked up busing tables at the only restaurant in town.

"Nobody talks about what happened here tonight. Not ever," Ty reminded them. They couldn't afford for anyone to discover even a part of their plan and piece things together. "Right?" he asked, wanting to hear them say the words. His heart pounded so

14

hard in his chest, he thought it would explode.

"Right," Hunter agreed.

And Ty knew they'd both protect her secret forever.

"Lilly?" Ty prodded. She had the most to lose if her uncle found out she was alive.

She nodded. "I'll never talk about it." Her gaze remained locked on his, her fingers toying with the little heart around her neck.

For that split second, they were in their own world. He stared into her brown eyes and suddenly everything was okay. They'd go back to his mom's house and he'd sneak into her bedroom so they could hang out and talk all night. They'd be together.

Instead she broke the spell. "I'll never forget what you guys did for me," she said to them both.

She hugged Hunter first and Ty waited, clenching and unclenching his fists.

Then she turned to him and pulled him tight. He held her for the last time, closing his eyes and fighting the fullness in his throat.

"Be careful," he managed to tell her.

She nodded, her hair soft against his cheek. "I'll never forget you, Ty. *Cross my heart,*" she whispered, the words for his ears alone.

ONE

The Hawken's Cove courthouse was a fixture in town, the old stone building the landmark by which everyone gave directions. Make a left at the courthouse and The Tavern Grill was on the right, along with Night Owl's Bar. Make a right at the courthouse and the gas station was on the corner. The ice-cream shop was across from the courthouse.

As a lawyer, Hunter spent his days haunting the courthouse when he was on trial and working in his small office located on the street behind the courthouse when he wasn't. Some might find it odd that Hunter remained in Hawken's Cove after the childhood he'd had, but the good memories outweighed the bad and his closest friend and the only family Hunter knew still lived there.

Hunter never considered moving anywhere else. But to keep his life interesting, he lived in Albany, twenty minutes from work and the closest thing to a real city he was likely to find in upstate New York.

He walked out of the courtroom at 4:00 p.m. and headed straight down the hallowed hallway toward the front doors. He'd won a hard-fought case today. An innocent man who couldn't afford expensive legal counsel had turned to Hunter and he'd done his best. These were the cases Hunter enjoyed. He only represented the rich and obnoxious so that he could afford to take on the pro bono cases he preferred.

After working endless hours for months on end, all he wanted to do was have a stiff drink and not have to use his brain for at least twenty-four hours. But as he passed the clerk's office, his gaze settled on a pair of long legs and vibrant pink high heels. Only one woman wore shoes that bright and in-your-face.

"Molly Gifford," Hunter said, coming to a halt beside his old law school nemesis. They'd vied for top spot at Albany Law. It still galled him to admit she'd won.

After graduation, they'd parted ways, with Molly leaving for a job in another state. But recently she'd moved to town and for the last month, he'd had the pleasure of checking out those incredible legs on a near daily basis. But her move here had been a surprise because Molly wasn't born or raised in Hawken's Cove. When he'd asked, she'd said something about reconnecting with her mother and not much more.

Molly shifted her focus from the court clerk she'd been speaking to and settled her brown eyes on him. "Hunter," she said, a welcoming smile on her lips. "I hear congratulations are in order."

Hunter wasn't surprised she'd already heard, but still, he was pleased. Hell, if she hadn't congratulated him he'd have told her himself. He wasn't much for modesty, not when it came to looking good in front of a woman.

"Word travels fast around here."

"A win's always a cause for gossip. I hope you're going to celebrate," she said.

The one thing he'd always admired about Molly had been her willingness to acknowledge another person's success. "I could be persuaded." Meeting her gaze, he leaned against the filing counter. "Join me for a drink?"

"Can't." She shook her head. Her blond hair fell in soft waves around her pretty face and the old familiar attraction kicked into gear inside him.

He wasn't shocked at her answer. He'd

ask, she'd decline. Even back in law school they played this old game. He knew his reasons for not pushing her harder. Molly was a *nice* girl and it had been a lot easier for Hunter to avoid anything serious with the not-so-nice ones. The ones who didn't expect much more than sex and fun.

Still, he couldn't resist the pull that caused him to keep asking Molly out anyway and now that fate had thrown them together again, he'd hoped she'd give him — give them — a chance. Because he'd finally figured out that he'd grown up enough to want to take one with her.

"What's your excuse this time? You have to give your dog a bath?" he asked her.

She grinned. "Nothing nearly as exciting. My mother's fiancé has a legal issue he wants me to explore. Which reminds me." She glanced at her watch. "I'm going to be late meeting him if I don't hurry. Maybe another time?" she asked and rushed to the door, leaving a whiff of intoxicating perfume in her wake.

He groaned, knowing he'd be tossing and turning tonight and not just because of her sensual scent. *Maybe another time?* were words Molly had never used with him before. In the past, no had always been a definite no until he'd asked the next time. His heart pounded harder at the possibility she'd opened up to him.

He turned to the court clerk who sat behind her desk eagerly listening in on the exchange. "So, is Molly's mother marrying someone local?" he asked, knowing Anna Marie was the woman with all the answers.

Anna Marie Costanza had been the clerk for longer than anyone who practiced law could remember. She came from a family who held important posts in town. One of her brothers was the mayor, another the town supervisor, yet a third a partner at the prestigious Albany law firm of Dunne and Dunne. They were connected and could provide assistance and answers to most questions anybody needed answered.

As for Anna Marie, she provided the main source of courthouse gossip but she also ran a tight ship. She and her brothers also owned one of the oldest boardinghouses in town. Anna Marie lived there herself, acting as the superintendent in charge of all things, and lucky for Hunter, Molly rented one of the units. Between the older woman's day job and her occupation as landlord, he'd bet she knew every last detail that was available about each local resident. Especially Molly.

"Yes sirree. Her mother's marrying a longtime resident of our fair town." Anna Marie leaned forward. "Aren't you curious as to who the lucky guy is?" she asked, obviously eager to impart the information.

"I was getting there," Hunter said, laughing.

"Her fiancé's Marc Dumont. I found out when Molly's mother filed for a marriage license." Anna Marie met Hunter's gaze and nodded slowly, giving him time to absorb the implications of her news.

As he did, Hunter's smile faded. Memories of a time when he was young and not as cocky as he liked to appear now kicked in hard and fast. He clenched his hands into tight fists, the old anger he worked hard to control, rising to the surface. He fought it down.

It wasn't Anna Marie's fault she remembered his connection to Dumont. There wasn't anyone who'd lived in their hometown who didn't know the story of how Lilly had disappeared, presumably running her car off a cliff and into the quarry below. Her body had never been recovered.

There also wasn't anyone who didn't know that Marc Dumont blamed her best friends, Hunter and Ty, for his niece's "death." He'd tried, without success, to

21

make the stolen car charges stick. But he *had* convinced the state to split the friends apart, taking Hunter away from Flo Benson's foster home.

Hunter had spent the year prior to turning eighteen in a state-run juvenile facility for troubled teens. His anger and resentment resurfaced and his attitude had gotten him into enough fights that he'd nearly ended up in jail. Instead he'd been forced to attend a Scared Straight program in a real lockup and the reality had turned him around fast, just as the program intended. He'd done so by using Lilly as motivation.

He'd hear her voice telling him that she wanted better for him than jail. But he still blamed Dumont for his stint in juvie just as he credited Lilly, Ty and Flo's influence for his turnaround.

Hearing Dumont's name still set Hunter's nerves on edge. "What's the old bastard after now, that he needs Molly's help?" he asked Anna Marie.

She pursed her lips. "Tsk, tsk. You know I can't be passing along privileged information."

Hunter laughed at the mock offense in the older woman's voice. He and Anna Marie shared a love of information any way they had to get it. "Have any court papers been officially filed by Mr. Dumont?" he asked.

Anna Marie grinned. "Well, no."

"Then what's privileged about a little courtroom gossip?" Hunter had a sudden, urgent need to know more about what Dumont would need a lawyer for at this point in his life, why he would involve Molly and who the bastard was using now.

"Good point. You are as fast thinking on your feet as they say. Are you sure you're too young for me?" she asked, playfully nudging him in the arm.

"I think you're too young for me. I'm afraid your energy would wear me out," he said, laughing. Though he didn't know her exact age, he'd bet she was in her midsixties and though she didn't keep up with the trends, she was spry in spirit.

She smacked the counter and chuckled.

"Come on, now spill what you know." He could see from the light in her eyes, she was dying to share her secrets.

"Well since you asked so nicely . . . I heard Molly talking on the phone earlier. Marc Dumont's getting ready to claim his niece's trust fund as his own."

"What?" Hunter asked, certain he'd heard wrong.

"Since it's been nearly ten years, he plans to go to court and have her declared legally dead. You know, seeing as how no body was ever found after her car went into Dead Man's Drift," Anna Marie said, mentioning the unofficial name the townspeople had given to the cliff and water below after Lillian Dumont's *death.*

Nausea washed over him at the thought. Not a day went by when Hunter didn't think of Lilly, that fateful night and his role in her disappearance. He'd always missed her, her laughter, her friendship. It helped that Hunter hadn't heard Dumont's name in years. The man was a subject Hunter tried to avoid and until today, it'd been easy. Dumont had remained under Hunter's radar for years, secluded in Lilly's old home and not causing any trouble. Now in the span of five minutes, Hunter discovered the man was going to marry Molly's mother and attempt to legally bury his niece so he get could his hands on the millions still held in trust for her.

His timing couldn't be worse. Just when Molly seemed to be softening toward the idea of dating Hunter, Dumont once again became an obstacle.

The bastard hadn't changed. He'd merely been in hiding, waiting for a time when the three friends believed their pasts were behind them, to resurface. The man had changed their lives once before. Hunter had a hunch none of them would survive this confrontation unscathed, either.

Tyler Benson wasn't a morning person. He'd rather work the late shift at Night Owl's than clock in on a nine-to-five day job. It helped that Ty rented the apartment above the bar from his friend Rufus, who also owned the establishment and appreciated Ty helping him out now and then. When he wasn't tending bar as a favor to his friend, Ty ran a P.I. business out of his apartment, as well as the bar and a small office across from the courthouse. The locals found Ty wherever he happened to be and he appreciated the flexibility and spontaneity of his life. Most of all he liked knowing he earned his own way at no one else's expense.

He made a decent enough living that he could pick and choose the cases he wanted to work, passing the easier ones on to Derek, a guy who'd gotten his P.I. license but was new to town and needed Ty's name to bolster his business reputation. Ty figured he was better off having Derek as an employee than competition in the small town, so the situation worked for them both. In fact, the business was growing fast and they needed to hire an administrative assistant and another P.I.

Ty poured a Bud from the tap and handed it to the guy who'd been keeping a running tab. He glanced at his watch. Only 7:00 p.m. but with October baseball in full swing — Yankees versus Red Sox — this place would be hopping within half an hour. Right now though, time was dragging by and he stifled a yawn behind his hand.

"In about five minutes you're going to wish life was as boring as you're obviously finding it now." Hunter, Ty's oldest friend, slid onto a stool across from him.

Ty grinned. "Somehow I doubt hearing about your day in court is going to get my juices flowing." He laughed and reached for the ingredients of a refined martini his friend had come to prefer over the beer of days past.

The other man shook his head. "Jack Daniel's. Neat."

Ty raised an eyebrow in surprise. "Something big must be going on if you're giving up your polished drink for harder liquor. And here I was just about to say congratulations on winning your case but if you were celebrating, you wouldn't be ordering whiskey."

Hunter's expression was clouded. Obviously, he was miles away, his thoughts definitely not on his big win today.

Ty figured he'd know what was bothering his friend soon enough. When Hunter had a problem to deal with, he usually mulled it over for too long before spilling his guts.

"Do you remember when I came to live with you and your mom as a foster kid?" Hunter asked.

The subject took Ty by surprise. "Yeah, I remember. But that was a long time ago and a lot has changed. You looked different then for one thing. Hell, you *were* different."

At sixteen, Daniel Hunter had come into the Benson home with a chip on his shoulder and an unwillingness to let anyone in. He'd already decided nobody in the world would care about him anyway. He'd been wrong on both counts. Hunter had spent almost a year with Tyler and his mother, becoming like family to them both.

Hunter nodded. "I've tried to be different. Better somehow."

Ty glanced at his friend, understanding his reasons. He'd fought hard to become an upstanding lawyer and member of the community and he'd succeeded. Tonight he wore dark jeans that looked pressed and new, along with a rugby shirt. Hunter's choice in clothing was a symbol of the man he'd become.

"You may dress the stuffed preppy part but you're still a street kid at heart," Ty teased. Which was why they'd remained tight over the years. "So what's going on that's forcing you to remember the past now?"

"Things. And it's not just that I need to remember, but I need you to go back in time, too."

"I remember Mom taking you in," Ty said.

"We were so different I thought you'd kill me in my sleep," Hunter said, his wry laughter interrupting Ty's thoughts.

"You're lucky I didn't." Ty grinned, the memory of Hunter's first night in the Benson home still vivid.

"The kid in the home I was in before yours kicked my ass after his mother left me in his room. You just tossed me a pillow and warned me not to snore," Hunter reminded him.

"You did it anyway." Ty laughed.

Outwardly they couldn't have been more different — Ty with his longer straggly dark hair and his mother's olive skin, Hunter with his sandy hair and paler skin. But the two had bonded. They were similar enough for an unlikely alliance to form because like Hunter, Ty didn't trust easily, either.

28

How could he when his father had set the pattern in a youth filled with broken promises? *I'll be at your game. I'll pick you up from practice.* If gambling and offtrack betting didn't distract him first, Ty thought bitterly. His father was consistently unreliable. Ironically, knowing he couldn't count on his old man hadn't prepared Ty for the ultimate kick in the ass.

He'd just turned nine the week before when his father had promised he'd pick him up from basketball practice. Ty hadn't been shocked when he'd been left standing out in the parking lot in the dead of winter. It wasn't the first time. So he'd huddled against a lamppost, knowing his old man would show up eventually full of apologies and excuses. When he didn't, Ty had finally dragged himself to the nearest business and called his mother who'd come immediately to pick him up. Together they'd discovered his father had taken off for good.

For the first time in his life, Joe Benson had left a note. He'd also left Ty cold, wary of trust and promises. Until Hunter had come into his home and then a short time later, Lilly.

Before he allowed himself to take *that* path, he turned to his friend. "So what's got you traveling down memory lane tonight?" Ty asked, pouring the whiskey into a glass and sliding it over to his friend.

Hunter smiled grimly. "You should pour yourself one, too."

Ty raised an eyebrow. "Why?"

Hunter leaned closer and spoke low and deep. "It's about Lilly."

Just hearing her name caused overwhelming emotions to rush through Ty and his head pounded hard. Neither he nor Hunter had heard from Lilly again after the night she left for good.

"What's going on?" he asked Hunter, needing answers.

Hunter drew a long breath before speaking. "Dumont's planning to have Lilly declared legally dead and claim her trust fund as his own."

Ty didn't wait for the words to penetrate before reacting, slamming his fist onto the top of the bar. "Son of a bitch."

All the old anger and resentment that Ty had spent years nurturing, then burying, welled up inside him once more. Dumont may have brought Lilly into Ty's life but he'd also been the reason Ty had lost her for good. He'd never forgive the man for that or for the abuse he'd heaped onto Lilly in the years before they'd met.

As the reality of Hunter's news set in, the past returned, surrounding Ty as if it were happening today. The blood pounded in his head, his feelings raw. First Hunter had come into Ty's home, somehow breaching the walls he'd erected since his father had walked out. Then Lilly had arrived and it was as if the small hole he'd made for Hunter had weakened his barriers and they'd come tumbling down. He'd paid for that over many long lonely years but he couldn't regret meeting or caring about Lilly.

For a short time he'd learned to open his heart. Ty had gone from a loner to a guy surrounded by his best friend and his best girl — at least that's how he'd thought of her at the time, although they'd never had the chance to really act on the feelings simmering below the surface. Maybe they'd been smart enough, even at their young age, to put the friendship first. Maybe time just hadn't been on their side. Ty would never know. Because too soon a letter came, indicating her abusive uncle's intent to have her returned to his custody, and the three friends had put their plan into motion.

"Hard to believe, Dumont has the balls after all these years, huh?" Hunter asked.

Ty glanced heavenward. "I wish we'd

looked ahead and seen this one coming."

Hunter rolled his eyes. "This from the man who insisted we never speak of the night again?"

"Shut up," Ty muttered, hating when his own words came back to haunt him.

But his friend had a point. Like a fool, Ty had thought if he never spoke about Lilly again, he'd be able to get her out of his system. Believed he'd be able to forget her.

Cross my heart. Her softly spoken words returned to him now. The last time he'd seen her, she'd promised she'd never forget him. As hard as he tried, he hadn't been able to block her out of his memory, either. No matter how painful he found it to think of what might have been, he'd thought of Lilly often. He still did.

From the minute he'd watched her plop his baseball cap on her head and walk off, Ty had wanted nothing more than to go with her. For days he'd struggled with the idea of taking off after her. But he'd stayed home because his mother needed him. Ty knew Flo couldn't handle her son running off so soon after Lilly had disappeared and she deserved better than two heartbreaks so close together. Three if he counted Hunter being taken away from them as well. But Ty had missed Lilly every damn day since.

Years later, he'd given in to temptation. Ty had made some cop contacts in New York and with their help, he'd done some surface digging for Lacey Kinkaid, the name they'd chosen. From there, it had been surprisingly simple to discover that she was alive and well.

Ty hadn't taken it any further. He hadn't contacted her. She'd obviously moved forward with her life and he couldn't see disturbing those ghosts. Ty himself had insisted on a clean break. And though he'd made that initial choice, she'd followed his instructions. She hadn't contacted him, not after she'd turned twenty-one and had nothing to fear from her uncle. And not years later when she was an independent woman capable of making her own decisions.

On the nights when he second-guessed his decision, he told himself that his feelings for her had been nothing more than infatuation or puppy love, as the parents of the runaway teens that he tracked now often labeled their children's hormonal emotions. He'd done some pretty fine convincing, too. She couldn't be as pretty as he remembered. Her skin couldn't be as soft. Her scent wouldn't still wind its way into his heart. All those things must have been an illusion built on the things Lilly represented. The wealthy heiress whose guardian had turned her out of her home, denied her her fortune, and left her fragile and in need of someone strong to take care of her.

Ty had willingly stepped in and filled the role, but deep down, he knew that Lilly was tougher than he gave her credit for and didn't need him as much as he'd wanted to be needed. She'd run away to the city and thrived there, proving she wasn't the fragile princess he'd put up on a pedestal. And thank God she wasn't, or else she wouldn't have survived, while he'd been living pretty well off of money his mother never should have taken.

"I knew this wasn't going to be easy on any of us," Hunter said. "But you're looking green. Are you okay?"

Ty cleared his throat. "I'm fine. How'd you find out about Dumont?" Ty asked.

"Indirectly through Molly Gifford."

"The chick you knew in law school?"

Hunter nodded. "I ran into her at the courthouse today."

"Has she agreed to date you yet?" Ty laughed, certain his friend had at least given it another try.

"No, but I'm making progress. Unfortunately the timing of her turnaround sucks.

Her mother's going to marry Dumont, which leaves her as my only link to information on the man." He shifted in his seat, obviously uncomfortable in the role he'd have to take on.

"No shit? Molly's mother is going to marry the bastard?"

Hunter's reply was to finish his drink in one gulp.

"Then you *are* going to have to turn up the charm."

"And she's going to see right through me," Hunter said and winked. But despite his cocky grin, he was obviously not pleased at the connection.

Ty poured his friend another shot. "But you'll do it to help Lilly?"

Hunter inclined his head. "Do I have a choice? We're tied together, the three of us. I helped her then and I'll help her now."

Because he cared about Lilly, too. In all the years of their friendship, they'd never spoken about Hunter's unrequited feelings or the competition between the men that never had time to develop. Another reason Lilly's return would be uncomfortable for all involved.

"So we're in agreement?" Ty asked. "Dumont has no right to the money." Ty bent his head from side to side, trying to work the stiff muscles in his neck but the tension remained. His life was about to change drastically.

"We're in agreement. But you were right. We should have thought about the future," Hunter said. "About her trust fund and what would happen years down the road. But we didn't. And now Lilly is going to have to deal with that part of her life."

Affecting all their lives in the process, Ty thought.

"Lilly needs to be told." Hunter spoke with quiet certainty.

"Lacey. She's Lacey now," Ty said, already forcing himself to begin the mental shift necessary to meet with the woman Lilly had become.

"Lacey needs to be told that Dumont plans to have her declared legally dead and live large on her parents' money."

Ty's head began to pound. Hunter's words reminded Ty that his mother had done exactly that.

Hunter eyed Ty warily. "That's not what I meant and you know it."

Ty shrugged. "Maybe not but it's true. We thought Lacey was just another foster kid, but she wasn't. My mother took money from Dumont to take Lilly in. Unofficially, off the books, off the record. He paid her to take his niece until he felt she'd learned her lesson and would come home easier to control."

"Your mother didn't know Dumont's reasons at the time. She thought she was helping out a man who didn't know how to handle his out-of-control niece and she was getting money to give you a better life in the process. He offered her an opportunity and she took it."

Ty nodded. He still dealt with what his mother had done. Still lived with a measure of guilt over the lifestyle they'd had, using money that had rightfully belonged to Lilly.

"You paid your dues, not that you owed any. Dropping out of college was self-punishment if you ask me. Who did you benefit?" Hunter asked.

"My own pride. I could look myself in the mirror each morning." It wasn't the first time they'd had this conversation but it was the first time Ty had explained because he sensed Hunter already understood.

Hunter nodded. "Fate's providing the chance for you to give Lilly back what she lost. Go find her and tell her to come back and claim her fortune."

Ty ran his hand through his too-long hair. He needed a cut, he thought, wishing he could focus on something so trivial.

"She has a lot of bad memories here." Ty took his friend's advice, pouring himself a stiff drink of his own. He gulped a sip of fiery liquid and savored the burn on the way down.

"She's an adult. There's nothing here that can hurt her anymore except old ghosts," Hunter said.

"Something we all need to deal with." Ty swirled the liquid in his glass.

"Think she'll be easy to find?"

"You know me when I'm determined." Ty forced a cocky grin and raised his glass.

The kicker was that he'd had no trouble at all locating her that first time. Lilly had been living as Lacey Kinkaid, but she used her real social security number and she legally filed taxes. If her uncle had tried to search again years later, after Lilly had become a successful businesswoman, he might have found her after all. He'd just had no reason not to believe she'd perished in the deep, dark waters that fateful night. Thank goodness for Lacey their plan had been a success.

Although Ty had found an address for her five years ago, who knew how many times she'd moved since then. Still, he wasn't too worried. He had his connections and his ways.

Hunter lifted his glass in return. "Good luck."

"Something tells me I'll need it," Ty said, tipping his glass to meet Hunter's.

The clinking noise that usually signaled a celebration sounded like a warning instead.

TWO

Lacey Kinkaid glanced at her newest employee, a young Spanish girl who spoke broken English and had no experience at doing odd jobs around New York City or anywhere else for that matter. But she needed the job badly and Lacey knew exactly what the desperation she saw in Serena's eyes felt like, prompting Lacey to hire her anyway. When she'd first met Serena, Lacey had also let the young girl sleep on her sofa, just as Marina, the woman who'd helped Lacey out way back when, had done.

She shook her head, pushing the past away as she always did when memories threatened to surface. The present was all that mattered and in the present, her job defined her. When Lacey wasn't doing some of the different jobs her clients required, she was smoothing over crises between employees and clients of her small company, aptly titled Odd Jobs.

"What exactly is the problem?" Lacey asked Amanda Goodwin, a client who used Lacey's services weekly and had been a valuable source of referrals.

"She," Amanda said, pointing her manicured fingernails toward Serena, "doesn't understand English. Her cleaning skills are wonderful, but her English isn't. I needed to explain something so I spoke to her in Spanish. She burst into tears and called you."

Lacey nodded. Serena tended to cry easily, which could cause problems on the job. "What exactly did you say to her? In Spanish, if you don't mind." Lacey kept a comforting hand on Serena's shoulder as she spoke.

Lacey had become close to fluent in Spanish during her early days in New York City. She'd discovered her high school Spanish had come in handy and allowed her to pick up the language easily, which helped, since she'd needed a job and the only person who'd hired her was a woman named Marina who ran a cleaning service comprised mostly of immigrant girls. What she didn't know, Marina taught her, tutoring Lacey at night so she could not only speak Spanish, but she could get her GED high school diploma.

41

After arriving in New York, Lilly had taken the name of Lacey Kinkaid and used it religiously out of fear of being found out by her uncle. Later, when she'd become an adult and wanted to form a business, she knew she needed to do things legally. Although she went by the name of Lacey Kinkaid, her legal documents still read Lilly Dumont. Few people questioned, less cared, and at this point, her uncle wouldn't think to look for her.

She glanced at her client, silently asking her to explain what was wrong.

"I wanted to tell her not to feed the dog." The other woman pointed to the Pomeranian, a dust-mop of a dog lying at her owner's feet. "So I said, *por favor no comas al perro*." Amanda folded her arms across her chest, obviously pleased with her ability to communicate with the hired help.

Lacey burst into laughter at the same time Serena began to wail in a torrent of rapid Spanish that even Lacey couldn't understand. She did happen to catch a few choice words which clearly indicated how upset and offended Serena was.

"You see? What's wrong? Why is she so upset?" Amanda asked.

Lacey pinched the bridge of her nose

before meeting Amanda's stare. "Because you said, please don't *eat* the dog instead of please don't *feed* the dog, which in Spanish is, *por favor, no les des comida al perro* — which actually translates to please do not give food to the dog," Lacey said, her Spanish grammar lessons coming back to her. "Serena's insulted because you'd think she'd do such a thing." Lacey swallowed another chuckle.

Amanda, meanwhile, who truly did have a decent disposition and treated hired help nicely, flushed in mortification. "I asked my daughter for help. She takes Spanish in school," the other woman explained.

At least Amanda was too embarrassed by her mistake to complain about Serena's overreaction, something Lacey would have to deal with later on. For now, Lacey repeated the mix-up to Serena in Spanish before turning back to her client.

"Don't feel bad. There's actually no real verb for *feed,* which probably resulted in things getting twisted around."

"I'm sorry you came all the way over here," Amanda said.

"I'm not. I wish all my crises could be resolved so easily." After making certain both Serena and Amanda were fine with her leaving, Lacey headed for home.

Her dog, Digger, met her at the door, her stubby tail wagging like crazy. Lacey liked nothing better than coming home to find her pet jumping up and down with excitement.

"Hey you," Lacey said, patting the dog's head.

With the pooch at her heels, Lacey tossed her purse onto the bed and hit the Play button on her answering machine. The only message was from Alex Duncan, an investment banker she'd met and recently become close to thanks to an introduction by a client. He treated her well, took her to Broadway shows and upscale restaurants, and bought her expensive things that reminded her more of her upbringing prior to her parents' deaths than her life since. He brought forth a longing for things she missed, like security and caring, luxury and stability.

He wanted to take care of her in the old-fashioned sense by providing her with a home and a family. Lacey had craved those things ever since she'd lost her parents. Her mom, Rhona, had been home every afternoon when Lacey returned from school and her dad, Eric, had tucked her into bed each night. Losing them had been traumatic, and had upended her entire world. In her innocence she'd turned to her uncle Marc and he'd betrayed her.

Other than Ty and Hunter, she hadn't allowed anyone to get close to her in years. But she desired intimacy with another human being. She needed affection and wanted someone to come home to each night. Alex was a good man. The best, really, yet he hadn't breached her barriers. And she hadn't accepted his marriage proposal. . . .

Not yet. Something she couldn't define was missing and no matter how much she cared about him, no matter how hard she tried, she couldn't quite say she'd fallen *in* love with him. They'd even been intimate for a while now but still, a deeper connection was missing.

But Alex understood she had a rocky past — though he didn't know all the details — and he was willing to give her time to come around because he loved her. And because he was convinced that love could grow over time. Lacey wanted to believe, so she hadn't given up on a future with him.

With a groan, she pressed the delete key on the answering machine and quickly stripped for a long, hot shower. She'd spent the afternoon food shopping for a busy working mother, then she'd walked an array of dogs down Fifth Avenue, before heading out to solve the crisis between Serena and Amanda. Lacey had been looking forward to some downtime all day. Time that didn't include worrying about her business or dissecting her feelings for Alex.

Half an hour later, she was wrapped in a terry robe and scrambling eggs, enjoying the low hum of music and cooking in her own kitchen, when the doorbell rang. Digger immediately began her obsessive barking and ran for the door.

Lacey sighed. She could only hope Alex hadn't decided to pay her a visit to talk things over. Shutting off the burner on the stove, she moved the frying pan away from the heat.

Then she stepped up to her door and glanced through the peephole. Alex had blond hair and wore suits or buttoned shirts. The guy outside her door had long dark hair, an old jean jacket slung over his shoulder and looked eerily familiar.

She blinked and focused on the man once more, recognition dawning. *Oh. My. God.* Ty.

With shaking hands, she opened her apartment door. "Ty?" she stupidly asked.

She'd know him anywhere. She saw him not only in her memories, but in her dreams.

He nodded but before he could reply, Digger began sniffing at Ty's feet and nudged his leg with her nose, begging for attention.

"Digger, off!" Lacey chided but the dog didn't listen.

Lacey had always thought she could judge a man by his reaction to a dog, so she grinned when Ty bent down and petted Digger's head. Ty obviously hadn't changed. He still had a soft spot for those in need, like she had been, Lacey thought. Which brought her back to the niggling question that lingered long after she'd left Hawken's Cove. Had Ty felt those same crazy feelings of desire and young love she'd felt for *him* or was she just another stray, like Hunter, that he'd taken under his wing and protected so well.

She glanced at Ty and realized in one quick instant that he still had the ability to affect her deep inside. Her emotions soared, from elation over seeing him again to a fuzzy warmth in her heart to a quickening in her belly that she hadn't experienced in years.

Enjoying the attention from a stranger, Digger lifted her front paws onto his legs, begging for more.

"Okay, you shameless hussy. Leave Ty alone," Lacey said, pulling the dog off of Ty.

"He's a she?" Ty asked, obviously surprised.

Lacey nodded. "She doesn't have a body any female would want, but she's a sweetheart."

"She doesn't have a name any woman would want, either," he said, laughing.

His voice had grown deeper, she thought, the husky sound providing a rush in her veins.

"I found her digging in the trash, hence her name. The poor thing was starving. I took her in, fed her and tried to locate her owners. No luck." She shrugged and scratched under Digger's chin. "She's been eating me out of house and home ever since." Digger was Lacey's in all her bad breath glory. She freed the dog's collar. "Go!" she directed and the dog finally ran into the apartment.

Lacey edged back so Ty could enter and he stepped by her, treating her to a whiff of warm, sexy cologne. Her body tightened at the unfamiliar, yet welcoming scent.

Once inside, she let the door slam shut and Ty turned to face her. He studied her without shame, his gaze swallowing her whole, his curiosity evident. She pulled the

48

collar on her fluffy robe together but nothing could change the fact that beneath it, she was nude.

Unable to resist, Lacey looked him over, as well. He'd been a sexy kid when she'd seen him last. He'd matured in the last ten years. His shoulders were broader, his face leaner and a somberness lingered in his hazel eyes that ran deeper than she remembered. He was all male and drop-dead gorgeous, Lacey thought.

And when he resettled his gaze on her face, she couldn't mistake the slight smile that tilted his lips. "You're looking good," he said at last.

Her face heated at the compliment. "You're looking pretty good yourself." She bit down on the inside of her cheek and wondered why he'd shown up now.

What exactly did fate, and even more, sexy Ty, have in store for her?

Lacey excused herself before disappearing through a doorway leading to what he assumed was her bedroom. She'd instructed him to make himself comfortable, something he'd have an easier time doing if she changed out of that bathrobe. Though the fluffy material covered her well, the deep vee left him wondering exactly what lay beneath the material while the short hem had revealed long, toned legs.

And that showed exactly where his thoughts had been since she'd opened her door revealing a womanly version of the Lilly he'd known. The same and yet different, more beautiful, more secure in herself, more for him to handle, Ty thought.

He'd been in lust with her when he was young, intrigued by the girl with the big brown eyes and daring nature. Only after she was gone did he realize he'd loved Lilly. First love, puppy love, no matter what he called it, losing her had been painful. They'd been denied the opportunity to explore what might have been and nothing and nobody since had even come close to making him feel as alive as Lilly had. She still did, if the spark inside him was any indication.

But the past was behind them and opening his mind or his heart to her now could only lead to heartache. She had a life here that didn't include him. She could have returned and opted not to. They'd each moved on.

Ty didn't need her to break his heart all over again when he'd established an easy way of life. He settled for sex, not love, with women who wanted simple relationships and who wouldn't complain when he grew bored, which he usually did. Lately he'd been hooking up with Gloria Rubin, a waitress at a bar he frequented when he didn't go to Night Owl's. She was divorced and liked it that way, but didn't want to take any man home with her while her son was under the same roof. He had an empty apartment, which meant their relationship was convenient if not special. But it worked.

Ty shoved his hands into his pockets and glanced around Lilly's living room in an attempt to get a feel for how she lived and who she'd become. He'd walked up three flights of dark stairs to reach her door but at least the neighborhood seemed safe enough and she had the ugly mutt for some sort of protection. The apartment itself wasn't small, it was tiny. Yet despite the size, she'd put enough warm touches around to make it feel like home, not a small cell. Simple floral posters were framed and lined the walls, while live plants filled the room. Colored pillows brightened up the sofa and a matching area rug lay beneath the table.

Noticeably absent were photographs of family and friends and for the first time, he realized she'd left more than just Ty and Hunter behind. She'd abandoned a life and tangible memories. She'd turned her back on money and material things. She couldn't have lived easily or well. All the more reason for her to return and stop her uncle from claiming what was rightfully hers.

"Sorry to keep you waiting." Her voice distracted him and he turned toward the light sound.

She rejoined him, this time wearing jeans and a plain pink T-shirt, both fitted, both showing feminine curves he couldn't help but admire. Her brown hair fell to her shoulders in damp waves, framing her porcelain skin, and her chocolate-brown eyes were still as deep and perceptive as he remembered.

"No problem," he assured her. "It's not like you knew I was coming."

She extended her hand toward the couch. "Why don't we sit and you can tell me what's going on. Because I know you didn't just happen to be in the neighborhood."

He sat beside her and leaned forward on his elbows. Despite the fact that he'd had time to rehearse his speech on the three-hour ride here, the words weren't easy ones. "I wish I had just been in the neighborhood because I hate what I have to tell you now."

"Which is?" she asked, remaining calm and composed.

"Your uncle is getting married," Ty said.

She shivered at his words, her revulsion at hearing about the man clear in her expressive face.

Unable to help himself, Ty reached out and covered her knee with his hand. He'd meant to comfort her but this first touch was electric and her leg flinched beneath his palm, telling him she was affected by his touch.

As for Ty, his body tingled and desire settled low in his belly. Damn, he thought. The old feelings were as real as ever, stronger even because he was older, wiser and he understood that his physical reaction was the tip of the iceberg. Below the surface, his feelings for her still ran deep and he had to remind himself she was just passing through his life. She'd passed through once before, as had other people he'd cared for and lost.

After his father had taken off, Ty shut down until Hunter and Lilly arrived. He'd opened up to them only to have Lilly desert him in the end. Though she'd had no choice in going, she had had the option to return after she'd turned twenty-one and became of legal age. Even if she came to Hawken's Cove with him now, it would only be to reclaim her money, not her old life.

Knowing that, Ty wouldn't be putting himself out there for her in a way that would guarantee heartache and pain again. He slowly removed his hand.

"What does the fact that my uncle is getting married have to do with me?" Lilly finally asked, meeting his gaze with a hooded one of her own.

"His marriage is an aside, actually. He's also decided to have you declared legally dead in order to get his hands on your trust fund."

Her eyes opened wide and the color drained from her cheeks, leaving her pale. With a groan, she closed her eyes and leaned her head back against the wall. "The man is such a prick," she said.

"That about sums it up." Ty chuckled at her apt description.

Watching her reaction to the news, he didn't know how he'd finish explaining the other reason he'd come. But then he reminded himself that although she appeared fragile and in need of protection, she had a deep internal strength that had served her all these years.

Ty cleared his throat and dove in. "You know this means you're going to have to come home."

Her eyes snapped open, her gaze one of horror. "No. No way."

He'd expected her initial resistance, at

least until she had time to think things through. "So you're going to just hand over your trust fund without a fight?"

She shrugged. "I've done fine without it."

He rose from his seat and began to walk around her small but cheery apartment. "I'm not going to argue the point. But it isn't his money to take. Your parents left it to you and you're still alive and well. It's one thing to leave the money untouched, another to let that bastard get his hands on it."

She inhaled deeply, her indecision and pain evident. "How's your mom?"

He eyed her warily. "We'll have to get back to the subject eventually."

"I know but give me a chance to chew on it for a little while. So how is your mother?"

He nodded, accepting Lilly's need for time. "Mom's fine. She has a heart condition now but with medication and diet she's the same old Mom." Ty tried not to let his tone change when discussing his mother but the first thing that came to his mind was the cash deal Flo Benson had made with Marc Dumont.

As a kid, Ty had been blind to the truth even when his mother had started to buy them nicer things. He'd remained in the dark when she'd surprised him with a car on his twentieth birthday, claiming she'd used her savings. He'd gone to college with much less in student loans than he'd thought he'd need, and once again his mother said she'd been saving. He realized now he hadn't wanted to see bad in his only parent, so he'd ignored the signs that something was wrong.

"How'd Flo take my — uh — disappearance?" Lilly asked. "It was hard for me, thinking about how much she must have suffered, believing I died while in her care." Lilly's eyes grew soft and damp at the memory.

Ty understood. He'd felt the same way. "Mom felt guilty," he admitted. "She blamed herself. She wished she'd kept a better eye on you."

"I'm sorry for that. I loved her, you know." A smile curved her lips. "And Hunter? How is he?"

A much easier subject, Ty thought. "He's fine. He's turned into a stuffed shirt. He's a suit-wearing lawyer, believe it or not."

"So he can argue and stand up for himself legally now. Good for him." She grinned, obviously pleased and proud of the news. "And you? Did you go to college the way we talked about?" she asked hopefully.

Ty and Hunter had shared a room while

Lilly had a bed in an alcove off the kitchen which Flo had turned into a comfortable nook Lilly called her own. Ty recalled sneaking into her bed one night and they talked until morning — about his mother's desire to see her son in college and his plan to fulfill that dream. Back in those days he'd been so focused on making his mother proud and repaying her for all she'd given him, he hadn't let his own dreams see the light of day.

He still wasn't sure what those dreams were since his plans were so tied up in his mother's. Lilly's hopes for him were based in the fantasy they'd woven as kids. Ty's life now was based in a different reality.

"I went to college," he said. "And then I dropped out."

Her pretty mouth opened wide.

"Now I'm a bartender."

She furrowed her brows, her curiosity and disbelief evident. "And what else are you?" she asked.

"A bartender's a good, solid job. What makes you think I'm also something else?"

She leaned in close. "Because you never could sit still and just tending bar would be too boring for you," she said, obviously certain she still knew him that well.

She did. "I'm a private investigator, too.

Now are you coming home or not?"

She exhaled, transforming in front of his eyes from secure female to exhausted woman. "I need time to think about it. And before you push me harder, you should know that maybe is as much of an answer as I can give you right now."

"I hear you," he said, his tone laden with understanding. He figured she'd need time and since Hawken's Cove was three hours away, he knew her indecision would mean a night or two in New York.

He rose and started for the door.

"Ty?" she asked, rushing after him, dog at her heels.

"Yeah?" He paused and turned too fast. She skidded to a halt, bumping into him, her hands coming to rest on his shoulders.

All the questions he'd lived with for ten years were suddenly answered. Her scent wasn't as sweet as he remembered, it was more sensual and warm, more enticing and inviting. Her skin glowed and her cheeks flushed as their gazes met and lingered.

She licked her lips, leaving a tempting moistness behind.

Understanding and yearning mixed together in one confusing yet arousing package.

"Where are you going?" she asked.

58

He'd looked into a local hotel but thanks to conventions and who knows what else, all the affordable places were booked. He'd packed his bag anyway and decided expensive or not, he'd have to take a hotel room because asking Lacey if he could bunk on her couch seemed like a damn stupid idea.

"To my car. I need to find a hotel."

"You could . . . umm . . . stay here," she offered, her hand sweeping in a grand gesture toward the couch.

He knew better than to say yes. But he couldn't deny the desire to spend what little time they'd have together getting reacquainted.

"I'd appreciate that." He glanced at the couch, hoping the damn piece of furniture was comfortable. Because having made his decision, he sure as hell wasn't.

"Good. I'd like to spend more time catching up," she said, her voice deeper and more throaty than before.

Or maybe it was his imagination overloading his senses. It didn't matter. Ty was in deep trouble, and probably something a whole lot more.

Lacey couldn't sleep. Ty was stretched out on her couch and her traitor dog, who usually slept beside Lacey, had chosen to bunk with her guest in the other room. The worst part was she couldn't blame the pooch for wanting to snuggle up against Ty's warm, hard body. She had the urge to do the same thing herself.

She'd missed him badly, especially in the early days, and seeing him again had opened the floodgates of feelings she'd kept walled off and in check. Her emotions were in complete turmoil. And Ty wasn't the only reason.

Memories of her family overwhelmed her, as well. Losing her parents had left a hole in her heart that had never been filled. Certainly her awful uncle hadn't helped ease the pain. Like Cinderella, who'd lost her father and been left with an evil step-mother, Lacey had been abandoned and betrayed at an age when she didn't know how to handle it. She hadn't even had grandparents to turn to, she recalled sadly.

Her parents had had Lilly later in life and all her grandparents had already passed away. Although her father had two brothers, Marc and Robert, her parents weren't close with either one. Only Marc, her single uncle, lived nearby. Robert had married and moved to California years ago, so it made sense that her parents left her with Marc. And at least she'd had a recollection of seeing her uncle Marc on the occasional holiday. There was no family on her mother's side because her mother had been an only child.

Ironically, the money Ty wanted Lacey to claim had been handed down on her mother's side for generations. Lacey was the sole heir. There might even be stipulations in the event of her death about the money going to her father's family. She didn't know. Because her parents had rarely discussed the inheritance. Instead her father always focused on his day job, the auto body shop he owned that specialized in restoring classic cars.

After her parents' car accident in hurricanelike weather, Uncle Marc had come to live in her family home and he'd taken over her father's business. And he'd loved the concept of the estate, the grounds, and playing lord of the manor. Lord of Lilly, she remembered bitterly.

From the beginning, he'd tried to make her obligated to him in any way he could. At first he'd been the kindly uncle and she'd fallen for his act. How could she not when at sixteen, she desperately needed someone to count on? But she'd noticed his drinking right away and she'd learned to stay far away the drunker he became. One afternoon she'd come home early from school and heard him on the phone discussing how he needed Lilly to sign her rights to the trust over to him while she was young or else he'd lose his chance to manipulate her in any way. By the time she turned twenty-one, he needed her to trust him enough that she'd sign anything he asked without question. Including the rights to invade the principal on her trust fund.

Even at sixteen, she'd understood the concept of betrayal and this was a big one. Anger and hatred had welled up inside her, and she'd decided then to make his life as difficult as possible. She'd become a rebellious teen. He'd responded by cracking down and becoming increasingly abusive in the hopes that she'd back down out of fear. When her behavior didn't change, he'd carried out a threat she never believed he'd implement.

He'd had her placed in foster care — temporarily he'd said — just long enough to scare her. He'd wanted her to be so grateful to come home that she'd not only toe the line, she'd be easy to control, trust fund and all. Thanks to Ty and Hunter, he'd never gotten the chance.

Back then Lilly hadn't been concerned with the legalities or with the money since she knew it wasn't hers until she turned twenty-one, as her uncle constantly reminded her. By then she'd had the beginnings of a life and enough inbred fear of her uncle to remain far away. She assumed the money had remained untouched and had been content to let it stay that way.

She swiped at the tears that had begun running down her face. Remembering her parents and all she'd lost was never easy, but recalling the time afterward caused her stomach to churn and the old anger and resentment to flare up. She'd gone from her parents' princess to her uncle's piece of property, something he could kick out of her own home on a whim.

That thought cemented her decision. Lacey didn't *need* the money her parents had left her. After all, she'd lived without the extras for so long, she rarely thought about them now. But there was no way she wanted her bastard uncle to profit from her parents' deaths. He'd run her father's business into the ground shortly after taking over, and he'd claimed ownership of her childhood home. She wasn't about to let him have anything more.

Lacey wasn't vindictive by nature. She had a life here that she was proud of, one she'd worked hard to build and maintain, which had prompted her initial reluctance to return home with Ty. But the thought of her uncle enjoying anything more at her expense churned her stomach nearly as much as thinking about her uncle and her past.

Ty was right. She'd have to go home.

THREE

Lacey climbed out of bed and slipped on her favorite pair of slippers, a fuzzy pair that were soft enough to feel like an old friend. She headed to the kitchen for a midnight snack, tiptoeing on the way, careful not to wake Ty. Careful not to stop and watch him sleep and risk rousing warm feelings for a man she no longer knew, but one she wanted to know again.

She poured a glass of milk, pulled the Oreos out of the refrigerator and settled into the corner she jokingly called her kitchen-ette. In reality it was a small table at the end of the entry hall.

"Mind if I join you?" Ty asked, just as she dunked her first cookie into the cold milk.

Without waiting for a reply, he sat in the only other chair that fit around the table, Digger curling at his feet. Ty was shirtless, wearing only his partially zipped jeans, unsnapped at the waist. A low light glowed from the kitchen, casting them in shadows, but even in the darkness surrounding them, she could see enough to admire how broad his chest had become, how drop-dead sexy he was.

She ran her tongue over her suddenly dry lips. "I hope I didn't wake you."

He shook his head. "I couldn't sleep."

"Me neither. Obviously." She gestured to her midnight snack.

"So you resorted to your old standby, cookies and milk?"

She slowly lowered the Oreo onto the table. "You remember that?" He'd often caught her snacking in his mother's kitchen late at night. That's how comfortable she'd been in his childhood home, she thought.

"I remember lots of things about you," he said in a husky voice.

"Such as?" she asked, her curiosity not the only thing that he aroused.

"Such as the fact that Oreo cookies are your comfort food. You like them cold and hard from the fridge even though you're just going to dip them into milk and make them soggy. And you keep the cookie in the milk for about five seconds so it doesn't get too soft. Like this." While speaking, he reached out, snagged a fresh cookie, dipped it into the cold milk, then held it out for her to taste.

She opened her mouth and bit down, the cookie partially crumbling, partially melting in her mouth exactly the way she liked it. Her lips brushed over his fingertip, the accidental touch causing an unexpected rush of physical sensation to sweep over her.

She laughed, keeping things light, and wiped her mouth with a napkin, but what she felt was anything but funny. Her breasts grew heavy and a pulse-pounding awareness thudded through her veins along with a heaviness between her thighs. She managed to suppress what surely would have been an orgasmic-sounding groan. Because somehow her comfort food had turned erotic and sharing memories with an old friend had become something much more sensual.

From the reciprocal yet clouded look in his eyes, she doubted that had been his intent. He was holding himself back from her now and she missed the closeness they'd shared when they were kids and they didn't think things through all that much.

There had been something special between them, something they'd never acted on, either because they'd been afraid to sever a friendship that represented the only stability in their young lives, or because neither quite knew what to do with what they were feeling. Maybe even back then, they'd subconsciously realized that sex alone wouldn't be enough.

Although Lacey had to admit, at the moment, sex sounded awfully appealing. Still, they'd never had the chance to scratch the surface of that first love, leaving them emotionally wanting more. Leaving *her* wanting more. She never really knew how Ty had felt, whether he'd really liked her or whether he just enjoyed being her hero.

At least now they were adults, capable of making grown-up choices and dealing with the consequences, she thought. Consequences that for Lacey included Ty showing up when she had an unanswered marriage proposal from another man.

"Tell me about the time after you 'disappeared'." Ty spoke, his voice a welcome distraction from both her thoughts and her desires.

Apparently he didn't intend to take things any further and she found herself feeling both disappointed and relieved at the same time. "Look around you. I've done okay." More than okay, as her business proved.

But as she spoke, she realized this was the

second time tonight she'd defended her small apartment and her life. For no good reason. Ty hadn't belittled who and what she'd become. She wasn't used to feeling defensive — usually, she was more than proud of all she'd accomplished.

Ty's presence reminded her of the good and the bad things in her past and forced her to face how *different* her life had turned out than what she'd envisioned as a child. It wasn't what her parents would have wanted, but given the reasons and the things she'd been through, Lacey felt sure they'd be proud, too. Which was just another reason Odd Jobs meant so much to her. It was something tangible she could point to that proved Lilly Dumont had survived.

Ty nodded. "You've done more than okay, but what I see now doesn't tell me how you got here."

She drew a deep breath. The past was something she preferred to keep there, but as her onetime coconspirator, Ty had a right to some answers. And just maybe, talking about it would help her release some of the pain she still held inside.

She glanced down at her intertwined hands, remembering the dark night with too much ease. "I walked for about half an hour and right outside of town, I met up with your friend. The one who'd stolen Uncle Marc's car. We drove to a place far enough away where no one would recognize me. Then I took a bus to New York City."

"Just like we planned."

"Right." But no one had planned beyond that. "I crashed on the bus and when we arrived, it was the next day. I had the small stash of money you and Hunter had given to me. I slept in a YWCA one night, a bus terminal another."

He winced.

She ignored it and kept talking. "I washed dishes and I got by. Eventually I met someone who cleaned apartments. She worked for a Spanish woman who hired immigrant girls. By that time, my hands were rough enough from detergent and water, so somehow I convinced her I could handle the work. That pretty much saved my life because I'd run out of free or cheap places to sleep and it was getting harder and harder to duck the johns and pimps in the bus and train stations."

"God, Lilly, I had no idea."

The raw distress in his voice touched a place deep inside her. She didn't want him holding himself responsible for something he hadn't caused. He'd saved her life and she'd never forget.

He reached out and grabbed her hand. Ten years too late and yet it was exactly what she needed now.

"None of us did." She curled her fingers around his, the warmth and strength giving her the motivation to continue. "But things got better after that. The woman who hired me — her name was Marina — let me sleep on the floor in her apartment until I found a dirt-cheap rental."

"How bad was it?"

She hadn't wanted to upset him but he'd asked. "The place came with company. There were cockroaches on the walls." She tried not to gag on the vivid memory. "And a drunk lived next door. He liked to wander the halls in the dead of night. The locks on the apartment door didn't work and the superintendent ignored my requests to fix it. I couldn't afford to pay for a locksmith myself so I'd drag a dresser in front of the door at night for security."

"God," he said again. He ran a hand over his face.

She didn't know what to say, so she remained quiet.

Finally he asked, "And what's your life like now?"

A much easier topic, she thought, and

smiled. "I run a business called Odd Jobs that caters to the working man or woman," she said with pride in her voice. "I have about fifteen employees depending on the day and their moods. We walk dogs, clean apartments, food shop, whatever the busy person needs us to do. Over time I've accumulated a loyal clientele and I've been able to increase prices. Things are going pretty well."

He grinned. "You've made an amazing climb."

The way she'd seen it, she had no choice but to keep going.

"I admire you, you know."

His words took her by surprise, but warmed her at the same time. Still, she wasn't looking for his pity or admiration.

"I only did what I had to do to survive. What about you?" she asked Ty.

She wanted to know why he had dropped out of college when that had been his goal for so long. And what explained the difference in his tone when he'd spoken of his mother? The shift had been subtle, but she'd noticed it just the same. She wondered what had caused it.

"Ty? What happened to you and Hunter after I left?" she asked, curious to fill in those years.

"That's a story for another day." He glanced down and his eyes suddenly widened, as he realized he still clasped her hand in his.

She wished he'd pull her up and into a long, lingering kiss. The kind she used to dream about when she slept in his house, his room a few feet away. And later, the kind that kept her warm at night when she thought she'd go crazy from fear and loneliness.

Tonight wasn't the first time she'd seen longing and desire in the depths of his eyes and it wasn't the first time she'd allowed herself to let the present disappear. Just like before, when they were together, little else mattered.

"It's late and we should get some sleep." He rose from his seat, lifting his hand away from hers.

Disappointment clogged her throat even as she appreciated his hold on common sense. Obviously she had none. "You still like to call the shots, I see."

He shrugged without apologizing for his controlling nature. "You have some big decisions to make and I'm sure sleep will help," he said, his voice softening.

"I've already decided." She nodded firmly, knowing she had no choice.

He raised an eyebrow. "You're coming home?"

Swallowing hard, she nodded. "But I just can't pick up and leave without settling some things here first."

"The business?"

"Primarily. I need to get someone to run things until I get back." Mentally, she'd already begun to make a list of people to call and things to do. "I also have neighbors that will worry. Friends and —" Alex, she thought, knowing he'd panic if she suddenly disappeared.

She knew she'd hate it if he just took off on her. They were beyond the dating stage. Way beyond. He wasn't the first man she'd been intimate with but he was the only one she truly cared for. Yes, she realized something was missing and being with Ty, she knew the sizzling sexual attraction was just one part of their problem. Or at least a part of *her* problem, Lacey thought. Alex obviously had no such issues.

He also had no idea Lacey had a past that could someday come calling, disturbing her life and rousing compelling emotions she didn't feel when she was with him, she thought, guiltily glancing at Ty.

"And what?" Ty asked, picking up on what she hadn't said.

She shook her head. "Nothing. There are just people who'd miss me and be concerned."

He let out a slow, patient groan. "I'm not dragging you out of here kicking and screaming. Take the time you need to get your things here in order. Then if you forget anyone, you can always call from the road." He paused, his eyes narrowing. "Unless there's someone important that you haven't mentioned?"

"Such as?" She hedged, knowing the coming conversation was going to be difficult.

He massaged his forehead with his fingers. "Boyfriend or someone you need to check in with?" His words sounded brittle as he spoke.

She drew a deep breath. "As a matter of fact, there is someone." Guilt immediately swamped her.

"I see," he said stiffly.

She'd been living on her own for ten years and had no reason to feel as if she'd betrayed Ty by seeing someone else. Yet looking into Ty's eyes, she did feel guilty. Terribly guilty.

"His name is Alex," she said, forcing herself to admit the truth and hopefully keep the other man real to her in the process. "And I can't just pick up and leave without getting in touch with him."

Ty inclined his head, the motion curt. "Well, nobody's stopping you from checking in with the important people in your life."

She swallowed hard, the sense that she'd somehow hurt him filling her with intense pain. "Fine. We'll talk more tomorrow, okay?"

Without answering, he strode past her and headed back to the couch. He lay down and Digger jumped on top of his legs, settling in.

"Hussy," Lacey muttered to her pet as she walked back to her room and closed the door behind her.

She wasn't comfortable with how she'd left things with Ty but then she wasn't comfortable with the state of her life these days. It was a tough thing to admit, seeing as how she prided herself on survival and doing well. But she hated feeling unsettled and her inability to commit to Alex was but one symptom.

A few short hours with Ty and already she sensed the difference in her reactions to both men. She shivered, knowing in her heart that difference meant something important. And knowing, too, that her time in Hawken's Cove would define exactly what.

Ten years ago, Lacey had left a life behind and hopped a bus for New York City with no idea what to expect there. Tomorrow she was about to go back to where it all began except this time, she knew exactly what awaited her. She tossed and turned for the rest of the night.

The only thing that kept her from changing her mind was her parents. If she didn't go back, nothing would be left of her family and their legacy. Nothing good, anyway. She owed it to them to take control of what was rightfully hers. She owed it to herself to finally put the past behind her by facing it, not running away.

Even if that past included Ty.

Ty awoke with Lilly's ugly mutt stretched out on top of him and the sun streaming in through the open window blinds in Lilly's apartment. He hadn't slept well but who could blame him? Between his smelly couch mate and Lilly's revelation that there was someone special in her life, sleep had eluded him.

It wasn't like he'd expected her to become a nun. Hell he hadn't been celibate, either. Nor had he come back to Lilly looking for a relationship of any kind. Yet when he thought of her with another guy, every protective instinct he possessed kicked into high gear. Those same instincts never took over when it came to other women, not even Gloria who he'd been sleeping with for the past few months. Yet those damn instincts were alive and well with Lilly, full-blown and making him crazy. Despite the fact that he had no right to feel anything at all.

He'd helped set her on the path to this new life, but she'd opted to stay in it. To not come home for the past ten years. To stay out of touch, secluded and alone. The best thing for everyone involved was to bring her home, let her handle her personal affairs and then allow her to return to New York City. To her boyfriend, her business, her life. Maybe in settling Lilly's past, he'd find a way to settle his own and move on. Because if seeing her again proved anything, it was that he needed to put her behind him, this time for good.

He glanced toward her still closed bedroom door. Since he was up first, he showered and changed before letting himself think about his growling stomach.

He glanced down at the mutt who'd followed him loyally around Lilly's apartment, going so far as to push open the bathroom door that wouldn't lock and lick his damp legs when he'd stepped out of the shower. "I wish I could feed you, but I don't know where your food is."

"She needs to go out first," Lilly said, stepping out of her bedroom fully dressed.

Ty cocked his head to one side. "I thought you were sleeping."

"I've been up since five. I showered and dressed before you dragged your lazy body out of bed at six-thirty."

So she'd heard him puttering around out here. "Have you eaten?" he asked.

She shook her head. "You?"

"Not yet."

"How about you come with me to walk Digger and we'll pick up something to eat while we're out?" she suggested.

"Sounds like a plan."

She hooked Digger on a leash, grabbed a plastic bag from a kitchen drawer, and together they walked down the flights of stairs, onto the front stoop and out to the sidewalk. The sun was just rising over the tall buildings and a chill hovered in the air.

Digger didn't seem to mind. She took off at a run, tempered by Lilly's hold on the leash, pausing only when she'd reached a small patch of dirt and a lone tree.

Ty shook his head and laughed.

"What can I say? She's a creature of habit," Lilly said. "And this is her favorite spot."

Once the dog had finished and Ty had taken the bag from Lilly to clean up and throw away, they took a more leisurely walk around the city. Everything was familiar to Lilly and she was familiar to most people they met. The kid at the Starbucks counter knew her by name as did the owner of the newsstand on the corner. Along the way, she pointed out some buildings where she worked and stopped to pet some dogs she knew from walking them during the week.

Ty had the distinct sense she wanted him to see her life, where and how she lived, firsthand. Now that he had, he knew for certain how well she'd done for herself and how content she was here in her city life.

He paused on the sidewalk. "So what made you decide to go back? What ultimately swayed you?" he asked.

She halted in her tracks beside him. "It's not a simple one thing." She bit the bottom of her lip. "As many reasons as I have not to go with you, I have at least as many reasons *to* go back."

"Any chance you'll share some of them?"

He tipped his head to one side, shielding his eyes from the sun with his hands. He wanted to get inside her head and understand what made her tick.

"You made most of the arguments yourself. I owe it to my parents not to let my uncle steal from them. I owe it to myself to stand up for what's mine. Most of all, I guess I think facing him will give me closure."

He nodded. "You never really put that part of your life to rest, have you?"

She shook her head. "I can't forget that I turned a lot of people's lives upside-down."

Some of those people, like his mother, had helped set things in motion, Ty thought. It was such a complicated issue because by taking Lilly in, his mother had ultimately saved her life. It'd also given them blood money, he thought.

He glanced Lilly's way. Her brows were furrowed in concern, her distress over the upset she'd caused obvious. He needed to reassure her that she'd done the right thing.

"Hey, those people cared about you. They did what they wanted to do. Nobody forced them and you have to admit, it was pretty amazing that we pulled it off." He grinned, the adventurous thrill of that time coming back to him.

She burst out laughing. "Leave it to you to turn it into an exciting caper."

He smiled grimly because up until the moment she'd walked out of his life, that's exactly what it had been.

Lacey nervously fingered the locket she'd hidden beneath her shirt. She'd worn the small piece of jewelry around her neck, only taking it off when she showered for fear of it slipping down the drain and being lost to her forever. She hadn't been wearing it last night because she'd just taken a long bath, but she'd placed the locket back around her neck this morning. She couldn't explain her reasons beyond sentimentality, but the one thing Lacey knew, she always felt better once she was wearing it.

Today in particular. As she'd begun to make arrangements to leave town, it was as if the small piece of jewelry gave her the courage to resurrect Lilly.

She needed that courage more than she'd have thought. Lacey had never left the city before. She'd never left Odd Jobs in someone else's hands unless she was too sick to work, something that was rare. Her days were defined by Odd Jobs and each client's needs and schedule. She was about to go on the second biggest adventure of her life.

One she wouldn't take without first making certain her business was in good hands until she returned. She chose Laura, one of her longtime employees, to be in charge. She provided the other woman with an updated list of clients, the schedule and some tips for dealing with their employees and their various personalities. She made the same list about each of her clients.

Then she'd taken care of the little things a vacation entailed, like asking her neighbor to take in her newspapers and check her mail, while letting her few friends know not to worry if they didn't hear from her for a brief time.

She'd packed for herself and Ty had thrown a bag of dog food into his car for Digger. All typical things people did before taking a short trip, except nothing about Lacey's situation could remotely be construed as *normal.*

Dreading the final phone call she'd have to make, she waited until the last minute to call and give Alex the news. While Ty watched television in the other room, Lacey dialed Alex's apartment, a phone number she knew by heart.

"Duncan," he said, answering the phone on the first ring.

"It's me." She gripped her fingers tight around the receiver.

"Hey, babe. How are you? I didn't expect

to hear from you until tonight," he said, pleasure warming his voice.

She didn't usually call him during the day because he was busy and she was rarely in one place for too long.

"I'm fine." Lacey drew a deep breath that failed to calm her nerves. "Actually, that's not true. I had a visitor last night. Someone from my hometown and I need to go back for a little while and settle some things. I know it's last minute but I'm sure you understand."

"I can't say that I do because I don't know a damn thing about your past, but hopefully you'll fill me in on the details when you get back. Because keeping secrets isn't good for a relationship and there's too much I don't know." He cleared his throat. "And I can't help you get past whatever's keeping you from saying yes if you don't open up."

She swallowed hard. "I know. And I'll tell you everything," she promised. What better time to share her history than once she'd faced it down?

"Good." He sounded relieved. "This visitor you mentioned. Is it anyone I know about?" he asked, obviously fishing for something before she left.

They both knew there wasn't anybody she'd ever mentioned by name. "No. I never told you about — him." She shut her eyes, hoping he wouldn't ask for more of an explanation.

She'd never told Alex about Ty because her feelings for him were too close to her heart. Too personal to share with anyone, especially another man.

"A *him* you've never mentioned." Alex's voice dropped lower, taking on an angry tone she'd never heard before. "Is he anyone I need to worry about?" he bit out.

"No." Lilly shook her suddenly pounding head. "Nobody you need to concern yourself with. He's just an old friend." She knew in her heart that last statement was a bald-faced lie.

She was worried about Ty and her renewed feelings. But how could she say that to Alex over the phone and then take off on him?

Lacey glanced up and saw Ty waiting in the doorway. Nausea swept through her as she realized what he'd overheard. In one day, her life had become overwhelmingly complicated.

He held up a hand and she covered the phone.

"The car's illegally parked out front," he reminded her.

She nodded. "I'll be off in a sec."

Ty turned and walked out, leaving her with his dark, hurt expression in her mind.

"Lacey?" Alex called for her attention, his irritation clear.

"Yes. I'm here."

"When you come home, we'll go to Nick's," he said of his favorite Italian restaurant. "And then maybe we'll check out Peaches," he said of his sister's dessert place in the Village.

"That sounds . . . nice." A bland word, she thought but it described how she was feeling — in direct contrast to the anticipation she felt about climbing into Ty's car and heading on an adventure with him by her side.

Oh God.

"Alex?"

"What, babe?"

She didn't want to leave him with the wrong impression and yet she didn't know what the right one would be. "When I get home, we'll talk. About a lot of things."

It was the best she could offer. For now.

FOUR

While Ty loaded her last-minute things into the trunk, Lacey sat Digger in the back seat for the car ride to Hawken's Cove. Knowing her pooch, the dog would pace the long seat nervously but after a while, she'd settle in and lie down for the rest of the trip. After sitting in the passenger seat and buckling herself in, Lacey steeled herself, not knowing what Ty's mood was now.

They hadn't spoken on the walk down from her apartment and her stomach churned with nervous jitters. Behind them, Digger paced the backseat, just as Lacey had thought.

Ty started the engine, then buckled his seat belt. "Are you sure you have everything?" he asked.

She nodded.

"So you're ready?"

"As I'll ever be," she said, her voice quivering.

He reached out and placed his hand on her thigh, surprising her with his touch. She'd thought he'd keep his distance.

"You can do this," he said in an obvious attempt to reassure her.

His palm was big and warm and his heat seeped through the denim of her jeans, branding her skin with his touch. His effect on her was immediate and electric. She swallowed hard, unable to deny the fiery sensations shooting straight between her thighs. She crossed her legs, which only served to increase the fullness which had settled there.

Needing an escape, she closed her eyes and he took the hint, removing his hand and shifting the car into gear.

Next thing Lacey knew, she woke up and glanced at the clock. Two hours had passed since they'd left the city. She'd shut her eyes in an attempt to escape her feelings and she'd fallen fast asleep.

She looked out the window at the lush green landscape rushing by. No more big buildings, no more hustle and bustle.

She shifted in her seat uncomfortably. "I need to make a pit stop next time there's a place," she said to Ty.

Ty lowered the radio which had been playing Top 40 and glanced her way. "She speaks."

Heat rose to her cheeks. "I can't believe I slept and you had no company the whole ride up here."

"Don't worry. I let Digger here climb in front and she kept me company." He winked and turned his gaze back to the road.

He'd obviously put her earlier phone conversation behind them and she was glad.

They had some time until the next rest stop, so she bent her knees beneath her and shifted toward him. "So tell me a little more about your life after I left," she said.

One hand on the wheel, he glanced over. He remained silent for so long she was afraid he wouldn't answer.

Finally, he said, "Your uncle went on a rampage."

She winced, pulling her knees tighter against her chest.

"He couldn't find you, which meant he couldn't get his hands on your money — not that he said as much. He just ranted and raved to Mom about how she'd obviously been neglecting the children in her care if his niece had been able to run away and get herself killed."

Lacey let out a sigh. "Then what?" She was almost afraid to ask.

Ty's knuckles turned white against the wheel. "He pulled some strings and had Hunter taken out of our house." Ty flipped on the blinker. "There's a rest stop coming up in half a mile. I'll pull over so you can go."

"Thanks. Digger will need it, too."

Silence followed and she knew Ty was avoiding finishing his story. "What happened next?" She needed to know.

"Hunter was sent to a state-run group home."

Lacey's eyes filled with tears and guilt clogged her throat. She'd been so caught up in her own survival, she hadn't thought about her uncle's reaction to her disappearance. Even later, when she had, she'd never considered that there was anything he could do to the people she'd loved and left behind.

And she had loved Hunter, as a best friend and as a brother. He'd been so vulnerable back then, though he tried to hide it. And he'd emulated Ty, needing that guidance to keep him from acting on his emotions and not common sense.

"How bad was it?" she whispered.

Ty shrugged. "You know how Hunter was. Without one of us there to temper him, he ended up in one fight after another. It took a mentor program with inmates at the local correctional facility to set him straight."

Lacey shivered. Reality was far worse than she'd ever imagined. "I could kill my uncle," she spat.

"Just showing up alive might do the trick." And to her surprise, Ty laughed.

She appreciated his attempt to lighten the mood, but couldn't bring herself to feel anything but anger and contempt for her uncle, sadness and pain for her friend.

Yet she recalled Ty telling her Hunter was a lawyer now, which lightened her spirits. "How did Hunter get from delinquent to attorney?"

Ty met her gaze. "With a lot of damn hard work. He set his sights on a goal and worked hard to get there." Pride tinged Ty's voice.

Lacey understood, admiration for Hunter filling her, as well. "Tell me more."

"There were some things Dumont couldn't control. Hell, maybe there were things he forgot to care about over time because Hunter lucked out. He had no juvenile record other than misbehavior and he was able to get his paperwork sealed when he turned eighteen. He put himself through college and then law school. He owes more in student loans than he makes in a year, but he's a damn good lawyer."

"Thank God he pulled himself together."

Lacey realized she was rocking back and forth and stopped the movement. "What about you? What was your story after I left?" she asked Ty.

"Since we've been sitting outside of this gas station for a good five minutes, I think you'll want to run inside." Ty pointed to the full service rest area. "I'll walk the dog."

She hadn't even realized they'd come to a stop. She lowered her legs and grabbed her purse. "I'll be right back. But don't think you can avoid the subject again," she warned him.

"My story is nothing as dramatic as Hunter's. Or yours." His gaze drifted away from hers.

Lacey shook her head in disbelief as she finally understood what bothered him about himself. "You feel guilty about it, don't you?" she asked. "Because you didn't suffer the same way, you feel guilty. That's why you avoided discussing it last night and you almost threw me out of the car without answering me now."

Ty ran a hand through his hair. "You've been gone ten years. You have no right to think you still can read my mind," he said, his words suddenly turning harsh and biting. "Especially since I'm not someone who was even worth mentioning to your *friend* Alex."

His tone hurt but she obviously *had* read his mind and he hated knowing she could still see inside him. She'd bet he felt she'd belittled him by never having discussed him with the man she was involved with.

She reached out and touched his hand briefly, enough to grab his attention before pulling back. "Some things, some people are too important to mention aloud."

Instead, they were to be held close to the heart and treasured, she thought, feeling a lump rise to her throat.

"You saved my life, Ty." Without second-guessing herself, she reached into her shirt and pulled out the locket he'd given her. "And when I crossed my heart, I meant it."

His gaze settled on the small gold piece he'd bought with his own money, his eyes opening wide in surprise. "That was a long time ago," he said gruffly.

She'd embarrassed him with the reminder. But she'd also eased the slap he'd felt over her conversation with Alex and that was all that mattered.

"This got me through some really tough times." She delicately fingered the treasured piece around her neck. "You got me through."

That long-ago night, she'd sworn she'd never forget him. And she realized now that no matter where she went or who she was with, she'd always had him with her — his strength, his courage and his caring.

She reached out and touched his cheek, forcing him to meet her gaze. "I never forgot you. Cross my heart," she whispered, before she turned and ran for the safety of the rest stop.

Ty and Lacey met up with Hunter at Ty's place as soon as they hit town. They entered through the back entrance off the bar. There were no awkward hellos when Hunter saw Lacey for the first time, Ty thought, watching stiffly as she bolted across the room and into Hunter's arms.

"It's so good to see you!" Her voice rose in an excited squeal.

Hunter pulled her into a tight hug. "You, too." He pulled back, looking at her with a grin. "You're still as gorgeous as ever."

She laughed and punched him lightly in the shoulder. "You're looking pretty good yourself."

"He works at it," Ty muttered.

He hadn't received such an easy greeting

and rationally he understood why. She hadn't expected to see him, so she'd been caught off guard. Once she adjusted to his presence, he'd dropped one huge bomb about her uncle.

Ty knew he was consoling himself with platitudes and tempering his jealousy, neither of which sat well with him. He was normally a guy who went about his business with few highs and lows. Man, things had changed.

Ty cleared his throat. "Hey you two, break it up. We have some planning to do."

Lacey turned toward them. "That sounds like old times. So how do you want to handle things?"

Ty stepped toward her. "I suppose the first order of business would be looking into the terms of the trust and finding out exactly what you need to do in order to claim the money." Ty glanced at Hunter. "Am I right, lawyer man?"

The other man nodded. "You're right. And I'll look into that as soon as possible. I'm going to need some help because I'm a criminal attorney."

"That's amazing," Lilly said, her eyes glowing with pride in what Hunter had accomplished.

Ty felt the same way.

"What kind of cases?" she asked.

"A little of this and a lot of that," he said and laughed.

"Don't be so modest," Ty said. "Hunter's well known around town. He's one of the biggest trial lawyers in the state. His clients are pretty high profile even for upstate New York standards."

Hunter actually flushed at the complimentary description. "I take those cases to make money so I can afford the pro bono ones for people who couldn't otherwise afford decent representation."

Lilly wrapped her hands around her forearms and nodded in understanding. "And I am so proud of you! I should have known you'd end up helping people."

His cheekbones flushed even redder. "Ty's the one who played savior while I went along for the ride. I guess I learned from him."

"Well as far as I'm concerned, you're both the best." She grinned at them both. "Thanks for looking into things for me," she said to Hunter. "I can't afford to hire anyone without depleting my savings."

"Which won't make a difference once you get the trust fund away from the bastard who calls himself your uncle," Ty said.

She nodded. "Still, having a friend to

depend on is so much easier."

"I've got an important trial next month, but I have some time now and I'll handle it for you." Hunter hoisted himself onto the kitchen counter, making himself at home, which considering how often he came by, he was. "So what will you do while I'm researching?" he asked Lilly.

Ty raised an eyebrow and glanced at her. "I'm curious about that myself."

She shrugged. "I thought I'd reacquaint myself with my hometown. I need to relax and maybe feel like I belong here again."

"I understand how you feel." And he sympathized. "But you can't just go walking around in broad daylight and risk alerting your uncle to your reappearance. You need to be discreet, at least until your uncle's been told that you're alive, well and intend to be rich."

"Man, I wish I could see his face when he finds out he's waited ten years for nothing." Hunter rubbed his hands together, his anticipation of the other man's downfall as understandable as it was shared by everyone in this room.

Lilly laughed but Ty heard the shakiness in her voice. For all her strength, she wasn't quite ready for the reunion. A few days of breathing room would do her some good.

"So how do you think we should let him in on the secret? I can't just walk up the front steps, ring the doorbell and say, *Hi, Uncle Marc, I'm home!*"

Ty grinned. "Maybe not, but I'd pay good money for tickets to that show."

"We'll have to go about this in a more subtle manner," Hunter said.

"And I take it you have the answer?" Lilly walked up beside him and leaned, one hip propped against the counter.

He nodded. "That I do," he said, cryptically. "But I'm not ready to explain just yet. In the meantime, you should lay low and relax."

"I think I can handle that. Starting now. I'm going to walk around out back. It seemed quiet enough. Digger, come," she called to her dog, who came running from her spot on the floor.

After hooking Digger to her leash, Lilly gave both Hunter and Ty an obviously forced smile. Then she walked out the front door.

Ty started after her, intending to catch up.

"Let her go." Hunter placed a restraining hand on Ty's shoulder. "We can't begin to imagine what she's feeling. Give her some time to deal with things."

Ty clenched his jaw as he turned around to face his best friend. "When did you turn into an expert on Lilly?"

"When did you turn into a jealous son of a bitch?" Hunter asked.

Ty groaned. "Is it that obvious?"

"Only to someone who knows you." Hunter ran his hand through his hair. "You have no competition from me. No matter how I felt about her once," Hunter said, shocking Ty by laying his feelings out there for the first time.

"Once and no more?"

Hunter nodded.

"Is that because you don't want to compete with me?" Ty asked, not comfortable with the direction the conversation had taken.

Hunter shook his head. "I may have felt that way once. Back when we were kids, I knew there was no way I could win against you. I'd never have even tried." He slapped Ty on the shoulder in a brotherly manner. "But those days are gone. If I had those old feelings, only our friendship would stand in the way. Not my insecurity."

Hunter's admission shocked Ty. He gave his friend credit for knowing his mind and admitting the truth aloud. "So what gives?" Ty asked.

Hunter grinned. "My focus is on someone else."

And Ty knew who. "Molly?"

"The woman's said no so many times I'm lucky I still have an ego left," he said, somehow managing a laugh. "But I keep asking her out anyway."

"Mind if I ask why the hell you haven't pushed her harder to say yes to a dinner?"

Hunter scratched his head. "Because until now, she was sending vibes that warned me to back off. And now that she seems more open to exploring the chemistry we have, Lilly's back and I have an ulterior motive for wanting to spend time with Molly."

Ty shrugged. "Explain the situation. Maybe she'll understand."

"Sure. And hell will freeze over *and* maybe she'll tell me why she's said no all those times when her body language was saying yes."

Ty tipped his head back and laughed. "Which means you'll never figure it out on your own. No sane man can read a woman's mind, no matter how much they think we can."

Hunter smiled. "Now that's the truth," he said, his smiling fading. "But by the time I get finished pumping Molly for information about Dumont, she's not going to want to give me the time of day." He walked to the refrigerator and opened a can of Coke.

"But you're going to do it anyway?" Ty asked.

"Yeah." Hunter downed half the can in a long gulp. "We're the three musketeers. I just keep telling myself that where Molly's concerned, I can't lose what I never had. Not that I won't give it a shot . . . But let's just say my expectations aren't high." He finished the can and slammed it against the counter.

Ty felt for his friend. The guy hadn't had any long-lasting relationships in his life, though like Ty, he had his share of women. And now the one he obviously could get serious about, he might lose. "Hey, man, how about we find another way to get information on Dumont and leave the field clear for you and Molly."

Hunter shook his head. "If she was that interested, she'd have gone out with me long before now. Lilly needs us and that's that." Hunter started for the door, then paused and turned. "But when it comes to anything other than my help, when it comes to Lilly, you're the *man*."

Ty groaned. Sometimes Hunter still showed signs of being the idiot kid who spoke up and thought later. Which was why Ty loved the guy like a brother.

He glanced at his friend. "Actually there's another *man* in Lilly's life and his name is Alex."

Hunter frowned. "Well, damn."

"Exactly." And since Ty wasn't one for deep conversation, he had no idea what to say now.

Hunter glanced at his watch, a gold Rolex he'd bought after winning a huge case for a wealthy guy accused of murdering his wife. It was his first step toward becoming a stuffed shirt hired by the hotshots.

"I need to get going."

"Molly?" Ty asked, figuring it was a rhetorical question.

He nodded. "I guess she's the best person to tell about Lilly being alive. I have no doubt she'll break it to Dumont. We can go from there."

"Think she'll just hand us the trust fund agreement?"

Hunter shrugged. "Who knows. Hopefully she'll tell us which law firm does have it."

"Good luck. You know where to find us when the deed is done," Ty said.

"You said *us*. Lilly's staying here?"

Ty nodded. "I didn't think she could afford a hotel. Besides, I didn't think she'd want to be alone."

"There you go again. Playing the hero. Making decisions for others. Except in this case, it's the right thing. The two of you under one roof ought to give you a chance to revisit the past and see what could have been. What still might be."

Ty shook his head. "Not a chance." Lilly had been a sweet girl who needed him. Now she was a grown woman who needed no one and had a life and another man waiting for her in the city.

"You know what they say. Never say never," Hunter said before walking out the door and slamming it behind him.

Hunter paused in the hallway outside Ty's apartment. He needed a minute to pull his thoughts together.

Lilly was home and looked better than ever. Ty was as sucker punched as he'd been way back when. And Hunter, well, his questions were answered. He'd been damn glad to see her, but only as a friend.

A friend he'd do anything for, not just for old times' sake but also because, as a lawyer, he'd become an advocate of the underdog. Faced with Dumont, Lilly was the underdog and Hunter wouldn't mind sticking it to the man who'd caused him untold pain. He just didn't want to cause Molly any grief in the process.

From the day they'd met, Hunter and Molly had been on parallel paths that just couldn't ever seem to cross. Back in law school, Molly barely took time from studying to do much of anything else. Hunter had been the same way, focused on succeeding. He'd been determined to graduate and make something of himself, mostly because his father had told him he never would. Once Hunter had done a one-eighty in juvie he'd decided to prove everyone who ever said he'd never be anything wrong. And he had, despite the father he'd run away from, and the mother who just didn't want him. And despite Dumont, who'd pulled Hunter out of the only home he'd ever known.

Despite it all, Hunter had succeeded. And he resented like hell the fact that Dumont would once again cause him to lose someone he cared deeply about. He and Molly never had a chance before and tonight Hunter's actions would ensure they never would. It wasn't that he put Lilly and Ty above Molly — he just could never betray his family. They were all he had.

He stopped at The Tavern and picked up a variety of things for dinner, including a bottle of wine, before showing up on Molly's doorstep. He walked up the driveway.

Just as Hunter had anticipated, Anna Marie, the court clerk and Molly's landlord, sat on her porch swing. Her graying blond hair was pulled up in a bun. Wrapped in a sweater, she enjoyed the cool September night air — along with the ability to scour the neighborhood for good gossip. Which Hunter knew he was providing.

Still, he strode up the walkway, stopping outside Molly's door. "Nice night out," he said to Anna Marie before he rang the bell.

"It's getting cold. There's a chill in the air." She pulled the heavy knit sweater tighter around her.

"Why don't you go inside then?"

"I might miss —"

"A shooting star?" Hunter asked.

"Something like that." The older woman winked at him and eased back in her swing. "What are you doing in town this late in the evening? I thought when you weren't in court or at work, you preferred your swanky apartment in Albany."

Hunter laughed. "I'm sure you already know why I'm here, so let's get it over with." He reached out and rang the doorbell with Molly's name beneath it.

Under Anna Marie's prying eyes, Molly opened the door, her eyes widening at the sight of Hunter and the grocery bag tucked under one arm. "Well, this is a surprise."

"Because I finally decided not to take no for an answer?"

She nodded but pleasure lit up her gaze and for a minute, he let himself enjoy it.

He leaned against the siding of the house, admiring her formfitting jeans and fitted long-sleeved shirt. A far cry from the suits she wore in court, she looked more like she had when he'd first met her at Albany Law. Except now that she was home alone, the bright colors that defined her were nowhere to be found. Hmm. Another intriguing part of Molly to figure out . . . Wouldn't that be a pleasure, assuming he was given the chance.

"Well, I can be persistent when I decide to be. So are you going to let me in? Or are you going to keep giving Anna Marie over here a free show?" He winked at the older woman who waved as she continued her swinging.

"When you put it that way, I have no choice." Molly pushed open the screen and Hunter stepped inside, shutting the door behind him. "Honestly, sometimes I think she's listening with a glass to the wall," she said, laughing.

"Do you live the kind of exciting life she'd

find entertaining?" he asked.

"Wouldn't you like to know." A sly smile curved her lips. "So what's in the bag?"

"Food."

She motioned for him to follow her up the stairs and into her home, stopping in the little kitchen area.

"I didn't know what you liked, since you've never allowed me the privilege of buying you dinner, so I've got a variety of specials from The Tavern." He proceeded to unpack a fully cooked steak dinner, a Tilapia fish entrée, and chicken Marsala. "I covered all the bases," he said.

Hunter knew he'd come a long way from the embarrassed, awkward kid that Ty had taken under his wing. Still, sometimes he was thrown back to the state of insecurity he experienced before he'd overcome juvenile detention.

But Molly didn't laugh at him. Instead she looked over each platter and inhaled deeply. "I'd love a little of each. How about you?"

That easily, she broke through his anxiety and they shared a meal. He asked about her parents and her life, but like a lawyer, she deflected his questions with ones of her own. They sparred and he enjoyed her company. But none of their conversation of-

fered him any openings to ask about Dumont.

"So Anna Marie tells me you know my
soon-to-be-stepfather," Molly finally said,
as Hunter handed her dishes and she rinsed
them clean.

She'd made it easy on him after all, giving
him the entry he sought. He shook his head
and laughed. "I forgot gossip runs both
ways."

Molly slanted her head his way. "Meaning?"

"Anna Marie was only too happy to feed
me information about your mother's up-
coming marriage. Then she turned around
and told you about Dumont and me."

"Actually all she mentioned was that you
shared a past. Care to elaborate?"

"Not really." He braced his hands on the
white Formica countertop. "But I suppose
if I want information from you about Dumont, I'm going to have to share what I
know."

Hunter knew the minute she realized his
dinner had been more of a ploy to question
her about Dumont than a ruse to get that
long-sought-after date.

Disappointment clouded her eyes. "So
you're not here just for the company." Molly
placed the dish towel on the counter and

turned to face him. "You know what, Hunter? You suck," she said, plainly. "We may have spent years tiptoeing around dating each other but I never pegged you for a guy who wouldn't just outright ask for something he wanted."

Unless he cared about the woman he wanted something from, Hunter thought. He had no answer for Molly. Not one she'd want to hear, anyway.

"So what do you want to know about Marc Dumont that's so urgent you showed up here tonight?" she asked, her disgust with him clear.

"Do you like the man?" He figured he'd start with basic questions and lead up to his big revelation.

Molly shrugged. "He seems like a decent guy. He may be my mother's soon-to-be fifth husband, but he's the first one who's brought me into the family instead of pushing me out."

The same man who'd thrown Lilly out of her own home now chose to give one to Molly. What a goddamn mess. Hunter hadn't known about Molly's history with her mother but now he had a clue. Like Hunter, Molly's family proved that sometimes having parents didn't guarantee a good life.

"Why do you ask?"

Hunter inhaled deep. "Let's say my past with Dumont doesn't paint him in a favorable light. But you like him?"

"Like I said, he seems decent. He makes Mom happy and he's been nice to me. But I can't say I know him all that well. The romance or whatever you want to call it happened pretty fast. Then again with my mother, all her romances happened fast. The marriages materialized even faster."

"Is your mother . . ." He sought for a delicate way to ask his next question, then decided what the hell. He'd blown any shot with this woman already. "Is your mother wealthy?" he asked.

Molly burst out laughing. Not the light ringing laughter that usually drew him but a loud, droll sound.

"God, no. Well, I take that back. My mother marries wealthy men, ends up divorced with a decent settlement, blows through the money and moves on to the next catch."

"Dumont's her next wealthy catch?" Hunter asked incredulously.

Molly nodded. "If he isn't now, he will be after he inherits his late brother's trust fund."

Which explains why good old Marc Dumont was the future husband who wanted Molly around. The man needed her legal skills to help him gain his fortune. And what better way to get it than to push his fiancée into renewing her relationship with her lawyer daughter? He'd endear himself to both Molly and to his soon-to-be wife.

Molly exhaled and pinched the bridge of her nose with her fingertips.

He stepped forward, placing his hand on her shoulder. Her skin felt hot and feverish beneath his palm. "Are you okay?" he asked.

"I'm fine. It's just a headache. I'd really appreciate it if you'd tell me what your connection is to Marc Dumont and why you're here grilling me about my family. It's not like you gave a damn before now," she said, her voice deep and gravelly.

"I always gave a damn," he said so low he could barely hear himself speak. "I just didn't know what to do about it."

"Well, I can tell you that showing up here with a meal and an agenda is one hell of a way to show you care."

He wasn't surprised by her words. She had a valid point. "You're going to have to cut me some slack here. I'm not exactly a pro at forming relationships."

She laughed. "You'd never know it from the courthouse rumors."

He wanted to treat her to a cocky grin but a real smile was all he could offer. "You said it yourself. All rumors."

He'd never had a relationship with a woman that involved his emotions. Unless he counted Lilly and he realized now that he'd loved her but he hadn't been in love. The truth came as a relief. He'd always be there for Lilly. He'd bail her out or help her in any way he could because they'd bonded years before.

Yet what he'd begun to feel for Molly was stronger than his feelings for Lilly because of what he sensed he *could* feel in the future — if he opened himself up to the possibility of being hurt. He'd betrayed her tonight. At this moment. Because he stood in Molly's house, in need of information to help Lilly, a woman Molly thought was dead.

The ironic thing was, the women were very much alike and Hunter could even see them being friends. In another life or in this one, if only things were less complicated.

But they weren't. And they'd only get more complex when Molly found out the truth.

FIVE

Hunter sat in Molly's kitchen, asking her to give him a break because relationships weren't and never had been his thing. He couldn't believe he'd laid it on the line that way but he had.

She placed one hand on the counter, her expression a mixture of disbelief and what Hunter wanted to think was hope.

For them.

She studied him. "Is that what we're doing here? Forming a relationship? Because I have to tell you, I'm lost."

He let out a groan. "Can I sit?" He couldn't answer her question until he'd told her everything. Then she'd have to decide what was or wasn't possible between them. And the story he had to tell her was a long one.

She gestured to a chair by the table and he straddled the wrought iron seat.

She pulled up a chair and warily sat down

beside him.

He used the time to steady his emotions since he rarely shared his past. "I grew up in foster care," he finally said.

Her eyes grew softer. "I didn't know."

He stiffened, waiting for the dose of pity women usually offered when they found out. The kind Hunter hated because it meant they felt sorry for him.

Molly tapped her fingers against the table, meeting his gaze. "I wonder if it was better than being carted off to boarding school when the stepfather of the moment was willing to pay the bills."

He laughed, grateful for her smart-ass reply. He'd sensed she was special. Now he knew for sure.

"So really, how bad was it?" Molly asked.

"Not that bad." He wasn't lying. "Especially the last place. You've met my friend Ty who works at Night Owl's?"

She nodded. "You introduced us last time I went with friends for drinks after work."

"He's my foster brother. His mother took me in and treated me like family. She did the same with another foster kid in the house. A girl." Hunter paused a beat, knowing this is where their understanding and bonding would end. "Her name was Lilly Dumont."

"Marc's niece?" Molly narrowed her gaze, the connection becoming clearer. "The one who died?"

"The one presumed dead," Hunter said, correcting her as best he could until he could ease into the truth. He leaned forward to explain. "Most people in town know the story but you didn't grow up here. And obviously Dumont's left out key pieces if he never mentioned my name to you."

Molly drew back, her shoulders stiff. "I'm sure he had his reasons. But since he's not here, why don't you fill me in?" she suggested with barely concealed sarcasm.

Already she was treating him like the enemy.

Hunter gripped the cool steel backing of the chair. His only hope of winning her over was with the truth. "You already know that Dumont's brother and sister-in-law died in a car accident."

Molly nodded. "They left a huge estate and millions of dollars in trust to Lilly and named Marc as her guardian."

So far their versions agreed, although Hunter assumed that was about to change. "Lilly was a scared girl when she came to live with her uncle. She'd just lost her parents and she wanted him to take care of her, and to love her. She thought he did, but it turned out that he only loved her trust fund."

He recalled Lilly's version of events, told late one night when the three friends had hung out on an old tire swing that hung from a tree in the backyard.

He glanced at Molly. Her expression remained skeptical and wary.

He decided to just continue. "His love and kindness had really been a way to manipulate her to gain access to her inheritance. It was the cruelest twist of fate. That's when Lilly became angry and rebellious . . . and Marc became vindictive. When he couldn't control Lilly with abuse, he had her placed in foster care in order to scare her into submission. It was the fear of going back to her uncle that caused her 'death'."

"No." Molly shook her head.

Hunter could almost see the unwillingness to believe washing over her in waves as she rocked in her seat.

"Marc said Lilly was difficult from the beginning. Unwilling to accept authority or the fact that her parents died. He couldn't handle her and had no choice but to hand her over to the state."

Hunter clenched his jaw tight, not surprised at the twisted version of events or the fact that Molly would buy into them.

"You said yourself you don't know Dumont all that well, so you can't possibly discount what I'm telling you."

Molly rose from her seat. "I can and I do. Marc said Lilly was wild and uncontrollable. He'd been single and didn't know anything about kids. He was at his wits' end when he sent her to foster care. Afterward he felt awful about his decision and wanted to take her back and start over, but she stole his car and —"

"He has no proof," Hunter said. "No proof that Lilly stole anything. All he knows is that his car ended up in the quarry below the cliffs and no body was ever found."

Molly stood towering over him. Eyes wide, she was obviously fighting against accepting his story, probably because it would upset the fragile peace she'd begun to find at home. A peace she'd probably dreamed about for a lifetime, he thought, understanding her better than she knew.

"Think like a lawyer, Molly. You're too smart to take Dumont's word at face value," Hunter said.

She rubbed her hand against her forehead. "I need some time. A few days to look into all this," Molly said without meeting his gaze.

He rose slowly from his seat. "You won't

need to look too far. You can just ask the source."

Molly moved her hand away from her face. "What do you mean?"

Hunter drew a deep breath, fortifying himself for revealing the news. "Lilly's alive. Any questions you have, you can ask her yourself."

Instead of looking incredulous, Molly merely shook her head at him. "You're reaching, Hunter. You may not like Marc, but conjuring up a story of Lilly Dumont's resurrection isn't going to work. I know this has to be about the trust fund. There's no way you can legally stop Marc from filing to claim the money."

"You're right. I can't. But Lilly can."

"You're serious." Molly lowered herself back into her chair. "She's *alive?*"

He nodded.

"You've seen her?"

"With my own eyes. She goes by a different name these days, but she's alive and well." He neglected to mention that he'd been in on the setup all along.

"Wow," Molly said. "Wow."

He placed his hand on the chair behind her, careful not to touch her, regardless of how much he wanted to. "So you'll let Dumont know his quest for cash is over?"

She rubbed her hands over her eyes again. "I'll tell him what you said. That's all I can do."

"Can I get you something? Water? Aspirin?"

She shook her head. "Nothing. I just need to be alone, you know?"

He nodded. She had a lot to process thanks to him, including the fact that he cared — if she chose to believe him.

She walked him back down the long flight of stairs. "Some surprise date," she said as he reached for the knob to let himself out.

He wasn't pleased with himself but a lot had come out tonight, at least on his part. What Molly chose to do with that information was up to her.

"You *do* know I always wanted to get to know you better. I've asked you out before," he felt compelled to remind her.

"But you never pressed the issue until now when you had an agenda."

"It's not *my* agenda."

Molly pursed her lips. "That's an interesting point. It's obviously Lilly's agenda."

"She goes by the name of Lacey now."

"And are you Lacey's lawyer? Because trusts and estates aren't your specialty." Molly's voice was purely detached and professional, a sign she'd withdrawn completely.

Hunter groaned. Lilly hadn't officially *hired* him but he assumed he was all she had. "I may have to get some help but yes, I'm her attorney."

She perched her hands on her hips. "Which puts us on opposing sides should Marc decide to pursue the matter."

Hunter raised an eyebrow at that. "He doesn't have a leg to stand on and I would hope you'd look at the issue from all sides before going in that direction."

"I'll discuss all options with my client," she said stiffly.

She appeared so hurt, so betrayed, he felt compelled to step closer. He wanted to apologize but showing weakness might cause her to think his case and claim were weak, as well.

Alone in the small hallway, she seemed very close and for Molly, very vulnerable. He reached out and tipped her head upwards. "Molly?"

Her tongue flickered out and moistened her lips. He wanted to kiss her and knew he couldn't.

"Yes?" she asked on a whisper.

"While you're discussing options with your client, you might want to ask him who he blames for Lilly's death. And what he did about it afterward."

She didn't reply.

"I'll check on you tomorrow," Hunter said, dropping his hand before he acted on his desire.

He'd never been farther away from Molly than he was now. The irony was huge. Just as his feelings for Lilly became clear, potentially freeing him for a real relationship, it was Lilly's return that prevented him from getting closer to Molly.

Without replying she turned and headed back upstairs to her apartment, her footsteps echoing as she went.

Hunter walked out.

Anna Marie had finally gone inside. Although he was relieved not to have to make idle chitchat, he realized she'd probably tried to listen in on their conversation. He hoped like hell her hearing aid batteries had died or else the old glass-against-the-wall trick hadn't worked. Otherwise she'd be blabbing to the world about his blown date with Molly. And Hunter's reputation as a stud, such as it was, would be shot to hell by nine-fifteen tomorrow morning.

Molly closed her door and leaned back against the wall, exhausted and wound up at the same time. She'd always had a thing for Hunter and she'd enjoyed the sexual tension that came along with their verbal sparring. Back in law school, she hadn't gone out with him because she'd been a woman on a mission.

She had no time for a real social life since she'd been determined to work hard, focus on school and become a self-supporting attorney. Unlike her mother, who needed a man to validate her existence and keep her afloat financially, Molly intended to be independent. Unfortunately her success had come at the expense of any real relationships.

But now that she'd moved to Hawken's Cove in an effort to renew ties and family connections, she'd mentally begun to open herself up to the possibility of a social life, a sex life.

With Hunter. But his walls were as high as hers. Even though he'd repeatedly asked her out, he'd never pushed. Now she thought she understood why. Foster care. She shivered. The reserve in his demeanor finally made sense to her. She couldn't see someone who'd been raised as he had, being willing to put himself on the line for rejection.

And Molly was by no means certain she

could move forward, either. Since she'd been a little girl, Molly had dreamed of a relationship with her mother. She'd wished for a mom who'd take an interest in her life, her friends, her schoolwork. Someone to talk to about boys, and hard times. Unfortunately, her mother had been too self-absorbed to worry much about Molly, who had been a mistake with husband number one. Her father was a wealthy California vineyard owner who Molly knew of but didn't really know. And he had another family.

But since meeting Marc, her mother's attitude toward Molly had changed and warmed, something she didn't want to risk losing. And she knew Marc would feel betrayed if she started anything with Hunter. She'd lose the beginnings of her newfound family closeness.

Which brought her back around to the quagmire she suddenly found herself in. Marc had definitely left gaps in his story about his past with his niece. Hunter's name had never come up, nor had Tyler Benson's. Yet both had apparently played a big role during that time. She bit down on her lower lip, wondering how Marc would handle it if she questioned him.

Then there was Hunter, who'd finally

stepped up and brought her dinner — an assortment of choices no less — yet had an agenda. He'd wanted to dig for information about Marc, as well as let her know Lilly was alive.

Where had Lilly been for the last ten years, Molly wondered. And why had she suddenly resurfaced now, just in time to stop her uncle from claiming her fortune?

Molly drew herself up and headed toward the telephone to call her mother and Marc, to see if they were up for an evening visit. Because she wouldn't have any answers unless she asked the right questions.

The late-afternoon sun shone through the blinds in Ty's apartment, but not even the bright light eased the feeling that Lacey was shut in. She hated being confined. She'd been on her own for so long, she was used to coming and going as she pleased. Instead, she'd spent the last three days sitting around and waiting for Ty to come home from work. True, she went out with the dog, taking frequent walks with Digger behind the building where Ty lived, but she was more isolated than she'd ever been. Being idle wasn't her idea of fun but she'd promised. In return, Ty and Hunter had assured her it was only temporary.

They didn't want her to be recognized by the locals and have to explain her presence just yet. Explanations would come soon enough. Hunter said he'd spoken with her uncle's lawyer and stepdaughter-to-be. He'd let Molly know that Lilly was alive and well, and he'd left it to the woman he claimed was his friend, to inform Marc Dumont of that fact. Lacey knew Hunter would have some news of her uncle's reaction soon, but still, she was antsy and on edge while waiting.

She missed her job and her routine. As a means of keeping busy, she'd spent the last few days cleaning Ty's bachelor pad, which obviously hadn't seen *clean* in ages. On the first day, she dusted, vacuumed, washed a stack of dishes piled high in the sink, and then straightened up. The man obviously never picked up after himself. On day two she worked on the closets and today, she was starting the picking up process all over again.

She wouldn't have thought it possible, but she found the whole messy bachelor pad thing kind of endearing, just like Ty himself. Lacey didn't know if Ty had a woman in his life — nor did she care to think about it right now — but she wondered if there was a female who stopped by and picked up after him when Lacey wasn't around. Nobody had called since she'd arrived. Nobody female, anyway, though Ty had had more than his share of clients leaving messages.

She picked up his sweats which lay beside his bed and placed them in the laundry basket, then continued with what had become her routine. Normally when Lacey cleaned, she was working for a living and the process was a distant, methodical one. She'd come by her job choice by accident and good fortune, but the occupation suited her. She'd always found solace in organization.

She couldn't say she found the same comfort here in Ty's place. Because along with cleaning up here, she discovered an intimacy she couldn't deny. One she never thought about when she'd taken care of other clients' homes.

She was learning how Ty lived day-to-day, what clothes he wore . . . what brand of boxers he preferred. Her fingers tingled when she touched his personal items, something else that never occurred when she worked at home. Ty made her think about the past, about a time when she'd felt cared-for and safe. And he made her think about the heavy-duty sexual attraction that she just didn't feel for anyone else. Not even Alex.

With that thought, Lacey decided she'd had enough of being surrounded by Ty — his scent, his things, him. A short walk would help clear her head. She whistled for Digger who jumped off the couch where she'd perched her lazy body and within minutes, Lacey started for the door, the dog at her feet.

A loud knock startled her and she glanced at the door warily. Ty used his key and Hunter usually called to let her know he was stopping by. She looked through the small peephole and sucked in a startled breath.

"Uncle Marc," she said under her breath. She wasn't prepared to handle him but she refused to run away, either. Those days had passed.

Drawing a deep breath, she opened the door to face him.

"Lilly," her uncle said, disbelief in his voice.

She folded her arms over her chest and nodded. In the silence that followed, Lacey took in his appearance. He'd aged. His hair had turned a silver-gray at the temples and he had deeper lines and creases in his slimmer, drawn face.

Digger sniffed at his feet, her nose digging

beneath his pant leg.

"Would you please get that dog away?" He stepped back to get away from her pet, but each time he moved, Digger went with him, nudging him and begging for attention.

Uncle Marc's aversion to Digger didn't say much about the man's character. Then again, she'd always known he didn't have much.

She could have initiated conversation but a perverse part of her didn't want to make this easy on him. She paused deliberately, watching the man squirm.

He glanced at her, his eyes pleading.

Lacey sighed. "Digger, come." When the mutt didn't move, Lacey pulled her collar so the dog had no choice but to get behind her. To prevent her from sniffing and further attempting to make her uncle's acquaintance, Lacey blocked Digger's way with both her body and the partially open apartment door.

"Thank you, Lilly."

"I'm Lacey now," she said to her uncle, feeling more powerful in her new life than she'd been in her old one.

Confusion colored his expression. "Well, whatever name you go by, I'm amazed. I simply can't believe it. I know Molly said you were alive, but . . ." He shook his head, his face pale. "I had to see for myself."

"I'm sorry to disappoint you, but it's true. Here I am, alive and well." She deliberately remained in the doorway, leaving him outside looking in.

He lowered his head. "I can understand why you'd think I'm disappointed, but it isn't true. I'm glad you're fine and I want to hear everything about where you've been for all these years."

"It doesn't matter now." She gripped the door frame tightly. Polite conversation wasn't on her agenda.

"I'd like to talk. Can I come in?" he asked.

"Only if you want Digger in your lap. She's a people dog," Lacey said.

He shook his head, resigned. "Okay, we'll talk this way."

Just as she'd expected, Lacey thought, doing her best not to grin. She had no desire to be alone with the man. She didn't care if her feelings were unreasonable or a holdover from childhood. She wasn't taking any chances.

"I've made a lot of mistakes in the past." He reached a hand toward her, then dropped it again. "But I want you to know, I don't drink anymore. I'm not blaming how badly things went between us on liquor, but it didn't help. I didn't know anything about being the guardian of a teenager."

She narrowed her gaze. "Any idiot could figure out that abuse wasn't the way to go. Especially since you only wanted my money —"

"That was your perception. I never said that specifically."

"Maybe not to my face." She pursed her lips. "If I hadn't come back, are you saying you weren't going to claim my trust fund by having me declared legally dead?" Nausea rose to her throat at the thought.

He shrugged. "Practicality dictated some-one take over the trust."

At least he hadn't denied it.

"Besides, your parents provided that if you passed on, the trust would be divided between myself and your uncle Robert. I was just following their wishes."

Once again, he reached for her arm, but this time he didn't retreat.

Her pulse pounded in her throat. Before he could touch her, Lacey immediately stepped out of his reach.

His gaze dulled at her rejection.

She wondered whether he really cared or if he was still an excellent actor. She'd bet on the acting.

"I didn't come here to talk about the

money," he said.

"Then why did you come?" Ty stepped up behind her uncle, surprising them both.

Lacey had never felt more relieved in her entire life. She'd handled her uncle but Ty's presence was more than welcome.

Ty stepped past Dumont and came up beside Lilly. He couldn't believe Dumont had had the balls to show up at his apartment to confront Lilly and Ty was glad he'd come home early and surprised the man.

"Are you okay?" he asked quietly.

She gave him a curt nod.

Relieved, he turned back toward Marc Dumont and wrapped an arm around Lilly's waist. From behind, he felt Digger push her nose between them until her head poked out through their legs.

Some protector the mutt turned out to be, he thought wryly. Though Ty wanted to believe Digger wouldn't have let anything happen to Lilly, he knew the dog was a lover not a fighter. As for Ty, he wanted nothing more than to protect Lilly, but once again she'd held her own. He had to admit, though, she'd looked awfully relieved to see him.

Now she leaned into him, her flesh soft and pliant, her fragrance sweet and tempting. He was proud of her for not showing any weakness in front of Dumont, he thought.

The older man cleared his throat. "I came to see for myself that Lilly — I mean Lacey — is really okay," Dumont said.

"You've done that and now you can leave." Ty stepped back, intending to shut the door, even if it was in Dumont's face.

"Wait. There's one more thing." Dumont reached into his suit pocket and pulled out a rectangular envelope. "It's an invitation. Two, really. One to my engagement party this Friday night and the other to my wedding next month."

Lacey accepted the invitation with trembling hands. She was obviously shocked, gripping the invitation so hard her fingertips turned white.

"I don't expect an answer now. Just know I'm glad you're alive. I'm sorry about the past and I hope you'll accept my invitation to start over."

"I'll think about it," she said, surprising Ty.

From Dumont's wide-eyed expression, Ty would guess she'd taken him off guard, as well.

"Thinking about it is all I can ask. I don't even deserve that much. But I'm going to have a new family and a fresh start. I'm hoping we can have that, too." Dumont shifted his gaze to Ty. "The apology and invitation includes you, as well," he said a bit more stiffly.

Ty merely nodded. He had no intention of acknowledging anything the man said. He figured that made Lilly a better human being than him. He didn't care.

In the wake of the silence that followed, Dumont turned and walked away.

"He's full of crap," Ty muttered, shutting the door behind them.

Lilly nodded. "How could he expect me to forget he had me placed in foster care at seventeen?" she asked, her voice shaking.

And Ty knew that foster care was one of the nicer things Dumont had done to her. None of them would ever get past the shift all their lives had taken as a result. "At least one good thing came out of it. You met me," he said trying to lighten the mood.

"And my life was never the same." Lilly turned toward him, a smile on her lips. "It seems that once again, your timing was perfect." She stared at him with wide eyes that were less vulnerable than when she was younger but no less compelling.

"I'd been running DMV searches all afternoon." The department of motor vehicles was computerized but no less bureaucratic.

He'd been searching for a missing husband and running checks on an alias his wife thought he'd use in various states. If Ty wasn't already jaded by life, his missing persons and cheating spouses cases would leave him sour on romance. Instead he was just ambivalent in general and wary of the damage Lilly could do to his heart — again.

Ty was a textbook case — fear of abandonment and rejection, caused by an unreliable father who'd taken off and a gut feeling that Lilly would do the same.

"Good thing it was damn boring work. I thought I'd surprise you and come home early to keep you company."

In truth, work that should have taken him no time had extended itself for hours because he'd been preoccupied wondering what Lilly was doing back at his place, knowing she couldn't possibly find much more to make sparkle and shine.

"Well you definitely surprised Uncle Marc. You should have seen his expression when he heard your voice behind him. His whole face turned pale."

Ty had wanted to take her mind off waiting for her uncle's reaction. He'd wanted to get her out of the stuffy apartment and make her smile. He still did. But first he had to take care of her uncle. So to speak.

"Give me one second." Ty pulled his cell phone out of his pocket and dialed Derek's phone number. "It's Ty," he said when the other man answered. "I need you to do me a favor. Call our friend Frank in Glen's Falls. Ask him to cover our active cases. I have something pressing I need you to handle." Frank Mosca owned a P.I. agency in the next town over. His business was larger than Ty's and he'd have the extra manpower.

"Name it, boss."

"I want you to tail Marc Dumont. Morning, noon and night. Get one of Frank's men to help if you have to, but I want to know what the guy's up to."

"Surveillance. I'll get right on it. I'd rather be out in the field than doing paperwork and traces anyway."

"It's all part of the game. You need to get comfortable with both." Although Ty agreed with Derek. He secretly preferred being out and about to sitting behind a desk. But until they found someone to hire who enjoyed the more routine aspects of their business, Derek was it.

"Maybe I can snag one of Frank's guys to come work with us." Derek laughed.

"No poaching. Call me at the slightest sign of anything out of the ordinary." Ty flipped his cell phone closed and turned his gaze toward Lilly.

"You're doing it again. You're protecting me."

He felt the heat rise to his face. "I'm doing what comes naturally. It's my job to be suspicious. Especially of that bastard," he muttered. "And especially when he's suddenly doing a one-eighty, acting like a repentant old man instead of the prick we know him to be."

Lilly grinned. "Well, I like seeing you in action." She smiled at him, her lips curved in a sensual pout, her mouth begging to be kissed.

He stepped forward. The years melted away, the desire for her was suddenly as real as it had once been. The light in her eyes told him the feeling was mutual. Something that strong and lasting couldn't be denied, despite all the obvious reasons they should both walk away.

But he didn't. From the moment Ty had laid eyes on Lilly again, he'd known he was a goner. Why bother fighting what he wanted so badly?

Putting the consequences aside for later, he lowered his head and let his lips touch hers for the first time. The old spark caught fire and burned between them. He kissed her, brushing his lips back and forth over hers, moisture and friction building. The play of his mouth, the eager movements of hers tempted him to take it further.

He slipped his tongue inside her mouth, filling his senses with everything she was. She let out a soft purr from the back of her throat and his body tightened with need and overwhelming desire. Sweet and warm, sensual and feminine, she curved her body into his, fulfilling every dream he ever had. And some that he hadn't.

Suddenly, Digger began to bark, jumping up and down on her stubby hind legs, begging for their attention. It wasn't the best way to be brought to his senses, but it did the trick.

He stepped back fast, still dazed but much more aware of what was going on around him. "That was —"

"So long overdue," she said, jumping in before he could get his actual thoughts together.

"That it was." Though he doubted those would have been his words of choice.

Mistake probably would have been more like it. He sure as hell didn't need to search hard for the reasons why. She had a guy named Alex at home and a life that didn't include him. Yeah, he'd known those facts going in, but in the heat of the moment, he hadn't cared.

He should have.

She laughed, but the sound was more of a tremor.

He felt certain she had her own share of regrets.

"You have to admit, we've been curious about what that kiss would be like for over ten years. And now we know." She turned and started to straighten up, fixing the blanket which already lay folded on the couch, obviously avoiding looking him in the eye.

Okay, so deep down she agreed with his unspoken assessment. The thought didn't make him feel any better.

"I'm thinking of taking Uncle Marc up on his invitations." She glanced over her shoulder as she fluffed a pillow.

His eyes widened. "You're kidding."

She shook her head. "I came back here to face the past and move on. I need to gauge his sincerity."

"I thought we agreed he's full of crap," Ty said, not wanting to think about her moving on any more than he wanted her getting anywhere near her greedy uncle or any other relatives who'd never lifted a hand to help her when she was a child.

She picked up the pillow, holding it against her chest. "We did. We still do. But I need to go, for my parents as well as for myself."

"You aren't going alone."

A relieved smile spread across her beautiful face. "I was so hoping you'd say that. So you'll be my *date?*" Her cheeks flushed red the minute the word flew out of her mouth.

Ty didn't think Alex, whatever his last name was, would appreciate the label, either. But Ty didn't touch the comment any more than he'd take the word *date* seriously. Once again she needed him, nothing more. Even if the kiss had been everything he'd ever imagined and one helluva lot more.

SIX

After seeing his niece again for the first time in ten years, Marc Dumont drove to work, ignoring Paul Dunne's phone call demanding a meeting. Marc didn't think they had anything to discuss. The man was a prick. Always had been. There probably wasn't a lot of difference between Marc and Paul, but Marc liked to console himself that he was at least trying to be a better man. Paul had no morals and no intention of reforming.

Marc thought of his niece. She'd grown into a beautiful young woman. When he looked at her today, he no longer saw his brother's spitting image, only her own strength and beauty. But back when he'd become her guardian, looking at Lilly had reminded Marc of all his failures.

At the time there had been many, the most glaring of which had been losing Lilly's mother to his brother, Eric. Marc had believed himself in love with Rhona but she only had eyes for Eric, who'd always been the golden child anyway. All things went his older brother's way. He'd won Rhona, started a successful vintage car business, and he'd married wealthy. Marc hadn't known about Rhona's money when he'd fallen for her but what a bonus. Of course it had become Eric's. His brother Robert merely went on his harmless, merry way while Marc seemed to bungle one relationship and job after another.

And when he looked at Lilly, Marc hadn't seen the woman he'd loved and lost, he'd only seen his brother. His competition. The person he had a chance to defeat one last time.

Marc used to blame his actions on drinking but he accepted the truth now. He'd allowed jealousy to rule his life and he'd made both decisions — to drink and to destroy his niece and steal her money, he thought, bile rising in his throat. But at least Marc was trying to make amends. Paul had no such desire.

Whatever Paul wanted from Marc now — and Marc knew for sure it had everything to do with Lilly's trust fund — he didn't want any part of the other man's scheme. The trustee had been siphoning money from the estate for years, as Marc had discovered during his first few months of sobriety. A time when he'd decided to take control of his life and see where things actually stood.

Paul, who'd known he could put anything over on a drunken Marc, claimed he'd intended to pay the money back before Marc inherited. A bald-faced lie if Marc had ever heard one. When Marc had threatened to go to the authorities, Paul had countered with a warning of his own. If Marc turned him in, Paul would expose Marc's lies and abuse of his niece. That left them in a stalemate, since Marc couldn't afford a public scandal now that he had a respectable job and the prospect of a future.

They'd both had too much to lose, so Marc had remained silent. After all, as soon as he inherited, the old bastard would be out of his life for good. Now there would be no inheritance and possibly no future if his fiancée bailed on him once she realized there was no money.

As for Paul Dunne, he was Lilly's problem. Once she took control of her inheritance, it was only a matter of time before she realized what had been going on for all these years. Then she'd have to deal with Paul Dunne, trustee. The thought gave

Marc little comfort.

He wasn't a saint, only a flawed man and a recovering alcoholic to boot. He couldn't help but admit everything would be so much simpler if Lilly had remained dead.

God, he needed a drink.

The engagement party for Lacey's uncle Marc was to be held in her childhood home. Her uncle had been living in her parents' house all these years, sitting by the fireplace in the den, eating in her mother's beloved kitchen, and those were just two of what she knew were many other personal violations. All things that had been easier to put out of her mind when she lived three hours and a lifetime away than now when she had to dress for her return.

Because Lacey dated a businessman, she owned a few nice outfits, but she hadn't brought them with her on this trip. She planned a quick trip to a mall in the next town over to buy something to wear. Hunter suggested she go with Molly — her uncle's soon-to-be stepdaughter.

Although Lacey was wary of the woman based on her relationship with Marc Dumont, she trusted her best friend's judgment. Hunter felt it important that the women meet and he believed they would get along well under any circumstances, including the one they found themselves in.

Lacey understood Hunter had dual motives. He wanted Molly to get to know Lacey and realize she wasn't lying about the man her uncle had been — and probably still was. He also, along with Ty, didn't want Lacey to be alone. Which was ridiculous since she'd been on her own for years.

Still, since it meant so much to them and since she missed having a close female friend around, Lacey had agreed to meet up with Molly at the local mall. It was hard to admit but she didn't have many close women friends. She worked but not in an office where she could meet people her own age. Her employees were mostly young women who didn't speak a lot of English and Lacey knew better than to make friends out of people who worked for her. Befriending her clients would have been as professionally ill-advised, and so other than Alex, she spent a lot of time alone. A part of her was looking forward to this shopping trip.

And not just for herself. Because when Hunter had spoken of Molly, Lacey had noticed a spark in his eyes she'd never seen before and his lips had curved into a smile. Hunter had a thing for this woman and Lacey wanted to see why. And she wanted to make sure Molly wasn't going to break her friend's heart. He'd been too good to her in the past and too protective of her now for Lacey not to feel the same way. She wanted the best for him and despite the other woman's connection to Marc Dumont, Lacey hoped Molly was it.

She met Molly outside the Starbucks in the mall. Lacey knew Molly immediately based on Hunter's description of a pretty brunette with a fondness for bold colors in her clothing and shoes. The other woman's bright red top was one indicator, but she still could have been anybody. Her unique-looking red cowboy boots gave her away.

"Molly?" Lacey asked, walking up beside her.

The other woman turned. "Lacey?"

Lacey nodded. "Nice to meet you. Hunter's told me a lot about you."

Molly swallowed hard. "Unfortunately I can't say the same. Most of my information's come from —"

"My uncle."

Molly treated her to an awkward nod.

"Let's shop," Lacey suggested. If she spent bonding time with Molly, she hoped the discomfort would ease and maybe they'd get to know one another better.

Lacey's idea worked. What had begun as

an awkward greeting changed over the course of shopping, lunch, and chitchat. Molly was warm and fun with a great sense of humor. Lacey enjoyed their day and now they sat at a table in Starbucks drinking lattes. They talked, if not like old friends, then not like adversaries, either. They hadn't discussed the past, which was fine with Lacey. She knew eventually she'd have to explain things, but just not right now.

Molly wrapped her hand around her grande-sized cup and met Lacey's gaze. "I love shopping," she said, relaxing in her seat.

"It isn't something I do much. Just for the basics," Lacey said. "I work too much to have time for shopping as recreation."

Molly smiled. "You're a saver, I'm a spender. I think it comes from not having a lot while growing up. I crave the luxuries, not that I can afford them. Thank goodness for credit cards," she said laughing.

"Amen." Lacey grinned. She had no intention of revealing she tried hard to charge little and pay off fast. She hated being in debt. She'd lived from hand to mouth for so long, she rarely let herself let go. Even though, these days, she could afford to do so now and again.

"I have to admit you're different than I thought you'd be." Molly's astute gaze appraised Lacey without shame.

Apparently it was time to discuss the past. "You mean because I don't have the word 'trouble' stamped on my forehead?" Lacey asked, laughing.

The other woman grinned. "At least not anymore."

So now they'd reached the crux of things. "I wasn't trouble then, either. What do you think of Hunter?" Lacey asked, the subject change not as off topic as it seemed.

Molly's brows furrowed. "I thought he was a good guy."

"He *is* a good guy. And you must still think so or you wouldn't be here with me, right?" Lacey asked. Molly's views on Lacey might be skewed, but if she trusted Hunter, she couldn't believe every lie Marc Dumont had fed her.

"I have many reasons to want to get to know you better. They don't all involve Hunter." Molly absently blotted some spilled coffee from the table.

Lacey knew her uncle was the *other* reason. "Do you want to know what happened back then? It might help you understand Hunter better."

Molly nodded, but she eyed Lacey warily, obviously uncertain of whether to believe whatever she was about to hear.

Lacey decided to keep the story short and succinct. She summed up her life, her time with her uncle, her stint in foster care with Ty and Hunter, and their elaborate plan to fake her death to prevent her from being returned by the state to her uncle's care. But she couldn't stop the occasional lump that rose in her throat or crack in her voice as she told the tale.

"My God." Molly stared at Lacey, shock etched on her face. "Three teenagers pulled that off?"

"Well, two of those teenagers had street smarts and one had connections." Lacey crumpled her napkin and tucked it into her now empty cup.

"You must have been desperate to have run off to New York alone." Molly's voice sounded distant, as if she were having difficulty comprehending. "And Ty and Hunter risked so much to help you. I mean if the police had found the car or linked them to the theft —"

"They didn't."

"But they had to have known there was a risk."

"We were kids. I'm not sure how far out any of us thought things through," Lacey said honestly.

She hated being reminded of how naïve they'd been, how little they knew about the ramifications of their actions. Molly was right. Despite how her uncle had turned on Ty and Hunter, they'd been damn lucky they'd gotten away with their plan.

"I guess what I'm saying is, both Ty and Hunter had to have cared about you a great deal to do what they did." Molly rose, empty cup in hand, and started for the garbage pail.

Lacey followed and they headed back into the mall. "We cared about each other," she said to Molly.

As Lacey rushed to keep pace with the other woman, she realized what had Molly so agitated all of a sudden. Molly was threatened by Lacey and Hunter's relationship.

The good news was that Hunter's feelings for Molly were obviously reciprocated. The bad news was that the other woman still hadn't come down on one side or the other when it came to Marc Dumont. For Hunter, Lacey and Ty, there was no middle ground.

"Molly?"

"Hmm?"

"Wait. Can we stop here and finish talking for a minute?" Lacey asked.

Molly came to a halt, folding her arms

149

over her chest.

"You don't need to worry about my feelings for Hunter or his for me. We're friends, that's all."

She shook her head. "I'm not worried. I was just realizing what kind of bond you must share, that's all."

Lacey reached out and touched Molly's arm. "Sometimes you form that kind of connection when you don't have anyone else."

"Maybe. But I saw something special in his eyes when he spoke about you."

"Which I'd lay odds is nothing compared to what I saw there when he talked me into going shopping with *you*." Lacey grinned. "I'm serious."

Molly sighed. "I'm sorry. I'm not usually so insecure but I'm not, I mean, I haven't been involved with a lot of guys and although Hunter's asked me out —"

"Often, from what I hear," Lacey interrupted.

Molly laughed. "Although he's asked me out often, he never pushed when I said no. It became like this game between us and we both enjoyed the tension."

"But neither of you ever acted on it."

She shook her head. "Not until the night after he discovered that my mother is about to marry your uncle. Then he showed up on my doorstep, food in hand and a lot of questions on his lips." Molly kicked her booted foot against the floor in disgust. "Before that he couldn't be bothered to push the dating issue."

"Well, you did say you'd turned him down before. And the Hunter I knew had —" Lacey bit down on her bottom lip fast. She had no business telling Hunter's secrets.

"The Hunter you knew what? Tell me about him," Molly urged.

Lacey frowned. She had been about to say the Hunter she knew had an inferiority complex and desperately needed others to love and believe in him. But what did Lacey really know about Molly? And how much could Lacey trust her with Hunter's past?

She drew a deep breath. "Hunter's a great guy. He's sensitive even though he tries to hide it and he needs people he can trust around him." And that was as much as she was willing to reveal. "But I'd bet if he shows interest, the slightest interest, it's real."

"After ten years apart you know him that well?" Molly asked.

Lacey nodded. "Like I said, he's my family." Ten years couldn't erase that feeling. "So forgive me for saying this to you. If you're playing a game, if you just like messing with the flirtation, then let it go. Don't bother acting the part of someone who's been hurt. Just leave him alone and let him move on."

Molly's eyes widened, partly in surprise, partly in admiration. "You're protective of each other. I respect that."

"You care about Hunter." Lacey decided they'd talked about so much, she might as well lay it all on the line.

"Our relationship is complicated," Molly said.

"Name one that isn't. The thing is, if you care about Hunter and you trust his judgment, then you need to know one more thing about our past."

Molly raised an eyebrow. "What's that?"

"After I left, Uncle Marc was furious that he'd lost any hope of gaining access to my trust fund."

Molly's shoulders stiffened.

Lacey refused to be deterred. "He was angry and needed to blame someone. That someone turned out to be Hunter and Ty but Hunter got the worst of it. Uncle Marc had Hunter removed from Ty's mother's home."

"How do you know Marc was behind his removal?" Molly asked.

Lacey remained silent.

"So it's like you said earlier about the car theft — there is no proof."

"Touché." Lilly smiled grimly. "But I think you need to allow for the possibility that there's truth in my story. In our story. Talk to Marc. Ask him. And talk to Hunter. I've never known him to lie."

A smile curved Molly's lips. "I'll do that."

They started walking again, this time toward the exit of the mall closest to where they'd parked. Lacey felt as though she'd accomplished a lot with Molly, from telling her the truth about the past to opening up the possibility of a relationship with Hunter. In her heart Lacey believed that even if Hunter had ever had feelings for her in the past, he considered her just a friend now.

They walked out the doors to the parking lot.

"Where are you parked?" Molly asked.

"That direction." Lacey pointed toward the area she'd left Ty's vehicle.

"Me, too."

They started toward their cars. Since it was a late weeknight, near closing time, and on a drizzly evening, it made sense that the lot was nearly empty. Although it was dark, the overhead lamps provided steady streams of light in all directions.

"I hope you're happy with the outfit you bought," Molly said as they walked.

"I am. I couldn't have bought it without you with me to tell me I looked good." She shook her head and laughed. "I'm just so nervous about seeing all the relatives for the first time, you know?"

"I can imagine."

Lacey saw her car straight ahead of her. She wanted to question Molly about the trust fund before she lost the opportunity. "Listen, I know you were going to help my uncle with —" Out of nowhere, a car careened toward them, cutting off her thoughts.

Lacey screamed and barreled into Molly, deliberately pushing the other woman toward the grassy embankment on Lacey's right. She rolled to her side and a nondescript car drove off in a squeal of dust, leaving both women shocked and shaking on the grass.

"Are you okay?" Lacey asked, panting as she spoke, her heart beating wildly in her chest.

"I think so. What happened?" Molly pulled her knees toward her, hugging her legs tight.

Lacey shook her head. Unexpected dizziness assaulted her. "I guess some idiot took a joy ride through the parking lot and aimed

for the only people around. Us. Whew!"
Lacey lay on her back and stared at the sky,
willing her pulse to return to normal.

"Did you notice anything about the car
that we can report?" Molly asked, joining
her on the ground.

"Other than the fact that it was dark out
and so was the car? No. I just saw that it
wasn't a New York plate as it drove off, but
that's it. You?" Lacey rolled her head toward
the other woman.

"No." Molly closed her eyes and exhaled
hard. "I can't get behind the wheel just yet."

"Me neither," Lacey muttered, shutting
her own eyes, too.

"When I came on this shopping trip I
didn't know what to expect. Who knew?"
Molly laughed, slightly hysterical. "Accidents happen, but that was way too close
for comfort."

"Lacey and Molly's Excellent Adventure."
Lacey shivered. Accident or not, she was
unnerved but good.

Ty decided to take his mother up on her
invitation to come over for lunch. With Lilly's return, they needed to talk. Ty stopped
by the office to check up on their borrowed
P.I. who was now handling the missing
husband case of Ty's, while Derek handled

surveillance on Dumont. Then he headed over to his mother's. He hadn't seen her since he brought Lilly back and he dreaded the conversation.

His mother still didn't know Ty had had a role in Lilly's disappearance and though she'd made her secret deal with Marc Dumont, that knowledge didn't make Ty's role in his mother's pain over the years any easier to bear.

She'd raised him and she'd done it alone. As she always said, she'd tried her best even if some of her choices had been misguided. With Lilly's return, Ty was forced to see his mother in a new light. She'd kept her secret from him and he realized now he'd kept his.

When he arrived, his mother was puttering around the kitchen. The decor had changed since Ty was a kid. The cabinets were no longer old stained wood but a modern white laminate and the once hideous yellow appliances had been replaced with shiny stainless steel. As always when Ty stepped into the renovated kitchen, he had to push aside the reality of where the financing for this upgrade had come from.

"Ty! I'm so glad you could come by." His mother greeted him with a huge hug.

Wearing an apron that signaled she'd been cooking along with a huge smile, she was the mother he loved and he wrapped his arms around her, too.

"You didn't have to cook for me. But I'm glad you did." He stepped back and surveyed the stove and its many simmering pots, inhaling the delicious aroma that filled him with warmth.

"I still love cooking for you. I made your favorite homemade tomato soup and a grilled cheese sandwich with butter on the bread." She smiled. "But I have to admit you're not the only reason I'm so busy in the kitchen."

Was it his imagination or did her cheeks flush before she rushed over to the oven to peek inside. "What's going on?"

"I'm cooking for a friend." She didn't turn to face him.

"You're cooking for a man?" he asked, surprised.

His mother had always claimed she was too busy to get involved again. Although he'd believed that line while he was growing up, a part of him had long suspected that she said it to protect his illusions of her as his mother. But he was a grown-up now and could handle his mother dating. In fact he'd much rather she wasn't alone.

"Dr. Sanford asked me out and I accepted. We went to the movies one time, dinner another. I'm cooking for him to-night."

Ty nodded. "I hear he's a good guy. Is it serious?"

"It could be," she said, trying to sound nonchalant. She busied herself pouring soup and serving their lunch before sitting down beside him at the table.

"Well, I'm happy for you," Ty said. Nobody deserved to be alone for all the years his mother had been.

His mother smiled. "I'm happy for me. And for you. Now tell me when you're going to bring Lilly by because I don't think I can stand another day without giving that girl a big hug and a kiss."

He'd known this subject was coming and he was prepared. "I know you missed her and you're relieved she's fine but before you see her, we need to agree on something." He turned his attention to his lunch. Any food was delicious as always when his mother prepared a meal. "This is excellent," he told her.

"Agree on what?" she asked, refusing to be deterred.

"The money remains our secret." He'd thought long and hard about this, and as much as he'd hated the lies that had sprouted between all of them, he couldn't

158

see any good reason to compound Lilly's pain by telling her the story that still haunted Ty.

Marc Dumont had met Flo in her position as school nurse. He'd overheard Flo discussing being a single parent and wishing she could give her son the quality time and things he deserved. Dumont had asked Flo to take his niece into her home and say she was a foster child from the state. In return, he promised Flo enough money to invest wisely in her son's future. To allow her to give Ty the things she'd wanted him to have, she explained, after Ty had uncovered the truth a few years ago.

"I don't see what good hiding it will do now," his mother said, frowning.

"Lilly already lives with the fact that her parents were killed and her uncle sent her to foster care. She doesn't know that you took an ungodly amount of money for the privilege."

His mother slapped her napkin onto the table. "Tyler Benson, you know good and well I loved Lilly like my own daughter. If she'd landed on my doorstep without a penny to her name, I'd have treated her as well and loved her as much as I love Hunter. And the state only paid me a pittance to care for and feed him." His mother turned

159

pale as she spoke.

Ty placed a hand on her more fragile one. "Calm down, please. It isn't good for your heart to get so upset." She had a heart condition and took medication, but since the heart attack years before, Ty was always nervous.

"I'm okay," she assured him.

Ironically it was her first heart attack and subsequent surgery during Ty's junior year in college that had led him to the paper trail regarding Dumont's money. He'd been temporarily in charge of her accounts while she was laid up and he'd discovered almost immediately that his mother had a ridiculous amount of money saved for a school nurse.

He'd gone to visit her loaded with questions and she'd revealed the whole sordid tale, grateful to have the secret out in the open. Once the truth had set in, so had Ty's reality — everything his mother had bought for him, everything she paid for, including college — had been at Lilly's expense. Not that she'd have been better off with her uncle, Ty understood that. But he hated the fact that he'd lived well, while she'd had to fake her death and run off to New York City. Alone.

"Are you sure you're not dizzy? Light-

160

headed? Anything like that?" Ty asked, focusing on his mother.

"No, I'm fine," she said.

"Good." He tried to believe her and relax. "For the record, I wasn't trying to say you loved Lilly more because of the money. All I meant was she doesn't need the additional burden of knowledge right now. That's all." He met her gaze.

Flo nodded. His mother still appeared paler than before and Ty decided a subject change was in order. "So tell me a little more about Dr. Sanford and his intentions."

"Andrew is a widower with no children. He's nearing retirement and he thinks he'd like to travel. I might like that, too," she said, her voice lightening.

Ty breathed a sigh of relief. With the subject change, her coloring returned to normal and she grew excited about Andrew Sanford. He wondered if he needed to meet the man who made his mother so happy.

Ty's cell phone rang and he unhooked his phone from his belt. "Hello?"

"Hey, Benson, it's O'Shea."

"What's up?" Ty asked Russ O'Shea, a cop he'd met during an investigation, who was now one of his poker pals.

His mother cleared off the table as he spoke.

"There was an incident at The Cove," he said of the local mall.

Every muscle in Ty's body stiffened. "What happened?" he immediately asked, knowing in his gut it had something to do with Lilly.

"Lilly Dumont and Molly Gifford had a close call with a car. Some bastard took a joy ride through the parking lot, narrowly missing them. A patrolling security guard showed up as the car skidded out of the lot. The women say they're fine. They dove out of the way just in time. Since it was Lilly, I thought you'd want to know."

"Thanks, Russ." Ty snapped the phone shut and rose from his seat. "Gotta go, Mom."

"Is everything okay?" she asked, concern in her eyes.

He nodded. "Russ wanted to fill me in on a tip in an ongoing investigation," he lied. His mother had just started feeling better. He couldn't burden her with this, especially since O'Shea said Lilly was fine.

Ty needed to see for himself.

His mother relaxed her shoulders. "Well, don't let me keep you then. I'm happy you came by. I just wish you'd do it more often."

He grinned. He saw her once a week, but called her much more often. "Sometimes I think mothers were put on this earth to remind their kids of all the things they don't do," he said wryly. "Thanks for the meal. It was delicious as usual." He kissed his mother on the cheek.

She touched his shoulder. "I love you, Ty. Everything I've ever done has been in your best interest."

"I love you, too, Mom and I'll bring Lilly by soon. She's been asking about you, as well." But until they'd seen Dumont's reaction, they'd kept her arrival quiet.

He took off at a slow pace so as not to alarm his mother but as soon as he was in the car, he hit the gas and practically flew home to Lilly.

Long after Ty left, Flo couldn't stop reliving the past. She sat in the kitchen nursing a hot cup of tea, thinking about all the things she'd done, right and wrong.

Her son still didn't understand why she'd taken money from Marc Dumont in exchange for Lilly coming to live with them. He couldn't fathom why she'd claimed Lilly was a foster child when she wasn't. But he also hadn't had to live his life without that extra cash. The money had done more than make life bearable. The little luxuries they had enjoyed, like the new kitchen, had come later. At the time the money had allowed Flo to have health insurance which covered the basics like strep throat, Ty's broken arm and ear infections. And later on the money had been a blessing when she'd had bypass surgery. Of course, the same money had allowed her to stay home and raise Ty instead of letting him turn into a latchkey child who would have been out at all hours getting into trouble.

Yet agreeing to Dumont's proposal hadn't been an easy decision, at least not until she'd stopped by the Dumont mansion and taken a look at the sad girl with big brown eyes who wandered the grounds lost and alone. Marc Dumont had claimed she was a difficult child who needed to be taught a lesson that his firm hand and guidance hadn't been able to accomplish. One look at Lilly and Flo knew the old bastard had been lying.

The girl needed love. Flo needed money to raise her son better. As far as she'd been concerned, it was a win-win situation. Dumont suggested she take a real foster child into her home to make Lilly's move appear legit. The state had been hesitant to give her a child when she'd been working so many hours but they'd finally agreed, and deep down Flo believed it'd been Dumont who'd pulled strings to make it happen.

Flo hadn't cared. The kids, Hunter and Lilly, needed her and in her heart, Flo knew she'd be making their lives better by taking them in. No matter that Lilly's situation wasn't on the books so to speak, her life had been happier with the Bensons than when she'd lived with her uncle. Taking the money didn't seem like such an evil thing.

Until Lilly had disappeared. Then Flo lived with guilt over not having watched the kids carefully enough that night. Over not having protected Lilly. Still, the money had changed hands and because Dumont was afraid Flo would reveal his scheme, he hadn't demanded she pay him back. But he had had Hunter taken away. Afraid that if she reported him to the authorities he'd do the same with her own son, Flo had learned to live with what she'd done.

She'd used the money on Ty after that, for better clothes, a better education. When Ty had discovered her secret, his anger had been a scary thing. He'd sold the car she'd bought him and dropped out of college. For a while, Flo had been afraid of losing her only child, but Ty had come around because they were family and they loved and supported each other. They always had and always would.

Still, Flo knew her son had been punishing himself all these years for his mother's choices. With Lilly's return, Flo hoped that would change and he'd find the happiness he'd been denying himself. The happiness he deserved.

SEVEN

Lacey needed a warm bath to soothe the body parts she'd hit on her dive to the ground. Still shaken, she drove slowly back to Ty's place after the mall security guard, who'd arrived shortly after the incident, had taken their statement. She dropped Ty's extra set of keys into a dish on the hall shelf, propped her shopping bags against the wall and headed straight for the bathroom. Not five minutes later, the tub was filled with soapy bubbles she'd picked up in the mall.

She climbed into the warm tub, eased into the bubbles, and laid her head against the back of the cold porcelain, letting the tension ease away. No sooner had she shut her eyes than she heard the slam of the front door and Ty's voice call out to her.

"In here!" she yelled back. She assumed he'd talk from outside the door but just in case, she glanced down, satisfied the bubbles covered her, barely but enough.

Without a knock or warning, Ty flung the bathroom door open wide. "I heard what happened at the mall," he said, talking fast.

"It was one of those freak accidents." She remained motionless, knowing if she lifted an arm to cover herself, she'd risk shifting the bubbles even more.

"But you're okay?"

She nodded. "I appreciate your concern but I'm fine. Exhausted and maybe a little sore, but fine."

He stood in the doorway and stared, his gaze drifting up her body, his eyes darkening as if just realizing that he'd walked in on her in the tub. Nude.

Of course she was very aware of their situation. Her body might be barely covered but she felt completely bared to his gaze just the same. Her breasts grew heavy, her nipples tightening into hardened peaks and between her thighs, a delicious tingling began and grew the longer his heated gaze lingered.

She swallowed hard. "Ty?"

"Yeah?" he asked in a roughened voice.

"Now that you know I'm okay . . ."

"Yeah. I'm out of here." He took a step back. Then another, slamming the door shut behind him.

Her heart racing in her chest, awareness

and desire awakened, Lacey drew a deep breath and dunked her entire head beneath the bubbled water.

Ty leaned against the bathroom door and breathed in deeply but nothing calmed his racing heart. Lilly was naked on the other side of that door, with nothing but bubbles covering her body. He'd caught teasing glimpses of bare flesh, enough to make his mouth water and his groin tighten with need. He didn't know how much more temptation he could take, with them both living under the same roof.

His cell phone rang and he gratefully snapped it open. "Yeah."

"It's Hunter."

"What's up?" Ty asked.

"There's a case that I've been working on that suddenly had the court date moved up. Which means I'm going to be busy round the clock for the next few weeks. I hate to tell Lilly I can't figure out her situation right now, but there's no way I can do it myself."

Ty ran a hand through his hair. "Is the fact that your case was suddenly moved up on the calendar legit?" Or had Dumont decided to somehow pull strings and get Hunter too busy to work on Lilly's behalf.

"There are date changes all the time. It's

part of the process. But the changes are usually adjournments or postponements," Hunter muttered. "Still I'm one step ahead of you. I've already asked Anna Marie about it and she said the information came into her office today via routine channels."

Ty scowled. He wasn't so sure. Could old Anna Marie be bought, he wondered. With her family credentials in town, he doubted it. Still it couldn't hurt to dig a little and digging was what he did best.

Legitimately moved up or not, Hunter had his hands full with this case, so Ty opted not to aggravate him more by questioning Anna Marie's reliability.

"Don't sweat it," Ty said. "I'll let Lilly know, but I'm sure she'll say there's no rush anyway."

"Well, I can give you a heads-up on something you can take care of without me. Lilly's parents filed the original trust fund and will documents with the law firm of Dunne and Dunne in Albany. Paul Dunne is the trustee."

Ty frowned. "Isn't he Anna Marie's brother?"

"Yeah. Are you thinking there's a connection?"

"I don't know what I'm thinking," Ty muttered.

"You sound like hell. What's going on over there?" Hunter asked.

Ty walked out of Lilly's earshot and into his bedroom, shutting the door. "I can't take it." He lowered himself onto the bed. "I can't live under the same roof with her another minute or I'm going to do something I'll regret."

Hunter burst out laughing. "That's what's bothering you?"

"Glad you find sexual frustration amusing."

"Before Lilly's return, you were getting a steady diet from Gloria, so I'd say there's more going on than frustration. Maybe you need to explore the possibilities," Hunter suggested.

And set himself up for guaranteed heartache when Lilly returned to her life? "No thank you. I've gotta get going," he said.

"You can avoid me, but you can't avoid Lilly," Hunter said helpfully. "Speaking of which, don't forget to give her my message and let me know if she wants me to hook her up with a trust and estates lawyer."

"Will do. One more thing."

"Yeah?"

"You might want to check in with your friend Molly." Ty had been so preoccupied with his own frustrations he'd forgotten to fill Hunter in on the incident at the mall, and did so now. "The cops have no leads except Molly and Lilly's quick glimpse of a dark car with out-of-state plates."

"Were they hurt?"

"They're both fine, but —"

A click sounded in Ty's ear and he found himself holding a dead phone in his hand. He laughed, knowing Hunter was already dialing Molly Gifford, a woman who, for whatever reason, wouldn't give him the time of day.

When it came to women, Hunter and Ty had a lot in common these days and as the old expression said, misery loved company.

But Hunter had given Ty no time to explain details, including the fact that Ty had an uneasy feeling about the so-called accident. He'd called Derek on his way home from his mother's. Derek, who'd been watching Dumont, said he'd been at home the entire time Lilly and Molly had been at the mall. The only thing Derek's information provided was an alibi. It didn't mean Dumont hadn't hired someone to do his dirty work.

For the second time in one week, Hunter found himself banging on Molly's front door, only this time he had a damn good reason to be here. He wanted to see for himself that she was okay.

What kind of idiot nearly ran down two women in a parking lot, he wondered. When she didn't answer, he banged again, harder this time.

"You could be a little more considerate of the neighbors," Anna Marie said, poking her head out her front door. "What's with the racket?"

Hunter groaned. "I hope I didn't disturb your dinner."

"You woke me from my prebedtime nap. I like to sleep so I can stay up and watch *The Tonight Show*. I love that Johnny Carson."

"It's Jay Leno now," he reminded her.

"Well, I preferred Johnny."

"Is Molly home?" he asked.

The older woman shook her head. "Not anymore. She came home earlier and was all shook up from nearly being run down at the mall. I'm sure that's why you're here."

"It is." And he wasn't surprised the town's main source of gossip had heard, as well.

"About twenty minutes later, she left the house again and hasn't been back since. You're out of luck unless you'd like to bide some time with me until Molly comes home?"

"Thanks anyway." He turned and started

back down the porch.

"Don't you want to know where she went?" Anna Marie called to him, speaking without waiting for him to answer. "I heard Molly on the phone and she mentioned going to have dinner with her mother."

He paused on the front lawn. He had to refrain from asking the older woman whether she'd obtained the information by holding a glass to the wall. "I'll just call Molly later."

"You could always stop by The Palace in Saratoga. That's where Molly went. With her mother and Marc Dumont," Anna Marie added. "I heard Molly say it's their new favorite *it* restaurant."

Anna Marie had heard right. The Palace was owned by a chef who'd relocated from Manhattan, opening an upscale establishment in the heart of downtown Saratoga.

It was a place a kid of Hunter's background didn't frequent easily. Just like Molly's family gathering was one Hunter had no business intruding upon. "I think I'll catch up with Molly tomorrow," Hunter said, ending Anna Marie's hope for more gossip to pass around today.

"Suit yourself." She stepped back.

"Anna Marie, wait," Hunter called to her before she could go inside.

"Yes?"

"The Barber case," he asked of the pro bono case moved up by the court. The one that would conveniently keep him from helping Lilly.

"What about it? I already told you Judge Mercer requested the change himself."

"Is it possible someone pushed the judge to move it up on the docket?"

Anna Marie shrugged. "I wouldn't think so since the original date is the start of his vacation."

"A sudden vacation."

"Have you ever met Mrs. Mercer? If she told me to jump, even I'd ask how high." She gave an exaggerated shiver. "The woman's one of the bossiest people I've ever met. She wanted a vacation and the judge agreed to the week she asked for. No questions asked."

Well, Hunter had plenty of questions. Unfortunately he also had a case to prepare for, which meant Ty would have to do the digging on this one.

"You should go inside. It's cold out here."

"I'm warm-blooded." The older woman grinned.

Laughing, Hunter headed back to his car. He'd call Ty from his cell phone in a few minutes, but right now, his thoughts were on Molly. If she had felt well enough to go to The Palace, she couldn't be anything more than shaken up from today's incident, he thought, relieved.

He called Ty and filled him in and then started the car. As he drove home, he found himself wondering if Molly enjoyed that kind of swanky new restaurant or if she'd merely gone along with her mother's choice. As for Dumont, Hunter wasn't surprised the older man accommodated his new wife-to-be. The Palace was the kind of place slime like Dumont would want to see and be seen. Whether he could afford it or not.

Lacey heard Ty pacing the floor throughout the early part of the night. She heard him on the phone with Derek who was apparently still conducting surveillance on her uncle, although to what end, Lacey didn't know. She didn't buy his nice guy act, either, but the near miss at the mall had been an accident. Her uncle was vicious but to run her down? She shook her head, unwilling to buy into that particular theory.

Although she wasn't tired enough to sleep, she'd decided to stay in her room until the heated feelings between her and Ty cooled off. She couldn't stop her body's reaction to him but she truly needed to turn off her mind. The problem was, she just couldn't.

When she was around Ty, she was reminded of the girl who'd gotten on a bus to New York City with no idea what awaited her there. She felt more bold and adventurous. More willing to admit that her steady, dependable relationship with Alex bored her sometimes. She shivered at the truth she didn't want to face. She might not be engaged to Alex, but she was involved with him on many levels. Enough to be considering marriage. Which meant she should not be thinking about making love to Ty.

But she was thinking about it. Often. Enough that she tingled between her thighs even now. There were reasons besides Alex to avoid her desires. Her business meant everything to her. It was her reason for getting up in the morning and what helped put her to sleep at night, exhausted and looking forward to the next day. And her business was in New York City, not Hawken's Cove.

But her business didn't fill the empty spaces inside of her. Only a home, a family and the security she'd lacked for most of her life would take care of those needs. Along with the right man.

Lacey had no idea if Ty was that man. And she certainly didn't know how Ty felt about her now. He kept himself closed off to her in a way Alex did not, and she had no idea if Ty was even capable of giving her all she needed. Even if he did desire her, he might not want the kind of life and future she envisioned for herself.

She punched her pillow and eased herself onto her back. But none of that stopped her from wanting him. And she had no doubt that with Ty, it wouldn't be just sex. He reached inside her, he always had. She realized now that she'd never gotten him out of her heart. Of course she'd been seventeen when she'd fallen for him and ten years later, she didn't know him at all. But she wanted to.

She wanted to be the girl who'd gotten on that bus and she wanted to see what her life and her future held.

Marc Dumont paced the floor of the ballroom area of what he'd come to think of as his home. It wasn't, of course. He had no rights to the mansion any more than he had rights to Lilly's trust fund. Not anymore.

Years of anger management sessions and Alcoholics Anonymous had brought him to this — from being a man on the verge of achieving everything he'd wanted, including a fiancée he loved and a future — to a man about to lose everything thanks to the sudden resurrection of his presumed dead niece.

He poured himself a glass of club soda. It wouldn't be easy being at this party with the cocktails flowing, but his fiancée insisted the guests would be disappointed without alcohol. He suspected she didn't want to encourage the talk and speculation caused by a dry party. So he'd just have to gear himself for one minute at a time instead of one day. Or one hour. The temptation to drink was still strong.

Stronger now that things around him might fall apart.

The house looked bigger and more imposing than Lacey remembered. No matter how many people were inside, to Lacey it still felt as lonely as it had after her parents died. As Ty drove her up to the place where she'd grown up, the lump in her throat grew larger, the fear greater.

If she closed her eyes, she could imagine her parents — her mother greeting her with a hug and a kiss, and milk and cookies after school, waiting for her father to come home after a long day at work. It didn't matter to him that her mother had money. He enjoyed a day's work and she assumed he hadn't wanted to live off his wife.

"Are you sure you want to do this?" Ty asked.

She glanced at him and forced a smile. If he could show up at the mausoleum dressed in a suit and tie, she could handle walking inside. "I'm a big girl now." She treated him to a lighthearted laugh.

He shook his head. "I'm not buying the act. We can turn around right now and nobody would know the difference."

"I would." But she appreciated his offer. "Besides if we left, then nobody would see how well you dress up."

In a powder-blue shirt and black sport jacket, he wasn't her rebel, but her knight coming to her rescue all over again. Still, even in her dreams, he'd never looked this sexy or this male.

"Thanks," he said gruffly. He inclined his head toward her. "Since you're looking pretty hot yourself, you're right. We should do this."

Her body tingled at his compliment. She was so glad he'd noticed. When picking out her little black dress, she'd had him in mind. When she'd looked into the mirror to view herself in the dress, she'd imagined Ty's eyes staring back at her. But nothing in her imagination had prepared her for the heated look he gave her now.

He slowly pulled his gaze away and back to the road, turning up the long circular drive.

Lacey turned her attention back to what awaited her tonight. A valet greeted them as they stepped out of the vehicle.

"Fancy." Lacey wondered how her uncle was paying for this party.

She knew he had some money of his own from whatever jobs he'd worked over the years but he'd never come close to matching her mother and father's wealth. The incoming money from her father's business was long gone. And though the upkeep on this house was covered by the trust, or at least that had always been her assumption, she doubted her uncle received a stipend once he no longer had Lilly to care for.

But since she didn't know the exact terms of the trust, all she could do was guess based on the information her uncle had given her when she'd lived here with him.

The assumptions would end, since she'd made an appointment with the law firm Hunter had told her had possession of her parents' will. Information was power and soon she'd have some in her hot little hands.

With Ty's hand on her back, they walked into the house side by side. Lacey's first glimpse told her the decor was exactly as she remembered. Gray-and-white marble floors, white walls and floral furniture all remained the same, but the warmth she recalled from her early childhood was missing. She wasn't surprised. Lilly had learned not long after her uncle moved in that people made a house a home — or an empty shell of one instead.

"Are you okay?" Ty whispered.

"Yes," she lied.

Everything about how she was feeling felt wrong, from her racing heart to the overwhelming nausea. She wanted to run away fast, which made her all the more determined to face down these demons and these family members.

"Lacey, I'm so glad you could come." Molly greeted them with a smile.

The other woman's friendly voice immediately put Lacey at ease. "Thank you. I'm not sure how I feel about being here," she said, allowing a nervous laugh to escape.

Molly reached for her hand. "It's going to be okay. I wanted you to see how different things are now. Come meet my mother."

Lacey glanced back at Ty who shrugged and together they followed Molly through the foyer and into the large living room. She might as well have stepped into a dream because instead of the austere atmosphere she remembered when she'd lived here with her uncle, there were people laughing and the same man who'd abused her now sat at the baby grand playing the piano and smiling.

She blinked twice but the sight remained. Maybe he *had* changed.

"Lacey Kinkaid, I'd like you to meet my mother, Francie. Mom, this is Marc's niece," Molly said, pointedly.

A pretty brunette dressed in what looked like a Chanel suit, grasped Lacey's hand. "It is such a pleasure to meet you. We're so glad you could come."

"It's nice to meet you, too. I wish you nothing but happiness," Lacey said, feeling awkward.

"Thank you."

"And this is Tyler Benson. He's Hunter's best friend. I told you about Hunter," Molly said.

Ty tipped his head toward the older woman. "Nice to meet you, ma'am."

"Lilly, you came!" Uncle Marc came up beside his fiancée.

Thankfully he was smart enough to keep a respectful distance from Lacey, no kiss on the cheek or attempted hug. "If you could be big enough to invite me, I decided I should come. I hope you and Francie will be very happy," Lacey said stiffly.

She felt Molly's eyes on them, watching the interaction.

"Thank you, dear," Francie answered for him. "I've got to go see where the champagne is. They're supposed to be walking around with a choice of Dom or Crystal." Molly's mother headed through the French doors, presumably to find the catering staff.

"Dom or Crystal. She does enjoy spending," Uncle Marc said wryly.

"She always has," Molly murmured.

"Then I hope you can afford her." Nobody could mistake Ty's point. He wouldn't be supporting his soon-to-be wife with Lacey's money.

"I passed my Series Seven stockbroker exam and I've been doing well with Smith and Jones," Marc said of a company in town.

"Well, we wish you luck," Lacey said, not knowing what else to say.

The older man nodded. "I appreciate that. Please mingle. Meet your relatives. They were all stunned to hear of your return."

"I'll do that." She turned, eager to get away from her uncle as soon as possible.

"Let's get a drink first," Ty suggested. Taking her off guard, he slipped his hand into hers and led her toward the bar.

"Does he know the whole story about

what we did and where I've been?" she whispered to Ty.

He shrugged. "I don't know how much Hunter told Molly, but I don't think he does. And I don't think it matters, either. It's not like he's entitled to answers."

Lacey smiled. "Now that I agree with."

Ty ordered from the bartender and soon handed her a glass of white wine.

She took a long sip of the dry liquid but the tension remained. "It's even harder being here than I thought it would be."

Ty wrapped his hand around her waist, his embrace secure. But there was nothing safe about how he made her feel because along with the comfort came a tingling sense of arousal and desire. A deep, all-consuming need that only he could fulfill.

"Breathe in deep and relax. And try to remember that you're not a teenager in this house anymore and you sure as hell aren't alone." He whispered the words into her ear, his voice deep and husky.

Without thinking, she leaned against his shoulder. "It's a good thing I'm older and wiser because I really am overwhelmed." No matter how much she tried to tell herself otherwise. "Your being here means everything to me."

"Have I ever let you down?"

She shook her head. Ty always came to her rescue. He loved playing the role of her savior. It didn't matter if it was as big a thing as rescuing her from returning to her uncle or someone in school giving her a hard time. Ty had always been there.

"Lilly!"

She turned to see a tall, balding man stride toward her. His features were an eerie mix of her father and her uncle Marc, making it easy to see the men were related. But so many years had passed, she had to be sure. "Uncle Robert?" she asked.

"You remember me?" he asked, walking up and taking her hands in his.

She nodded. "A little. But the family resemblance made it easier." She shifted toward Ty. "This is my father's other brother," Lacey explained. "And this is Tyler Benson, an old friend," she said, the word *friend* a pale description of what Ty was to her.

"A pleasure," Uncle Robert said.

"Likewise." Ty studied the man as they shook hands.

"Where's Aunt Vivian?" Lacey wouldn't recognize her but she did remember he'd been married.

"I take it you haven't heard." The other man's eyes glazed over and Lacey realized she'd touched a sad subject. "She had a stroke a few years ago and she requires constant care. She's in a facility back home."

"I'm sorry."

"No need. It's part of life," her uncle said.

Obviously he'd had years to come to terms with his wife's situation.

A few seconds of awkward silence followed.

"Lilly and I were just about to get some fresh air." Ty broke the tension and nudged her forward with his hand.

"It was nice seeing you," Lacey said to her uncle. She shot a grateful glance at Ty. She'd been uncomfortable with her uncle who was virtually a stranger.

So were the rest of the guests who must be friends of her uncle and his fiancée because Lacey knew no one. She and Ty stepped outside onto the terrace, which thanks to the nice autumn weather, had been opened for the party.

"My mother used to play bridge with friends out here," Lacey said. She inhaled, forcing cool, fresh air into her lungs and immediately felt more centered. "I don't know what I was thinking, coming here."

Ty leaned against the railing. "You needed to see the house, the people. Gain some closure. It's understandable if you ask me."

She inclined her head. "I'm going to go to the bathroom. When I get back, would you mind if we left?" she asked, already knowing the answer.

"Yes, I mind. I wanted to stay and shut down the place," he said, grinning.

"You're a laugh riot." She playfully poked him in the shoulder. "I'll be back in a few minutes."

"I'll miss you." He met her gaze with a sizzling one of his own.

Surprised and pleased, she turned and wound her way through the crowd, heading for the bathroom. Not the powder room downstairs but the one in the upstairs hall, directly outside the old bedroom where she'd grown up.

EIGHT

Molly watched Tyler Benson over the rim of her Diet Coke glass. Lacey had walked toward the doors seconds before, leaving Ty alone. Drink in hand, he wandered around the room crowded with guests. Like Hunter, Ty was obviously a man who kept to himself and in this crowd, Molly couldn't blame him.

Coming here hadn't been easy on Lacey or on Ty. The past probably surrounded them until they wanted to choke on it, Molly thought. But they'd come. And she was grateful.

She might be silly, but she hoped they could all come to a peaceful coexistence just as she prayed her mother was finally marrying for love and not money. She wondered which wish, if any, had a chance in hell of coming true.

She walked over to Hunter's best friend. "Ty?" she asked, capturing his attention.

He turned. "Hello again." He greeted her with warmth.

She enjoyed studying people and Ty, with his dark hair and hooded expression gave off a rebel-like attitude she couldn't mistake. He was guarded and she understood why.

"Enjoying yourself?" she asked wryly.

"I'm hanging in there." She caught a hint of laughter in his voice.

"Well, I'm glad you could make it."

"Thanks." He placed his empty glass on a passing waiter's tray, then shoved his hands into his pockets.

"I heard you had a little excitement at the mall the other night."

She nodded. "I'm still shaking." She still saw that car coming at them. Good thing Lacey had such quick reflexes, she'd thought over and over since then.

"I can understand. Mind if I ask you something?" Ty gestured to an empty corner of the room where they could speak in private.

"Of course not." She stepped toward the area he'd suggested. "What is it?" He had her curious.

Ty leaned close. "How'd Dumont take it when you told him about Lilly being alive?"

She tried not to stiffen. She attempted not to become defensive. She tried and failed even though he was entitled to have that question answered and a whole lot more. But the truth was, Molly didn't have the answers he sought. She'd asked Marc the bare minimum — what she could handle hearing and no more. Molly hadn't considered herself a coward but faced with losing the inroads she'd made with getting closer to her mother and having a family, she discovered she was definitely a coward and more.

"Why do you want to know?" she asked Ty warily.

"Because," Ty said.

"Because isn't an answer and you know it."

He gave her a curt nod. "Because the last time something happened that screwed up Dumont's plans, he reacted. Lives were changed as a result. And he might be playing the role of the good, repentant uncle by inviting Lilly here, but I'm not buying into it. And I intend to make sure she doesn't suffer again because of some revenge scheme he has going." Ty ran a hand through his hair and leaned against the wall, his gaze locked with Molly's.

She admired his defense of Lilly and wondered if anyone would ever love her enough to look out for her that way. She'd certainly never experienced it before, not even as a child, which probably explained why she fought to keep her mother's love now.

"Let me tell you something," she said, focusing on Ty's words. "You and Hunter might think I've been taken in by Marc's charms but I haven't been. I weigh facts and I make up my own mind." Except this time she hadn't asked. But Ty didn't need to know that.

He grinned. "That's good to know."

"What's got you smiling all of a sudden?"

"You're feisty."

"So?"

"You could give a man like Hunter a run for his money," Ty said, his dark mood lifting just for a moment.

She was shaken by his perceptive words. "We're not talking about me and Hunter."

Ty nodded. "I wish we were. That kind of conversation would be much more fun."

She had to laugh, then, because he'd mentioned Hunter, she decided to tell him the truth. "Look, I went to Marc and told him Lacey was alive, just like Hunter expected me to do."

"And?" Ty prodded.

She drew a deep breath. "He was stunned. At first, he was angry, then he controlled it," she said, remembering. "Finally, he asked me to leave so he could be alone. I did. That's all I know." Molly brushed her hand over her black dress, smoothing out nonexistent wrinkles. Then she toyed with the fringes on her bright lavender belt.

That conversation had been one of the most painful she'd ever had, mostly because of all the questions she hadn't asked. She couldn't look at Ty head-on knowing what Hunter claimed Marc Dumont had done to him and to his friends. And she hated feeling selfish because she had every right to the close-knit family she desired. Didn't she?

Marc had become an important part of Molly's life. A father figure of sorts, someone who seemed to want her around. After a lifetime of being pushed away by the adults in her life, that mattered. Even as she struggled to reconcile the monster these people claimed Marc had once been with the man she knew now.

Molly glanced at Ty. "You have to understand that I met Marc at a different stage in his life. He said he goes to an AA meeting every week and I believe him. And yes, I know getting Lacey's money was a part of his plan when he proposed to my mother, but he seems accepting of how things are now that Lacey is alive."

"Okay," Ty said at last.

"That's it? That easily?"

He pushed himself off the wall and straightened. "I know you believe what you're telling me, and that's good enough for now. Just watch your back," he said by way of warning.

"Not to worry. I can take care of myself."

He glanced at his watch. "Lilly's been gone awhile."

Molly glanced toward the doorway. "Why don't you go find her," she suggested.

Because she could definitely use a stronger drink.

Ty felt bad about grilling Molly, but he'd needed to push her in order to gauge her honest reaction to Dumont and to the situation they all found themselves in. He'd also been assessing her for Hunter's sake. Ty was looking out for his best friend who had strong feelings for this woman. Her mother was marrying into a snake pit and he wondered where Molly fit into the family.

Which brought him to another question. Where in the world had Lilly disappeared to in this monstrosity of a house? Ty couldn't imagine what she was feeling now any more than he could envision growing up in a place like this. The house was a mansion, the grounds seemingly endless. He wondered if Lilly could separate the later years she spent here from her childhood and remember the place held good memories, too. Either way Ty was certain the absence of her mother and father made this visit extra difficult for her now.

After he checked the downstairs bathrooms, he climbed the long stairs in the foyer and began searching the empty rooms upstairs. There were bedrooms that looked as if they'd been closed off for years. He'd look in, find it empty and move on. At the end of the hall, there was a double door that must lead to the master bedroom suite and he started heading in that direction.

Although there was a crowd downstairs, the low hum of voices receded as he walked further away. As he came closer to the master suite, he realized there was another bedroom adjacent with a light shining from inside.

Bingo, he thought. He slowly opened the door and stepped inside.

Lacey sat in the middle of her old twin bed, a stuffed animal she'd been forced to leave behind in her arms. She'd spent the time since she'd walked out of the party wandering the old rooms upstairs. Not much had changed, except for the master bedroom. That Marc had transformed into a bachelor's room with dark colors and old wood furniture. She remembered her parents' bleached-wood, light-blue-painted furniture and she immediately began to cry.

Not quiet tears but big, gulping uncontrollable sobs, caused in part by being in her own home, surrounded by strangers. It had been years since Lilly had fallen apart or even let herself become so immersed in memories that she cried. She couldn't afford to be weak when she'd needed to be strong in order to keep going on. Forward. Living life no matter what stood in her way.

But the complete change of her parents' room had thrown her badly and when she closed her eyes, the memories of all she'd lost flooded through her.

"Lilly?" Ty asked quietly. "I've been looking for you."

She opened her eyes and met his somber gaze. "I got distracted," she whispered, her fingers digging into the ratty fur of her old stuffed pet.

He strode forward and seated himself beside her. "Your old room?" he asked.

She nodded.

"It hasn't changed," he said, glancing around.

"I know. Either he didn't have the money or . . . I don't know why."

"Are those ladybugs on the walls?"

"Red, white and royal blue ladybugs," she said proudly. "I chose the wallpaper with my mom." Lacey bit down on her lower lip. "She said bright colors would keep me cheerful all the time."

He looked around some more. "Looks like a happy place to grow up. Was she right?"

"Until she and my father died." Without warning, Lacey swung her feet off the bed and stood. "Let's get out of here, okay?"

"You're the boss." He rose, following her lead.

"Don't lie. You don't let anybody call the shots," she said.

"Unless it's you," he muttered.

Or at least those were the words she thought she heard him say as she turned off the light, then shut the bedroom door behind her for the last time.

Lacey stood by Ty's side as he gave the valet the ticket for his car. Instead of focusing on the night she'd had, she thought about Ty instead. The valet in a green jacket appeared, driving Ty's nondescript American car. Not a sports car, not a truck, just a car. Ty tipped the other man and climbed inside. Lacey followed him in, settling into the passenger seat.

As he pulled down the long driveway, she took in the strength and air of authority he brought to everything he did. For the hundredth time, she admired his handsome bone structure and sexy mouth that held a tiny dimple on the right side when he smiled. Which wasn't often enough, Lacey thought.

Ty was as complex as the things that surrounded him were simple. He was a deep man who kept his feelings inside but who gave of himself just by being there. He seemed to sense and show up when she needed him, and he knew when to give her space. Ten years apart and he knew her better than she even knew herself.

Lacey leaned her head back, feeling the tension seep out of her body the further from the house he drove. "I realized something tonight," she said softly.

"What's that?"

She took a breath and rolled her head toward him.

"It's not a house that makes a home, it's the people who live there. That big house was full of strangers and the living room wasn't the same place where my parents and

I spent Christmas by the fireplace. Without them there, the place is just an empty shell of something that once was." Her voice quivered but along with that realization came a sense of calming peace.

He glanced over for a brief second and treated her to an understanding smile. Whenever he looked at her like that, like she was the only person on earth who mattered, her pulse soared and shivers of awareness danced through her body.

"That's a huge revelation," he said, his voice gruff.

She nodded. "It let me leave that house behind because I know I'll always have my parents with me. In here." She placed her hand over her rapidly beating heart.

"I'm really glad you're okay. I know it's been a rough night."

She laughed. "That's putting it mildly."

"So what now? Do you want to go back to my place?" he asked.

She shook her head. She'd much rather avoid being alone with him in the close confines of his apartment. The sexual tension was getting so thick she couldn't stand it. "I'd rather drive around for a while if it's okay with you."

"My pleasure."

She hit the power window button and let

fresh air into the car. He did the same and soon they were driving fast, the breeze blowing around them and the radio cranked up loud. She let the cold air whip her hair onto her cheek, enjoying the rush of adrenaline flowing through her system. Half an hour passed in silence and when Ty ran out of back roads and highway exits, he headed for home.

"For the most part, things around town look pretty much the same," Lacey said as they drove down Main Street and turned the corner that led to his apartment around the back of the bar.

He nodded. "You know what they say, the more things change, the more they stay the same." He parked in his usual spot behind the building and after getting out of the car, she followed him up the stairs to his apartment.

He shoved his key into the lock and let them inside. It felt strange not to have Digger greet them with her pathetic whining and begging for attention but Lacey hadn't wanted to leave the pooch home for hours in a place that was still new to her. And because the hardwood floors and area rugs were part of the charm of his rented apartment, Ty had readily agreed with Lacey's idea to ask Hunter to take the dog for the night.

Ty started for his bedroom, in what Lacey thought was an obvious attempt to escape any awkward moments between them. She couldn't blame him. They weren't on even footing, nor did they have an understanding of any kind. All *she* knew was that she liked being here with him.

With Ty, she felt like she was home. She always had. "Ty?"

He turned at his bedroom door. His hand gripped the frame as he faced her. "Are you okay?"

She shrugged. "Sort of."

Because not only had she spent the evening reliving the happy memories with her parents and the painful ones inflicted by her uncle, she'd also reflected on the mistakes she'd made along the way in living her own life. "I've done a lot of thinking tonight. Uncle Marc's not the only one who made mistakes."

Ty stiffened. "No way do you think you're responsible for what happened with him because if you do —"

"No. No. My mistakes came later on." She drew in a deep, calming breath. Of all the errors in judgment she'd made, the biggest had been turning her back on the people she'd loved. Those who'd taken her into their homes and their hearts. Those who'd taken risks just by helping and loving her.

She clasped her hands together in front of her. "Do you think your mother would want to see me or is she angry because we let her think I'd —" She trailed off, finding it difficult to finish the thought but since she'd done the deed, she forced herself to face it. "Is she angry because I let her go on believing I was dead?" Her throat swelled with a mixture of guilt and pain.

Ty's worried expression turned into a smile. "I happen to know for sure that she'd love to see you. And before you ask why I didn't bring you to her sooner, I was waiting for you to ask first."

She narrowed her gaze. "Why?"

"Because I knew you'd ask when you were ready," he said simply, proving once again how well he understood her.

"I guess I needed to put the ghosts of my past to rest and I did that tonight," she said, the realization giving her a strength she hadn't known she'd been missing.

The thought filled her with pride in herself. Pride in the person she was becoming because she sure as heck was still a work in progress, Lilly thought wryly.

He nodded. "To be honest, I wasn't sure

you'd want to see my mother at all."

She shook her head, his words making no sense. "Why wouldn't I want to see Flo?"

Ty remained by his bedroom door, mere feet from Lilly but far enough from temptation to have this conversation without reaching for her. Touching her, whether out of need, compulsion or even sympathy would lead to far more. At this point he knew it as well as he knew his own name. If he allowed her to touch him both emotionally and physically, he didn't know how he'd deal with life after she left. For Ty, a guy who rarely let feelings get in the way, coping with the fact that he felt so strongly for this woman was driving him insane.

Somehow he turned his attention to their conversation about his mother. "I didn't know which category of memories Mom fit into for you," he said honestly. Though Lilly had a big heart, he'd wondered if in some way she grouped his mother in with the awful memories she'd rather tuck away and not revisit. "After all, from your perspective, you were in foster care."

He chose his words with care, refusing to be a party to his mother's lie — if he could help it. He still didn't think Lilly needed to know the ugly truth. Sometimes lies of omission were the kindest ones. But should the truth ever come out, he didn't want Lilly to be able to say he perpetuated the lie after her return.

"Your mother was one of my better memories." Lilly's soft smile hit him in the gut. "Just like you are."

That did it. He'd spent the evening keeping his distance in every way he could. From the moment she'd stepped out of his guest room wearing a simple but elegant black dress and a pair of high heels that accentuated her long legs, he knew he'd better build his walls higher. It hadn't helped. When he'd found her in her old bedroom, arms curled around a stuffed animal, he'd had to stop himself from lifting her into his arms and carrying her out of that house and away from those people.

Instead he'd opted to let her find her own inner strength. She'd put her demons behind her, telling him he'd been right. Except now, she wasn't just independent, she was sure of herself and what she wanted.

And she obviously wanted him.

He swallowed hard, trying like hell to focus on their conversation and not on how her tousled hair fell sexily around her face or how her cheeks had turned pink from the breeze.

He cleared his throat. "Well, now that

everyone knows you're alive, you can just stop by my mother's any time before you go back to New York."

And that was the kicker, Ty thought. She'd be going home to a life she enjoyed. Hadn't she said as much from the moment he'd found her again? No matter how important she claimed he was to her, Lilly's new life didn't include him.

"I'll definitely go see Flo." Lilly nodded, decision made. "I didn't get a chance to thank you for coming with me tonight. Whether you knew it or not, having you there made the night bearable."

"I'm glad and you're welcome."

Without warning, she stepped forward and wrapped her arms around his neck, hugging him tight. "You're the best," she whispered, her breath soft and warm in his ear.

He was also damn aroused and getting more so by the second. Her breasts pushed against his chest and her cheek brushed lightly, enticingly against his. The moment quickly turned from gratitude to so much more.

She lifted her head, questions in her dark eyes. As she moved, her long, lithe body molded to his. Her nipples tightened and as if there were no clothing between them, the tight peaks pressed into his skin.

A low, need-filled groan pushed up from the back of his throat.

Her eyes opened wider, a soft rush of uneven breath escaping.

"Ty?" She ran her tongue nervously over her lips, moistening them.

His body envisioned all sorts of possibilities and his ever analytical mind wasn't helping. It raced with the pros and cons of saying to hell with caution and giving in to what they both wanted.

He knew the moment he gave in and he understood his reasons. He already knew he'd never get her out of his heart, so why not enjoy what she offered?

If she was offering. He was no longer a child unable to cope with loss or desertion, nor was he the young man too stupid to go after the girl he loved. What he was, was an adult capable of having an affair and moving on afterward.

Yeah, right. But just because he knew better didn't mean he intended to stop himself and regret it for the rest of his sorry life.

He looked into her passion-filled eyes. Passion for him alone. "Lilly, I need you to be sure, because if we start something right now, there's no way I'm going to be able to stop." His words were as much a warning to her as notice to himself.

This would be it.

There would be no turning back.

"Oh."

She waited, saying nothing more as his heart beat out a rapid, nervous rhythm.

He reminded himself that if she walked away now, he'd be no worse off than he was last night and the night before that. Hell, other than needing another ice-cold shower and suffering from even less hours of sleep, he'd probably be a lot better off. Because then he wouldn't know what it felt like to make love to Lilly. To lose himself in her soft, moist flesh as he'd been dreaming of night after night.

"It's probably a mistake," she said at last, her voice soft.

"Definitely," he agreed. Not that his aching body would agree.

She drew a deep breath and still he waited.

"On the other hand, I've wondered for so long." Her fingers slid upwards through his hair.

Her hands were warm against his scalp and his nerve endings tingled as she playfully tugged and massaged with her fingertips.

He let out a long, slow groan. "I've wondered, too. I've asked myself what you'd feel like when I pulled you against me like this." He cupped his hands around her, feeling the indent and definition of her waist, wondering what she'd feel like naked and writhing against his hardened groin.

She remained silent and despite the passing of years, he knew what she was thinking. Knew she struggled with the decision. He remained silent, wanting the choice to be hers. Wanting any regrets or morning-after thoughts to be hers alone, not something he'd induced thanks to his own state of pent-up yearning for this woman and this woman alone.

Because despite how still he stood, he was damn close to exploding. If she gave him the green light, he figured he'd barely make it past the couch to his bedroom a mere few feet away. He'd worry about his own regrets later and he knew he'd have more than a few.

"Lilly?" He was asking for her decision, begging actually, his voice a ragged sound he barely recognized.

"Ty," she said softly. Seductively. Sincerely.

His groin responded, increasing the pressure as he waited.

She didn't disappoint him. Without breaking eye contact, she reached onto her tiptoes and pressed her lips directly against his. She was hot for him, her mouth insistent, her lips telling him she was as eager as he. He slid his tongue inside, gliding back and forth, tasting her sweet heat for what seemed like an eternity, tongues tangling, dueling, embracing in a desperate bid for completion the likes of which he'd never felt before.

She pulled his shirttail from the waistband of his pants, settling her palms against his back. He loved the feel of her small hands caressing and kneading his skin. He loved the feel of her. He bit down on her neck to show her just how much.

"Mmm. Do it again," she murmured on a low purr.

He obliged, grazing her with his teeth until she moaned with pleasure. His groin throbbed and he broke into a sweat.

Little buttons rose up the length of her dress and he started working on them, one by challenging one.

"There's a zipper in the back that might make it easier," she said, her eyes glittering with amusement.

He hurt too much to laugh. She turned and lifted her hair, revealing the tiny zipper and her slender neck.

He slid the hook down along her back but instead of sliding the dress off her shoulders, he first leaned forward and pressed his lips against her bared skin and lingered, nibbling at her soft flesh.

She shuddered and let out an erotic-sounding groan. He wanted to hear that noise again but this time he'd be inside her. Just not yet. He was beginning to discover how much he enjoyed foreplay with Lilly.

"You like this."

"Mmm."

Approving of her answer, he kissed her neck again, this time sliding his tongue over skin he'd tasted. He alternately nibbled and soothed until she writhed with pleasure, stepping backwards until her bottom came into direct contact with his straining groin.

He closed his eyes, savoring the desire building inside him. His hips jutted forward and he nearly came then.

He slid his hands around until he cupped her breasts from behind and discovered her nipples were drawn into tight peaks, begging for his attention and his touch. He didn't know what she looked like nude though he'd imagined many times and dreamed about it even more. He needed to find out.

He turned her around before pushing the dress off her shoulders and watching as it pooled around her ankles on the floor. Reality proved even better than his dreams. Her breasts were fuller than he'd thought, her black bra pushing her breasts upwards until they appeared to overflow the lace-edged cups. Her face was flushed, the blush spreading down her neck to her chest and he couldn't tear his gaze away.

She cleared her throat and his gaze shot upwards, meeting hers.

"You could say something," she said, her embarrassment sweet and endearing.

"I might be speechless, but I'm not too stunned to do this." He picked her up and carried her into his bedroom. The way he'd always dreamed of doing.

NINE

Ty's bedroom had been his sanctuary since Lilly had come to stay with him. After tonight, he wouldn't be able to escape her anywhere in his small apartment. Her scent and her touch would be with him wherever he went.

He strode into the room and placed her onto the mattress which dipped under their joint weight.

She pushed herself back, upwards against his pillows. "Is there a reason I'm the only one undressed?" She tossed the challenge his way, her hot gaze raking over him.

He grinned. "If you ask me, you're still wearing way too many clothes," he said, and eyed her, too, enjoying the sight of her in just a skimpy bra and panties. His gaze slid down her flat stomach and long legs, ending at her bare feet.

His erection strained against its confinement and he couldn't deny she'd made a good point. He sat back and began unbuttoning his shirt, just one piece of clothing blocking him from getting closer to Lilly. He dropped his shirt onto the carpet before working on his pants. Undoing the button, he then hooked his thumbs into both the waistband of both his slacks and briefs, and together he threw both items into the pile along with the shirt.

To complete his mission, he added his socks, as well, then turned to face her.

She slid her tongue over her lips, her wide eyes pinned to his erection. His body was as hard as a brick, his need for her reaching the point of no return, yet he knew they'd never have these firsts again. And they'd waited too long to rush things now.

"Now who has too many clothes?" He cocked his head to one side, tossing the challenge back her way.

Her cheeks were flushed but a slow, seductive smile curved her lips as she reached for the front clasp of her bra. She turned her fingers to unhook the catch, shimmied her shoulders and let the garment slide down her bare arms. She dangled it from her fingertips in a deliberate show before adding it to the pile below.

Lilly held his attention completely, his gaze fastened on her freed breasts, creamy white mounds of tempting, full flesh, ready and peaked for his attention. But when he slid closer and reached out to remove her panties himself, she laughed and smacked his hand.

"I'm a big girl now," she reminded him.

And how, he thought as she wagged a finger in a chiding motion. But apparently Lilly wasn't finished and he sat back to enjoy, his cock hard and erect, desperately waiting to slide inside her wet flesh.

"I also figured turnabout is fair play. You tortured me, I'm going to do the same to you," she said, teasing him.

She slid her fingers into the thin edges of her panties and wiggled them down her legs, slowly revealing the swirl of dark hair hidden beneath the silk. Her hips swiveled from side to side and finally when the last scrap of clothing joined the others on the floor, Ty reached his breaking point.

He exhaled a long groan and pulled Lilly down onto the comforter, aligning his body fully, blessedly on top of hers. Skin against skin, no barriers, nothing between them, he kept his body's needs at bay and held on to the moment he'd longed for, for what felt like a lifetime.

A sweet sigh echoed from the back of her throat and he'd never heard a more satisfying sound. She was meant to be in his bed and in his arms, arousing him and making him feel whole. He ran his hands through her hair, kissed her mouth, and ground his hips into hers, but his body told him he couldn't possibly last.

"Hang on," he said, pushing himself over toward his nightstand where he had protection in the top drawer.

"Convenient," she said. Her eyes had clouded over.

"Lilly —"

She shook her head. "That came out all wrong. Of course we need protection. I just wish we'd . . . that we . . . that you . . ." The words were obviously lodged in her throat.

"Say it," he urged. Though he knew what she was thinking, he needed to hear the words anyway.

She tipped her head to one side, her hair brushing her shoulders. He reached out and curled one strand around his fingertips, hoping the contact would give her courage.

"It's just that I wish you'd been my first," she said, the words coming out on a pain-filled whisper.

He nodded, understanding completely. He wasn't a man of many words, but she deserved to know what was in his heart. "I wish you'd been mine, too."

God, how many times had he had that thought over the years and how gratifying to know she'd felt the same. He hadn't been the same after she'd gone. He'd been left with the sense that he'd lost something not only precious but important in ways he couldn't understand.

And now he was about to.

He leaned close and brushed his lips over hers and immediately lost not just control, but his sense of time and place. All he remembered was ultimately coming over her at the same time he hooked one leg around hers, widening her legs, making room for himself in the molten heat awaiting him.

He slid one fingertip inside her, spreading her sexy juices over her thick, dewy folds. Her hips rose without warning, that triangular dark expanse he'd eyed earlier jutting upwards, pulling his finger deeper inside her tight, wet sheath. He no longer wondered if she was ready for him. He knew, just as his shaking body informed him he was ready for her.

He paused only long enough to cover himself with protection before bracing his hands on either side of her head and poising his body over hers.

"Would you rather be on top?" he asked her, taking himself by surprise.

He'd never wondered with any other woman. Never cared to ask, no matter what position they happened to be in, because sex was sex. As he'd always sensed would be the case, anything with Lilly was so much more.

"Anywhere, any way with you works just fine for me." She forced her heavy eyelids open as she spoke.

The honest feelings he saw there blew him away.

"Besides, I'm assuming this won't be the one and only time tonight, so I'll have my chance to experiment later." Once again she surprised him.

Damn but he enjoyed her. Everything with Lilly was just right.

He nodded and eased himself inside her for the first time. Slowly, bit by excruciating bit, he pushed into her, his body straining as she gradually widened just enough for a perfect fit. His cock pulsed and his body fought against the way he held himself back, giving her time to accept and to *feel*.

Heaven knew he'd never felt anything so intense in his entire life. "Are you okay?"

She bent her knees higher, pulling him further inside. "How's that for an answer?" she asked, her voice sounding husky and deep.

He got the point. He pulled out slowly and she moaned, her body shaking and trembling beneath him, squeezing him tighter in order to hold him inside and prevent him from pulling out completely. She had no reason to worry. All he'd wanted was slick passage and he got it, diving back into her with more force. More caring.

She lifted her hips to meet his, her small mound grinding into the base of his shaft. Arousal and desire peaked, his body's needs driving him out of his mind. He pumped into her, feeling every inch buried inside her. Then he pulled out, depriving them both again, deliberately building momentum and need. In and out, in and — without warning she crossed her ankles behind his back, anchoring herself against him so she could lift her behind off the bed and lock her hips tight against his.

She wanted pressure, so he gave her pressure, twisting and turning his hips, meeting her motions, until together they found the perfect rhythm. The one that brought them higher and higher, closer and closer to climax.

Beneath him, she whimpered with need, her soft sounds begging him to give her release. He slid one hand around and found the place where their bodies met, the moist wet spot that let him tease her just enough.

"Ty, Ty, Ty."

She came apart where he'd always wanted her to, in his arms, calling out his name, triggering a gut-wrenching climax of his own. His body tensed and then complete pleasure washed over him in waves of desire he never wanted to end.

And as he finally came back down and fuzzy awareness returned, he collapsed on top of her, her name on his lips.

Lacey tossed and turned. Beside her, Ty slept soundly and she envied him the ability. After making love with Ty, not once but twice, she had too much on her mind to sleep and she lay back against the pillows, trying unsuccessfully to relax.

She gripped the comforter and pulled the blanket tighter around her, inhaling deep. The musky scent of sex and Ty filled her nostrils. Suddenly he snored, a discovery that nearly made her laugh aloud. She turned to study him as he slept. How many times had she dreamt of watching the man she'd fallen in love with at seventeen, asleep after they'd made love?

She didn't know where things between them were headed. She wasn't sure she wanted to know. For now she just wanted to enjoy but she couldn't begin to do that until she'd taken care of some personal business back home in New York.

It was late, a little past eleven. Normally Lilly was preoccupied with her career, but not tonight. She'd been checking in daily with the woman in charge of Odd Jobs while she was gone. It helped that Odd Jobs operated on the same schedules, if not weekly then monthly, which enabled someone to oversee things while the daily tasks ran smoothly. Knowing all was well allowed her to keep a clear mind while she stayed here in Hawken's Cove.

It also allowed her to focus on Ty and what making love with him meant. It meant she had to deal with Alex. She owed him that much.

She climbed out of bed and quietly walked into the guest room, shutting the bedroom door behind her so she could talk in private. Her stomach churned as she dialed his number and it rang. Once, twice; he answered on the third ring.

"Hello?" he answered, preoccupied but not groggy from sleep. Alex normally worked at home until midnight and she knew she wouldn't be waking him now.

She licked her bone-dry lips. "Alex, it's me. Lacey."

"Hi!"

She imagined him pushing himself up against his ivory colored pillows, folders and work spread out over his bed.

"I can't tell you how good it is to hear your voice. I was beginning to think I'd have to send a posse after you," he said, the words meant to be funny but his tone was anything but.

Once again she heard the anxious edge in his voice. She supposed she couldn't blame him since she'd been deliberately vague on her sudden trip and she'd only checked in with him once.

"Nothing that drastic is necessary, I promise." She gripped the small phone against her ear.

"When are you coming home?" he asked.

"Soon. I have an appointment Monday morning that I have to keep and I should know more after that." She'd managed to get the secretary of Paul Dunne at Dunne and Dunne, the trustee of her parents' will, to fit her in for an appointment.

At first the secretary had insisted there were no open appointments for a few weeks, but Lilly had explained she was in town for a short time and she couldn't possibly wait that long. The woman had squeezed her in, though Lacey could tell she hadn't been exactly happy to do it.

"Well then hopefully I'll be seeing you by the end of the week," Alex said, his mood obviously cheering at his interpretation of her news.

"Umm." Her heart lodged in her throat as she formed the words she had to say next. "About seeing me again. We need to talk about that."

Lacey hated to break things off with him over the phone. She owed him better and she'd explain more when she returned home, but after tonight with Ty, everything had become clear in her mind. She couldn't continue to leave Alex dangling without an answer when she knew where her heart belonged.

Even if she and Ty never made love again, Lacey had to end things with Alex. There wasn't room for another man in her life. There never had been.

"What is it?" Alex asked, his voice curt, as he obviously sensed bad news to come.

"I'll explain more when I see you, but since being here, things have changed for me." She curled her legs beneath her. "Actually they haven't changed as much as they've become clearer."

"Stop pussyfooting around and say what you're trying to say."

She stiffened at his words, but she continued. "I know now why I haven't been able to commit to you. It has to do with unresolved feelings for people here."

"We all have unresolved things in our past," he said in what she could only call a patronizing voice. "So wrap those things up and come home. You'll feel better once we're together again."

She ran a hand through her hair. He wasn't hearing her and her frustration grew, mainly because she hadn't wanted to hurt him by having to spell things out too plainly.

He'd left her with no choice. "Alex, I'm sorry to do this over the phone, but we're over."

He let out a harsh laugh. "Oh, no, we are not."

She reared back. "Excuse me?"

"What I meant was, you need to think about what you're saying."

"That's all I have been doing since you asked me to marry you. Thinking. And the truth is, I shouldn't have to think about my answer. If I loved you the way you deserve to be loved, the answer would have been automatic." Sadness filled her, for all the fun they'd had and the caring they'd shared, but she knew in her heart that she was finally doing the right thing for them both.

"Lacey, please stop talking nonsense. Whatever's going on in your hick hometown —"

"Hawken's Cove is *not* a hick town." Surprise and a small pang of hurt rose inside her.

Well, what did she expect? She'd broken things off with him by phone. Had she thought he'd understand and wish her a long happy life?

She'd just never heard him be so nasty before. But she'd never disagreed with him until now, either. At least not on something so monumental.

"Well, obviously the people there are messing with your head. You'll come to your senses as soon as you return."

"Don't count on it," she said, clenching her jaw tight.

He made a tsking noise. "Nobody will ever love you as much as I do." His words sounded more like a threat than the lie she knew them to be.

"Alex, I'm sorry. I care about you and you deserve so much more than I can give. You'll see that one day and you'll thank me for coming to my senses before we made a mistake," Lacey said, trying to maintain her dignity in the face of his hurt and anger.

"I doubt it. And I don't believe for a

minute that we're finished."

She shivered at his words. "You're wrong. We are *over,*" she said, needing him to hear it one more time. "Goodbye, Alex." Lacey disconnected the line and placed the phone on the bed.

Her head throbbed badly. She made her way quietly back to the bedroom, tiptoeing as she let herself back inside. She climbed back under the covers and snuggled deep into the pillows, inhaling Ty's comforting scent.

She assured herself she'd done the right thing. She'd told Alex the truth as soon as she knew it herself. There was nothing more she could do. Time would heal his pain over her rejection.

She glanced at Ty, then rolled closer and wrapped her arm around his waist for comfort. Because time would also tell her what her future held.

Ty pulled the frying pan out of the cabinet and greased it with oil, preparing for his pathetic version of an omelet, then placed the pan on the stove. He opened the refrigerator to retrieve the eggs and came up empty. Muttering a curse, he searched the kitchen for something to make for breakfast but the cabinets were empty, too. There was no cold cereal because he'd finished a box of Cheerios yesterday, no milk because Lilly lived on milk and cookies, and he remembered now there were no eggs because she had finished those, too. He had promised to pick up some things after work but he'd forgotten all about making the stop.

He was too used to living alone and not answering to anyone. Most mornings he grabbed coffee and a bagel at the place next door to his office. Most mornings he didn't awaken wrapped around Lilly, too content to move.

The longer he'd lain beside her, his groin pressing into her back, the more aroused he became. Aroused and content at the same time. Two scary enough prospects to jolt him into reality and force him out of bed.

He couldn't allow himself to get too used to feeling good. To having Lilly around. He knew all too well how quickly things changed and not for the better. She'd be gone before he knew it. So he decided he was better off padding around his cold kitchen cooking instead of wishing for things that couldn't be.

One last glance into the refrigerator and he knew he had to hit the grocery store if they wanted to eat. Besides, the pooch would be back soon and she needed more food, he thought, looking at Digger's empty bowls. He glanced around at his kitchen, the frying pan on the stove, the dog dishes on the floor, and then turned toward the bedroom where a beautiful woman lay sleeping in his bed.

Ty grabbed his jacket and headed out in search of food, fresh air and hopefully some sanity along with it.

Hunter pulled Digger along the sidewalk in front of Night Owl's bar. The dog stopped for every odd smell and Hunter wondered how Lilly walked her dog every morning and still made it to work on time. He'd been at it for a solid forty minutes and she still hadn't done her thing.

Considering he'd woken up face-to-face with Her Smelliness as he'd come to call Digger, he couldn't wait to return the dog to her owner.

"Hunter?"

He heard his name being called and turned to see Molly stepping out of the new Starbucks that had opened next to the bar.

"Hey there," he said, his heart picking up speed at the sight of her in tight blue jeans and a gold long-sleeved shirt with matching gold scarf that picked up the highlights in her hair.

She glanced down at Digger who'd begun to sniff at Molly's feet. "Did you adopt a pet?" she asked.

"Hell no. The mutt is Lilly's. I'm on my way to return her and be free."

A grin tipped Molly's lips. "Aaah, so females confine you?"

"Did I say that?" he asked, laughing.

"Just call it a woman's inference." She took a sip of her coffee.

"How was the party last night?" Hunter asked.

While she'd been at the party with Ty and Lilly, Hunter had been surrounded by takeout Chinese food cartons and legal files. He'd been working late, pulling together a defense for a man accused of stealing a car, which had led to someone's death. In the end, Hunter's strategy came down to relying on his client's willingness to take risks in the hopes that the jury bought his story.

Molly shrugged. "It was okay. Parties aren't really my favorite thing to do but everyone seemed to have a good time." Her gaze shifted away from his.

He wondered if things at the mansion had been as happy as she'd like him to believe. Ty and Lilly would tell him for sure. "I've got to get Digger the Dog here back home, but I was wondering —"

"Yes?" Her eyes grew wide.

"I don't have much free time right now because my case has been moved up but a man has to eat and it's pretty lonely having to do it alone." Leveling with Molly wasn't easy but last night he'd decided he had no choice.

"Is that your lame way of asking me on a date?" she asked.

"As a matter of fact, it is. And not one of those joking questions where you can blow me off to paint your toenails," he said, his tone as serious as he felt at the moment. "And not a meal I'm going to bring by your place so Anna Marie can listen in and take notes. A real date with real conversation."

Last night, as Hunter had worked out the defense plan for his client, Hunter's thoughts had strayed to Molly and the parallels of his case to his life. Could he ask another human being to take chances when Hunter was unable to do the same? He'd decided then and there to go after what he wanted, risking the rejection he'd been avoiding for years.

He just hadn't thought he'd have the opportunity so soon. But as Lilly's return reminded him, life was about taking chances.

Despite the dog pulling on the leash and his own desire to run before she could answer, Hunter took one more risk and reached for Molly's hand. "So what do you say? Dinner?"

She surprised him by nodding. "I'd like that."

He glanced down at their intertwined hands. "Me, too."

The dog began tugging harder, obviously not happy about being ignored. He didn't know how to break it to Digger but Molly was a lot better looking — and better smelling — than she was.

He gestured to the dog. "I need to bring her back home. Pick you up at seven tonight?" he asked Molly.

"I'll be ready. Just tell me this is a casual kind of date because I'd really rather not dress up if you don't mind." She swept a hand across her jeans. "What you're seeing is the real me."

The always confident Molly spoke hesitantly, as if her dressing down might change his mind. Instead it turned him on more.

"So . . . would pizza and a beer be your idea of a good time?" he asked. "Because that's more the real me than the guy in the suit you see every day." He glanced her way and winked, enjoying the flush he brought to her cheeks.

She laughed. "Thank God." With a wave, she took off down the street, leaving him staring after her, watching the sway in her step as she walked.

He yanked the leash, pulling Digger away from a wrapper someone had left on the sidewalk and turned the corner toward Ty's. But he couldn't take his mind off Molly and the fact that they were finally making progress in the getting-to-know-one-another department, no matter how small the steps.

He walked up the stairs and Digger immediately bolted ahead of him, pulling the leash out of his hands. "And here I thought I treated you pretty good," Hunter muttered as the dog bolted to get away from him. "At least some women are beginning to appreciate my charm."

Digger rose onto her hind legs and scratched at the door, her urgency to get inside ridiculous if it weren't so pathetic.

He knocked on the door and when nobody answered, he pulled his spare key out of his pocket. "Ready or not, here I come," he called, hoping like hell he wasn't about to walk in on his two best friends in an embarrassing situation.

He glanced down, planning to slide the key into the lock when he realized the door was closed but not shut tight. "What the hell?"

Someone had jimmied the lock and once he turned the knob, the door opened wide. Smoke immediately hit him in the face, nearly knocking him over. Digger, who Hunter had already lost control over, bounded into the smoky apartment before Hunter could stop her.

"Lilly! Ty!" Hunter bolted into the apartment but smoke burned his eyes and forced him back out. His heart pounded in his raw throat and panic swept over him.

"Is anyone there?" he yelled before drawing a deep breath.

Nobody replied. He hit the door with his elbow. The smoke was too thick and dense for him to make it inside but he was determined to try. Before he could make his next move, he heard barking and a loud noise, as if someone had bumped into something.

"Lilly?" he yelled, loudly.

Next thing he knew, Digger bolted toward him, with Lilly stumbling behind her dog.

Hunter grabbed Lilly's arm and pulled her out of the apartment. With Digger by their side, they ran for fresh air outside, banging on other tenants' doors as they went.

Lilly fell onto the grass, coughing, while Hunter called 911 from his cell phone.

"You okay?" he asked, while Digger licked her owner's face.

Lilly struggled to rise but he gently pressed her back onto the ground. "Rest," he ordered. He glanced toward the building, grateful to see other tenants already on the sidewalk.

"What happened?" Lilly asked.

He shrugged. "Beats me. I was bringing your pooch back home. I knocked on the door, no one answered, so I let myself in and was bowled over by smoke. Much as it galls me to admit anything good about Her Smelliness, she just might have saved your life."

"You saved my life, too. You showed up just in time." Lilly exhaled hard and followed it up with a hacking cough. She grabbed her dog and hugged her hard, pulling the furry body against her chest.

Hunter's adrenaline was still pumping through him like crazy. Before he could reply, fire engines sounded loudly and the red truck pulled around back.

What the hell had happened, he wondered and hoped they'd have an answer soon.

Because if he'd spent another minute talking to Molly, he might not have reached
Lilly at all.

TEN

Ty turned the corner by Night Owl's and saw trouble immediately. A fire engine sat in front of the building and smoke billowed out from the windows of the apartments. Panic swamped him.

Milk, eggs and groceries forgotten, he ran toward the building screaming Lilly's name.

"Ty! Hang on, man. She's right here."

Hunter's voice broke through Ty's panic. He glanced over and caught sight of them beneath a tree, far from the building where the firefighters were working.

Relief filled him but his racing heartbeat didn't slow. "What happened?" Ty echoed Lilly's question.

"That's something we'd like to go over with you," Tom, the fire chief said. He lifted his hat off and wiped his sweaty forehead with the back of his hand.

Ty shook his head. "First tell me everyone's okay."

"Everyone's okay," Hunter and Lilly said at the same time.

Relief flowed through him and when Digger began to paw at his shoes, Ty scratched the dog's head.

"The fire started in your apartment, Ty, so why don't you run through your morning with me," the fire chief said.

Ty narrowed his gaze. "I woke up early and went to make breakfast. I couldn't find any eggs so I went out to buy some things and came home to pure chaos."

"Lilly?" Tom asked. "What about you?"

"I didn't sleep well last night," she said without meeting Ty's gaze. "I fell asleep so late, I was still out cold until Hunter came by with my dog. They woke me up just in time."

"So, Ty, you took out the frying pan and left it on the stove?" Tom asked.

Ty nodded, thinking back to the early morning. "I put some oil into the pan, went looking for the eggs and came up empty."

"Who uses oil to make eggs? You're supposed to use butter or margarine on the pan," Lilly said.

"An ignorant bachelor uses oil," Ty muttered.

Tom scratched his head. "So you didn't turn on the stove."

236

"No." The hair on the back of Ty's back prickled, giving him chills. "I *never* turned it on."

"I had to ask, even if I have known you forever. I'm guessing you didn't jimmy your own lock, either."

"Someone jimmied the lock? You mean someone broke in?" Ty asked, anger and fear fueling his raised voice.

"Ty —" Lilly put a calming hand on his arm.

The chief nodded. "There's evidence that someone broke in."

"Fingerprints?" Ty asked, his thoughts immediately going to Lilly's uncle.

The chief shook his head. "Don't know yet."

"Is anything missing?" Ty asked.

"Nothing obvious but you'll have to let me know."

Ty nodded. His gut told him nothing would be missing. Whoever had jimmied the lock wanted something and it wasn't anything he could carry out with him, Ty thought, glancing at Lilly.

As soon as the cops and firemen left, he'd call Derek but Ty knew Dumont hadn't been around here at all. If he had, Derek wouldn't have been far behind. He'd never have let the man get near Ty's apartment door.

"Why didn't the smoke alarm go off and wake me?" Lilly asked.

"That was one of the first things we checked. It was disconnected. So one of two things happened. Either you made another stupid bachelor move and pulled the batteries out last time it went off while you were cooking, or whoever broke in disconnected it. So which is it?" Tom raised an eyebrow in question.

"It wasn't me," Ty said through gritted teeth.

"I had a hunch you'd say that." Tom smiled grimly. "The police'll do their jobs once we finish ours. Right now I need to go talk to some of the other tenants. Don't go too far and let us know where we can reach you," he said to them. "Lilly, you make sure you stop by the ambulance and let the paramedics check you out," he said before walking away. "I'll be in touch."

Ty inclined his head, waiting for the other man to leave so he could talk to Hunter and Lilly. "Lilly, did you hear anyone inside the apartment?"

She shook her head. "I never even heard you leave. I told the chief the truth. I had a hard time falling asleep and once I did, next thing I remember was Digger barking and licking my face. I woke up coughing, I saw the smoke and ran." She hugged her knees against her chest, obviously still shaken.

So was he. When he'd seen the fire engines and the smoke, his heart nearly stopped when he realized Lilly might still be inside. The sun shone in the sky yet he still didn't feel its heat or warmth.

"It was Uncle Marc, wasn't it?" Lilly asked softly, petting Digger who lay still in her lap.

"It's possible," Hunter said.

On that note, Ty raised a finger indicating they should wait. He pulled out his cell phone and dialed Derek. A quick conversation with the other man confirmed Ty's hunch. Dumont hadn't left his house all night. Thanks to Derek's binoculars and his position on the road, he could see the older man in the kitchen as he and Ty spoke.

"Thanks." Ty flipped his phone closed and glanced at his friends. "I've had Derek tailing your uncle since the day he showed up at my apartment to see you. He had an alibi for the incident at the mall and he was also home all last night and this morning." Ty shook his head in frustration. "He could have hired someone, but we're not finding any proof. He's not being sloppy."

"But he isn't succeeding at hurting her, either," Hunter said.

"No he's just scaring the living daylights out of me," Ty said.

Lilly trembled and Ty pulled her tight against him. "Hang in there," he whispered into her hair. "I need you to think back to that night at the mall. When the car nearly ran you and Molly down. Could the car have been aiming directly for you?"

She lifted her head. "Yes. I mean, it was coming for us. I dove into Molly to get us out of the way. But I thought it was a prank. A kid driving recklessly. Something."

Anything other than the truth. That her uncle hadn't changed after all. Only this time, he didn't just want her trust fund. He wanted her dead in order to claim it.

Marc was thirsty and water wouldn't quench his need. Neither would soda, juice, coffee or anything else so bland. He needed a good, stiff drink but he fought the desire threatening to engulf him and drag him under.

Nobody told him sobriety would get harder as the years passed. Nobody ever mentioned he'd never forget the taste of alcohol, *any* kind of alcohol or that he could crave it in his sleep. And the worst part was, nobody understood. Just when his life had begun to turn a corner, everything around him was suddenly closing in.

He stood in his private office and stared at the answering machine, glaring at the offending piece of equipment. He hit the Play button to hear the messages one more time.

"We need to talk and it has to be soon. Don't defy me on this or else." Paul Dunne, the trustee and manager of Lilly's money in the years since Marc's brother died, issued a directive in his pompous voice.

The tone clearly said, "I'm in charge and you're not." Paul's arrogance and control over the purse strings had sent Marc to the bottle more than once back in the days when Lilly had lived here. Now Marc merely gripped the glass filled with tonic water tighter in his hand.

"Hi, it's Robert," his brother said. "Vivian's taken a turn for the worse. She needs round-the-clock care even in that hospital. I can't take another mortgage on my house. I need the money. You said we'd have it but that was before Lilly showed up alive. Now I'm desperate. My practice is dwindling and I can't afford the malpractice insurance it takes to keep it going anyway —" A loud beep cut off Robert midsentence.

A large lump settled in Marc's throat. He

knew how his brother felt. He knew desperation. The next message filled him with it.

"Marc, darling, it's Francie. I'm in New York City. I took a trip there to look for wedding gowns. There's one that is just exquisite. You said I could have anything my heart desires, regardless of the cost. I do hope that hasn't changed." She pointedly paused, the silence giving him chills. "Call you later, love."

The machine clicked off, leaving him alone in his office. A place and a state of mind he'd be in for eternity without the money. The sad part was, Marc no longer wanted or needed the money for himself. Along with getting rid of alcohol, he'd learned to get rid of the greed and jealousy that drove him for much of his life. If only the others in his universe felt the same.

Lacey held it together while the paramedics did a needless exam, and she was grateful when they let her go without so much as giving her oxygen. Hunter took off for his office, promising to check in on them later. The fire department allowed Lacey and Ty to go back into the apartment to collect their things, but as they'd predicted, everything smelled like smoke. There wasn't anything salvageable to take with them and she was shaken by the fact that they had to leave everything behind. Lacey was forced to remind herself that all of her things were still safely at *home.*

But where was home, she wondered now. Where did she want home to be? Here with Ty? In the one place she had people she loved and cared deeply about? Where her only family member wanted her dead?

Or in New York where she'd established herself and the business she loved? But what she was beginning to realize was that she kept herself detached from everyone and everything in her life.

Only when she'd come back to Hawken's Cove, did Lacey begin to *feel.* She felt both the good — like making love with Ty and renewing friendships and making new ones — as well as the bad — the fear of her uncle and the loss of her parents. But at least she felt alive, no matter how beside herself she happened to be at the moment.

She managed to hold herself together while she and Ty did a quick run through Target to pick up a few spare outfits and necessities. And she kept her composure while they drove in silence to Ty's mother's house where they were going to stay until his place had been aired out and cleaned, top to bottom.

By the time they drove up to the curb and parked, Lacey was hanging on by a thread. Still shaken up from nearly being killed and the realization that her uncle actually wanted her *dead,* she was exhausted and near tears.

So when Flo Benson opened her front door and stepped out to greet them, Lacey jumped out of the car leaving Ty behind, and ran up the front lawn, throwing herself into the other woman's open arms.

An hour later, they'd showered — separately, darn it, and Flo had fed them both, much as she'd done when they were young, Lacey thought.

She finished the last of her chicken soup and rose to help clear the plates.

"Uh-uh," Flo said. "Let me fuss over you. It's been way too long since I had the chance." Ty's mother began her cleaning, using the same efficient manner she'd always had.

She looked well, too, despite having had heart surgery a few years ago, as Ty had told her during a cookies-and-milk session late one night.

Lacey glanced at Ty. He met her gaze, his lips curving into a sexy grin. "I told you she missed you." He inclined his head toward his busy mother.

"Yeah. I missed you, too," she said softly, speaking of Flo, but also of Ty and this place.

Lacey glanced around, focusing for the first time. The appliances were different, a modern-looking stainless steel. They used to be a disgusting yellow, but she recalled the old room fondly despite the putrid color.

She had to admit she liked the new look and it made the kitchen appear more spacious and homey. "The house looks good," she said to Flo.

While showering, Lilly had noticed the bathroom had been refinished, as well. Flo hadn't had much money when Lacey had lived here, but either her circumstances had changed or Ty helped his mother, which wouldn't surprise Lacey. He was a good man.

"Thank you, honey." Flo caught Ty's gaze, then smiled at Lacey.

Over coffee, they made small talk, nobody bringing up the dreaded subject of Lacey's disappearance all those years ago. She knew someday they'd have to talk about it, but for today she was happy to just be here.

The rest of the day seemed to pass in a blur and when it came time to settle in for the evening, Flo insisted Lacey take Ty's old bedroom. He didn't argue and Lacey knew better than to fight with the two of them. She'd never win. She unpacked the few items she'd picked up at the store and joined Flo and Ty again in the family room for some television, but exhaustion swept over her much earlier than usual.

She stretched her hands over her head and yawned aloud, covering her mouth in the nick of time. "Excuse me," she said, stifling a laugh. "I am wiped out."

"It's no wonder considering what you've been through today," Ty said.

Lacey knew he was talking about more than just the fire itself. Neither of them had brought up the issue of her uncle. Although they'd have to talk about it soon, she needed a clear head first so she could focus and make decisions. "I'm going to turn in," she said, rising from the couch.

Ty's gaze followed her movements. All evening, they'd acted like old friends, neither touching the other, neither letting on to his mother that they'd been intimate last night and Lacey wanted to be again. She wasn't hiding their relationship out of a sense of shame or regret, but only because Ty seemed to want to keep his private life private.

But she ached to feel his arms around her

and to know he cared. That *he* wasn't filled with regrets of any kind.

"If you need extra towels or blankets or anything, just let me know," Flo said.

Lacey smiled. "I will." She turned and headed to Ty's old room, her thoughts jumbled and in turmoil.

Thoughts about Ty, her life and her future.

Flo Benson watched the beautiful young woman disappear down her back hall and she listened for the sound of the bedroom door shutting before she turned to her son.

"So what are you going to do to make sure you don't lose her again?" Flo asked.

Ty raised his eyebrows. "I don't know what you're talking about. Now that we've reconnected, Lilly will always be in my life," he said, a diplomatic nonanswer if she'd ever heard one.

Flo picked up the television remote and shut off her favorite show. "I am not talking about friends keeping in touch with friends and you damn well know it. You've been in love with that girl since the day she moved in here. Now I'm asking you what you're going to do about it?"

Ty rose from his seat and stretched. "What I'm *not* going to do is discuss my love life with my mother."

"So you admit you love her?"

He rolled his eyes much as he'd done when he was a child. "Don't read anything into my word choice," he warned her. "I think I'm going to turn in, as well."

Flo nodded. "Whatever you say. But I can tell you one thing. Few people receive second chances in life. I suggest you don't let this one pass you by."

"I'll take it under advisement," he said wryly.

Clearly he was humoring her. "So how long before your apartment is ready for you to move back home?" she asked.

He shoved his hands into his pockets. "Good question. I'm hoping four or five days max. It needs to be aired out, then I have a cleaning crew coming in." He shrugged. "We'll be out of your hair soon enough."

She grinned. "That's not what I meant and you know it. I'm happy to have you for as long as you need to stay. But I'm guessing the couch is going to be uncomfortable after a night or two." Her perceptive gaze met his.

"Quit fishing for information," he muttered, shaking his head.

He leaned down to kiss her good-night and strode out through the doors leading to the small alcove where Lilly's bed had once been. Flo had long since replaced it with a pullout sofa.

With both Ty and Lilly under one roof, life felt full again. It felt right. In Flo's experience, life never stayed perfect for very long. She shivered and headed up to bed, hoping against hope this time would be different.

Hunter picked Molly up at seven o'clock and together they headed to The Pizza Joint on Main Street. Anna Marie wasn't sitting on the porch swing and with a little luck, Hunter hoped she wasn't home to watch them leave. He was pleased to see not only was Molly wearing jeans and a long-sleeved black V-necked shirt but a pair of red cowboy boots that did amazing things to his libido.

Because he liked touching her, Hunter kept his hand on her back as they walked into the old-fashioned restaurant. He passed the sign that said Please Be Seated, choosing an empty booth in the back. He had his first time alone with Molly in years and he didn't want to be disturbed.

He gestured for her to slide into the booth first, then instead of sitting across from her, he edged in by her side.

"Make yourself comfortable," she said, her eyes gleaming with questions at his seating choice.

"I intend to." Not only did he want to take full advantage of whatever time they had together, he didn't want her to mistake his intent. He'd decided to gamble on Molly and he wasn't going to do things halfway.

"Can I get you folks something to drink?" a waiter asked, pad and pen in hand.

"Molly?" Hunter glanced her way.

She wrinkled her nose in thought. "Light beer. Whatever you have on tap is fine," she said.

"Regular for me. Tap's fine for me, too." Hunter couldn't help but notice the choice had flowed off his tongue easily.

For the first time in a while, he'd given no thought to ordering a martini or one of the premium vodkas he'd begun drinking as a statement maker. One that said *I've arrived.* With Molly, Hunter didn't feel the need to prove anything to her other than the fact that he cared. That said something important, he knew.

"I heard what happened at Ty's apartment today." Molly shifted in her seat, too aware of the man sitting beside her. She could barely concentrate thanks to the tingling in her leg where his thigh touched hers.

Hunter inclined his head. "It wasn't pretty. I got there just in time."

She placed her hand over his. "I'm sorry. I can't imagine what you must have gone through thinking your friends . . ." She shivered, unable to continue.

The waiter interrupted with their beers, placing them on the old wooden table and handing them menus, as well. "I'll be back in a few minutes," he said.

"I love their pizza." Hunter flipped the menu over to the back, focusing on the words and not on her. "I'll eat any topping you like, so just choose."

"Someone doesn't want to talk about the fire." Molly reached out and placed a hand over his. "Just know that I'm glad your friends are okay."

"My family is okay."

His words settled in her belly, telling her as nothing else could that he didn't have feelings for Lilly. At least not the kind that were a threat to Molly. Her stomach flipped with excitement and relief.

Taking his cue to change the subject, she picked up her menu. "So how do mushrooms sound to you? And maybe some onions and pepperoni?" she asked.

"Sounds delicious." He pulled the menu

out of her hand and placed their order.

Then he turned his full attention her way. They shared a large pizza and relived old law school stories. They laughed about professors Molly had forgotten all about and by the time he'd paid the check, she realized she'd smiled more than she had in ages.

He drove her back to the house and walked her to her front door. Her stomach fluttered making her feel like a teenager on her first date.

"Would you like to come in? I could make a cup of coffee or we could have an after-dinner drink," she offered. When they weren't discussing his past or Marc Dumont, they had a lot in common and she didn't want her evening with him to end.

Hunter placed one hand on the door frame and looked into her eyes. "I'd like to."

"But?"

He let his fingertips trail down her cheek. "But I don't think we should push our luck." A sexy grin tipped his lips. "We had a good time. Let's do it again soon."

She smiled. "I'd like that." A lot, she thought.

She dug into her purse and pulled out her keys, glancing up at the same time he leaned down and brushed his lips over hers.

His mouth was warm and enticing, his kiss as sweet as it was arousing. She reached up and cupped his face in her hands, the new position allowing a deeper kiss. The minute her tongue touched his, he groaned and took over, sweeping inside her mouth with demanding energy. He kissed her like he cared and she'd had too little of that in her life until now.

She heard a scraping noise and then Anna Marie's voice. "Isn't that what's called an inappropriate public display of affection?" the older woman asked.

Hunter jumped. Molly stepped back and hit the wall.

"It's only considered public if you have an audience. We didn't," he said to the older woman.

Anna Marie slammed the window shut tight.

"I really need to move," Molly said, laughing.

Hunter grinned. "That's a little drastic. How about next time you can walk me home?"

She leaned her head back, meeting his gaze. "Albany, right?"

"Close enough to drive in twenty minutes, far enough away from prying eyes." He gestured toward Anna Marie's side of the building with a nod of his head.

Molly put her key in the door, her hands still trembling from the impact of their kiss. "I'll have to take you up on the offer one day."

"I'm going to hold you to that," he said. And with a brief wave, he took off, leaving Molly wishing he'd taken her up on that cup of coffee after all.

ELEVEN

Ty knocked once on Lilly's door and let himself in without waiting for her to answer. They needed to talk. Most of all, he needed to just be with her and know she really was safe. But when he stepped inside and shut the door behind him, he realized she was lying on top of his old double bed and was fast asleep.

He smiled and sat down beside her, watching as her chest rose and fell. Her face was so peaceful, so beautiful. His heart ached just looking at her. Far from getting her out of his system by making love with her, he'd only fallen harder and deeper. He reached out and brushed her hair off her cheek, letting his fingers linger on her soft skin.

He wondered what she thought about them being together last night. And he was curious to know how she'd handle that boyfriend of hers now that she'd been with Ty. All questions he wanted answers to, even though he sensed none of those answers mattered. Not to Ty's future.

Whether or not she remained with the guy, she had a business back home that meant everything to her. A life that she'd created without him. What did she have here? Painful memories and an uncle who seemed to want her dead. Ty doubted his pull could overcome those obstacles.

For now they had more important things to think about than *them.* Their priority now had to be in proving her uncle was behind the two attempts on her life.

A few phone calls earlier confirmed that although someone had broken in, there were no fingerprints to go on. No leads. Ty knew someone had to have been watching Lilly, waiting for an opportunity to strike. Ty's grocery trip this morning hadn't been routine so unless someone had been outside his apartment, they wouldn't know or anticipate Ty leaving Lilly alone. The police were investigating but that didn't give Ty comfort as long as the culprit was still out there.

The only thing they had going for them was that her uncle was turning out to be an inept killer. Thank God.

He decided right then and there to call his assistant and turn his business over to

Derek for the time being. Until this mess with Lilly was resolved, Ty wasn't leaving her side.

Starting now, he thought, setting himself on top of the covers and pulling a pillow beneath his head. Then he wrapped one arm around her, snuggled her curves into his and settled in for the night.

Next thing he knew, the sun shone through the open window blinds. Beside him, Lilly lay facing him and when she stirred, her knee came into contact with his thigh.

She opened her eyes, looked directly at him and a warm smile curved her lips. "Well, this is a surprise," she murmured.

"I came by to lure you into the kitchen for milk, cookies and late-night conversation but you were fast asleep."

"So you decided to stay." Laughter danced in her brown eyes, her joy at finding him here obvious.

Pleasure surged through him. "It is my room."

She laughed. "Well at least I know now why I slept so well."

"I'll take that as a compliment," he said as he caressed her cheek with the back of his hand. He didn't see any reason to scare her by telling her he planned to be her twenty-four-seven bodyguard. "Seriously, are you okay?" he asked.

She nodded. "The paramedics said I'm fine and after your mother's cooking, I'm even better."

She obviously didn't want to get into detail, but they had to touch on some important things. "I wasn't talking about physically."

She swallowed hard. "I know. I'm trying to avoid thinking about it," she admitted.

"I wish that was the answer." He paused, then asked, "Do you have a will?"

She blinked in surprise at his question. "Well, yes. I wrote one recently. Alex said anyone who owns a business needs to plan for all possibilities."

Alex. Another conversation they needed to have. This time it was one *he* wished to avoid. Coming from Lilly, the man's name reminded him better than anything else that she had another life, and everything inside him froze.

Ty cleared his throat. "A will ensures all your possessions will pass the way you want. Which means you need to claim the trust right away. As soon as you do, your uncle will have no claim to it. He'll have no reason to kill you in the hopes of getting his hands on the money." He spoke in a clipped, businesslike tone.

Then he rose, intending to get out of bed. They were too close, too cozy for comfort.

She touched his back, her hand warm through his shirt. "Ty, listen —"

"Your appointment is in the morning, right?" he asked, cutting her off.

"Yes. And we'll talk some more about the trust fund and about my uncle later. Right now I need you to hear me out." She paused. "Please," she said, her tone plaintive.

He never could deny her anything. He lay back, propping his hand beneath his arms as he stared at the ceiling. "I'm listening."

She breathed in deep. "I called Alex after you fell asleep the other night."

He turned to look her way. In her Target flannel pajama pants and men's T-shirt, she looked so soft and vulnerable, he had to remind himself he was the one with his head on the chopping block.

"I broke it off with him," she said, taking him off guard.

Ty tried not to overreact to the news. He couldn't allow himself to get his hopes up that her decision would affect his life. But he couldn't control the kernel of hope lodged in his chest.

A flush stained her cheeks as she explained, "Despite what happened between us, I'm not the type to cheat."

"I know." With her words came the realization that he hadn't been in touch with Gloria at all. Not once since Lilly's return. He had some nerve being upset about her love life when he hadn't put his own in order.

She bit down on her lower lip, pausing in thought before continuing. "After being with you, I couldn't pretend he didn't exist and I couldn't go on the way I'd been doing, either."

"And how was that?" Ty asked.

"Well, I'd been avoiding giving Alex an answer on his marriage proposal and now I know why."

Marriage, he thought, his stomach churning. "I didn't realize it was that serious."

Her eyes remained solemn, her expression even more serious. She nodded. "It was an important relationship in my life. I can't deny that." She toyed with the comforter. "I don't have many close friends in the city. My job just doesn't lend itself toward meeting people and I'm not a bar person. Alex and I had a lot in common, at least on the surface."

Ty hated hearing about the guy, yet he also knew he needed to listen if he wanted to know what made Lilly tick. "So why didn't you say yes before I ever showed up?"

She smiled grimly. "He's a good man and he loves me. And he could give me a warm, secure future. But I always knew something was missing."

He wondered if he'd regret asking his next question. "And what was that?"

"He wasn't you." She reached out, touching his cheek with her hand. The simple gesture reached past his barriers and into his heart.

Every instinct he possessed told him to back off. Ty prided himself on possessing good, solid instincts but he wasn't surprised Lilly was able to overcome them. With a groan, he rolled over and pulled her into his arms, his mouth coming down hard on hers.

He felt her desperation in her kiss and in the frantic way she ripped at his clothes, her desire as strong as his. Only when they were naked, hot skin against hot skin, did he let himself calm a little. Enough to remind himself that he wanted to feel every last minute he had with her.

And he did, all the way from foreplay to climax, when he lost himself inside her moist, wet sheath, her fingers digging into his back. They lay together for a while, savoring the moment before he headed to the bathroom briefly then returned and climbed back into the warm bed.

She curled right back into him. "I can't believe you had protection," she said, laughing.

He grinned. "The firemen said to take anything that's important because I might not get back into the apartment for a while." He shrugged. "I took what was important."

"You're so bad." She snuggled backwards, her behind pressing into his groin, which had already begun to harden again.

"No, I'm good. And smart." He pressed a kiss against the back of her head.

"And egotistical," she said, teasing. "But we need to get going."

So much for a second round, he thought wryly.

"Will you come with me to meet with the trustee?"

"I already put Derek in charge for a while. Until we figure out who's behind the attempts on your life, I'm not leaving your side."

He only wished she'd never want to leave his.

"I appreciate you," she murmured.

As she dozed off again in his arms, he wondered why that couldn't be enough.

Lacey showered and dressed quickly. Now, as she and Ty were led to the office of Paul Dunne, the man who'd been trustee since the death of her parents, she couldn't help but shiver.

She knew from just the fact that he'd been left in charge, that he was someone her parents must have trusted. She also knew she had no relationship with him then or now. She hadn't thought much about that fact back when she was a child, but she did today. Paul Dunne had left her in her uncle's care and if he'd checked up on her at all, he'd done so from a distance. He'd probably taken Marc Dumont at his word that Lacey had been a problem child. Understanding things didn't leave Lacey feeling charitable toward the older man even if she didn't know him at all.

The woman who'd greeted them in the reception area knocked on the closed door and stepped inside, leaving Lacey and Ty waiting in the hall for a moment before she stepped out again. "Mr. Dunne will see you now."

"Thank you." Lacey walked inside, Ty right behind her.

An older man with gray hair and a navy power suit rose to greet them. "Lillian, it's a pleasure to meet you at last." He came around the desk and clasped her hand. "I was so relieved to hear you're alive after all this time. You must tell me where you've been all these years."

Lacey forced a smile. "The past is the past. I'd rather look to the future," she told the man. "Isn't that why we're meeting? So you can explain what my parents' wishes were and how things will work from here?"

He nodded.

Lacey took that as her cue and seated herself in one of two large chairs across from his old wooden desk. Once again, Ty followed her lead and took a seat in the other chair. Lacey folded her hands in her lap and waited for the trustee to speak.

As if sensing her discomfort, Ty reached over and covered her hand with his stronger, warmer one, offering her his strength. She appreciated it more than he realized.

The older man cleared his throat. "I'd be happy to get started. However I'd prefer to discuss these matters in private," he said, his gaze settling on Ty.

Dunne obviously wanted Ty to leave the room, but Lacey decided she was calling the shots. She was too nervous to remember

anything said in this room today and another set of ears would help her recall it.
Besides, Paul Dunne's cold aura gave Lacey
the creeps. And the last reason she wanted
Ty here had everything to do with the
strange things happening around her lately.
She'd be with people she knew well and
trusted or none at all.

"Ty stays," Lacey insisted.

Dunne nodded. "As you wish." He settled
into his chair and pulled out a blue-backed
set of papers. "These are your parents' final
wishes."

He read through the basic terms of their
will and she discovered that in addition to
the huge sum of money in the trust, her
mother and father's house would also revert
to her. Stunned, Lacey barely heard the rest.

Finally the older man finished. "Do you
understand what I just read?"

She shook her head. "I'm sorry. Can you
repeat that?"

"The gist of it is you must claim the
money in person on your twenty-seventh
birthday or any time thereafter. Should you
die prior to that date, the money is divided
between your father's brothers Robert and
Marc."

Lacey shook her head. "That can't be
right. Uncle Marc always said I would

inherit at twenty-one." In fact he'd counted on her signing the handling of her money over to him by then; the day she overheard that conversation was still vivid in her mind.

Beside her, Ty remained silent.

Paul Dunne steepled his fingers and met her gaze. "I can assure you these are your parents' wishes. I can't imagine why your uncle would have told you otherwise."

"Probably because he was hoping he could have convinced her to trust him enough to sign her money over to him when she was younger," Ty muttered in disgust.

Lacey nodded in agreement. Ty's reasoning made perfect sense, but the trustee shook his head.

"Lillian, you must admit you were a difficult child. I'm certain if your uncle misled you it was only because he knew someone with your — how shall I say it — your lack of maturity needed him more than you understood."

She pushed herself out of her seat. "You're condoning his lie?" Not to mention validating what she'd already thought of Paul Dunne. He was a disinterested paper pusher who hadn't given a damn about her as a child any more than he did now.

"Of course not. I'm just offering a possible explanation. Your uncle's lies were uncalled for. Assuming things happened as you remembered them. Isn't it possible that with the trauma of losing your parents, you were confused back then?"

Lacey stepped forward at the same time Ty rose and pulled her backwards until he had an arm wrapped around her waist. "I think speculating about the past is useless. What Lilly needs now is for you to explain to her what the next steps are for her to claim the money on her twenty-seventh birthday which is —"

"Next month," she said, suddenly becoming more aware of the other parts of her parents' will. "Why twenty-seven? Isn't that an odd number?"

Paul straightened his papers. "It isn't uncommon for parents and guardians to delay the distribution of money to their children until they've grown up. In this case, there are yearly allotments paid out of the interest on the money that came due each year. Those were designated for the care and upkeep of the house and land and were paid to your guardian, Marc Dumont. Your guardian also had the right to request money at the trustee's discretion for your care."

Lacey did her best not to snort at that last comment.

"But to answer your question, the reason you can't claim the money until you turn twenty-seven is that your parents wanted you to have time to really live. They wanted you to go to college, or Europe, etc. while you were young. Once again, the interest would have paid for those things according to the trust agreement. They wanted you to learn about life before inheriting. Otherwise they feared you might go through the money unwisely."

"Little did they know how things would turn out," she said to Ty.

She ran her hands up and down her arms. Her parents had wanted her to have valuable life experiences and she'd had more than they could ever have imagined. Instead of college, she'd ended up in New York City barely surviving thanks to her uncle, her so-called guardian.

Ty pulled her close, his strong presence the only thing holding her up.

"Still, isn't twenty-seven an odd number? Wouldn't they have picked a number like twenty-five? Or thirty?" Ty asked.

"Your mother was a sentimental woman. She met your father at the age of twenty-seven. They married on April twenty-seventh." He shrugged. "Your father lived to indulge her," he explained.

"That makes an odd sort of sense," Ty said.

Hearing about her parents caused a lump to fill her throat and Lacey could only nod in agreement.

"So on Lacey's birthday, she can come here and sign the papers?" Ty asked, obviously understanding that she was unable to ask coherent questions herself.

"It's a little more complicated than that, but essentially yes. She signs and the papers need to be filed with the bank. Then she'll be able to access the money." He cleared his throat. "Now if you two will excuse me, I have another appointment I must prepare for."

Lacey was not ready to be dismissed. "Just how much money are we talking about, exactly?"

"Well there has been fluctuation of interest rates over the years." Paul Dunne fidgeted with his tie. "But approximately two point five million dollars."

And Lacey knew she only had to stay alive long enough to claim it.

They exited Dunne's offices and Ty led her out onto the street. He knew she'd been shaken by all she'd heard, especially the fact that she'd inherited her parents' home. He knew better than to bring up the subject now. She needed time to digest the information.

Ty stopped at a drugstore next door to the law firm and bought her a bottle of water before they settled into the car.

"You okay?" he asked, as he opened the bottle and handed it to her.

She nodded and drank some. "Surreal doesn't begin to describe things, huh?"

"That's one word for it."

She gripped the bottle hard. "The terms of the trust are proof. Uncle Marc is out to make sure I don't live to see my twenty-seventh birthday."

He let out a groan, hating to agree with her. He had no choice. "I don't see how it could be anyone else. But he's not going to touch you."

She grinned for the first time since walking into the office. "What would I do without you?" she asked, impulsively leaning over and kissing him on the cheek.

He sure as hell didn't want to find out, but they both knew she'd survive just fine. She'd already proven she could.

He turned his attention to starting the car. "I say we go back to my mother's. You can hang out with Digger, rest a little this afternoon and come with me to Night Owl's later on. I have to work the night shift and you need to get out among people."

"Ooh, a night out. I can't wait!" She perked up a little, her shoulders straightening at the thought. "Think I can help out, too? I'm so tired of not being busy."

Another sign this little idyll between them was soon coming to an end, Ty thought. "I'm sure you can convince the guy in charge to let you do some work."

Because that guy in charge tonight happened to be him, and he couldn't deny her anything. Including a return to New York City and the real life she loved.

Marc had taken the morning off from work to have his tuxedo fitted for his wedding, which was still scheduled for the first of next month. Of course, he still hadn't told his soon-to-be wife that Lilly's birthday a few days before that would effectively ensure he not only had no trust fund, he also had no place to live. Lilly would inherit the mansion as she rightly should, and he'd be out on the street. He couldn't imagine her allowing him to stay on and he'd never ask for the privilege. He certainly hadn't earned any rights at all.

He'd already been viewing luxury rentals closer to Albany. His salary allowed for an upscale standard of living, thank goodness.

He just didn't know if upscale would be enough for Francie, for whom nothing ever seemed to be enough. Marc didn't know why he loved her but he did. Flaws and all. Perhaps losing her would be his punishment for past sins, he thought, not for the first time. He also loved her daughter Molly and felt certain he'd lose her, as well, just as soon as she accepted the ugly truth about his past with Lilly.

He pulled into the long driveway leading to the house and immediately realized he had company. The black Cadillac indicated an ominous visitor. One he'd been deliberately ignoring since receiving the message demanding an audience. Marc had nothing to say to Paul Dunne. As far as Marc was concerned, the man had dug his own grave by siphoning funds from Lilly's estate over the years.

Marc pulled his car up beside Dunne's and stepped out into the cool fall air.

"You've been avoiding me," the other man said.

"That's because we have nothing to discuss."

The other man raised an eyebrow. "Apparently you aren't living in reality but I plan to enlighten you, starting now."

Marc slipped his keys into his pocket.

"You know what? I don't have time for this." He turned and started for the house.

"Make time." Paul stopped him with a hand on his arm. "Lillian cannot live to see her twenty-seventh birthday."

Marc rotated slowly. "Are you insane? Embezzling money is bad enough. You're looking to add murder to your list of accomplishments?"

Paul let out a laugh, his eyes filled with crazed determination. "Of course not. I intend to add it to yours."

"Now I know you've lost your mind." It took everything inside of Marc not to show his own panic at the man's words. He needed to stay calm and outtalk him, but first he had to discover what Paul Dunne had in mind.

Marc paused, deliberately remaining silent, waiting for Dunne to explain.

"The girl can't inherit. It's as simple as that."

"Why? Because as soon as she does, she'll find out about the missing money and have you arrested and thrown in jail?" Nothing would make Marc happier.

"Because I'd much rather have you inherit the shrinking pot of gold. I have as much on you as you have on me. Which means I know you won't report me to the authorities," Paul said with too much satisfaction. He rubbed his hands together, not due to the cool weather, Marc knew, but because he was certain he had the upper hand.

Marc swallowed hard. He wanted all the facts on the table. No surprises. "What is it you think you know?"

Paul grinned, his expression pure evil. "I know you lied to Lillian about the age at which she'd inherit so that you could manipulate her into signing her money over to you, her kindly uncle. And when that didn't work, I know your real personality came out and you abused the poor girl. And I know you basically sold her to Florence Benson."

Marc leaned against the trunk of his car for support.

Paul glanced up at the clear blue as if in thought.

Marc doubted he needed the time to think. No doubt he was just prolonging the agony.

"Oh, did I mention that I'm well aware of how you manipulated and bribed people in the foster care system to have Daniel Hunter removed from the Benson home. Essentially I know everything about you."

As Marc thought about everything he stood to lose, his job, his reputation such as it was, and his fiancée, fear crept through him, slowly at first before exploding inside his head. "Fine," he spat. "We're at a stalemate. I won't report you and you won't report me."

"Good. Now let's discuss getting you to the point where you inherit, not Lillian. You need to take care of her. *For good.*"

"Hell no," Marc said, nausea swamping him. "I'd rather let you spill what you know and take my chances with what you can and cannot prove than do your dirty work."

Paul straightened his shoulders. As if he sensed Marc's fear, he stepped close, suffocating him with his presence. "I've already tried to handle things on my own but I've discovered that when you hire someone, they need to have something at stake or else incompetence rules."

"You had someone try to run her down at the mall? And set fire to Tyler Benson's apartment?" Marc asked, realization dawning.

Paul neither confirmed nor denied the accusations but Marc knew he was dead-on.

"You're disgusting," he muttered.

"Practical, just as you used to be. Lack of alcohol has dulled your edge."

Marc shook his head. "It's made me human."

The trustee shrugged. "You just see to it that Lillian suffers an unfortunate accident or I will. And just who do you think they'll blame when she dies? Her uncle, of course," he said without missing a beat. "After all, your *reformation* must be an act. You wanted the money all along, as I'll have to tell them. And you need the money now to support your greedy wife or else you'll lose her. That's motive if you ask me. Oh, and don't worry about your brother. I'll see to it he gets enough inheritance to care for his wife. He won't question anything beyond that. Robert was always scatterbrained. He doesn't even know how much was in the actual trust fund."

An old rage raced through Marc as he recalled the years of dealing with this man. Whenever Marc needed money, he'd have to go through Paul. Marc had asked Paul for money years before, and the other man had complied, using the interest in Lilly's trust account. Marc had paid Florence Benson with the money. It was no wonder the other man made it a point to find out what Marc had needed the money for.

Beneath his suit, Marc broke into a heated sweat and the desire for a drink to numb the pain was all-consuming.

"I really need to be going. No need to make a decision now. You can get back to me. Lilly's birthday isn't for a few weeks." Paul patted Marc condescendingly on the back.

Marc shrugged off his touch.

"If you remain a good boy, you can console yourself with the fact that you won't have to go through alcohol withdrawal in jail. That wouldn't be pleasant at all." Paul turned and headed for his car, settling himself inside and starting the engine.

He waved as if they'd had a social visit, then pulled down the long driveway, leaving Marc alone to ponder his fate which looked bleaker by the minute.

Marc was cornered and the bastard knew it. All choices led to the same result. He could do as Paul asked and never be able to look himself in the mirror again — which probably wouldn't matter since he'd end up in jail — or he'd wind up there anyway thanks to Paul Dunne's so-called proof and the other man's stellar reputation in the community.

"Damn." He kicked his foot against his tire, accomplishing little perhaps except breaking his toe.

He winced at the throbbing pain and slowly walked to the house. At one time, the mansion had represented everything he'd wanted out of life. Today the old house merely stood as glaring proof of what jealousy of his brother had done to Marc's life. How ironic, now that he could no longer stand to look at the place, he was destined to get his wish and lose the house and a whole lot more.

Unless he could find a way to outwit Paul Dunne. It was either that or cave in to his demands. What a choice, Marc thought. Unfortunately it was nothing more than he deserved.

TWELVE

Later that night, Ty stood behind the bar at Night Owl's, filling in for Rufus so he could go to his son's Back to School night. The place filled quickly and he appreciated how many people remembered Lilly and stopped to talk to her, making her feel welcome. He was glad she didn't have time to think about trust funds, her uncle, or someone trying to hurt her for at least a few hours.

When his cell phone rang, he glanced down and saw Derek's number. He picked up, told Derek to hang on, then turned to the other regular bartender. "Hey, Mike. Hold down the fort for a minute, will you?"

The guy nodded, freeing Ty up to take the call. He glanced at Lilly who was deep in conversation with Molly. Certain she was in good hands for a little while, Ty walked into the hall and closed himself in the quiet back office.

"What's up?" he asked Derek.

"I think we got ourselves a break." The other man's excitement hummed through the cellular lines. "Dumont had a visitor around 11:30 this morning."

Ty seated himself on the top of Derek's old desk. "Finally. Who was it?" he asked, his own adrenaline increasing.

"I didn't know at first so I had Frank run a check on the license plate and get this. The vehicle belongs to Paul Dunne, of Dunne and Dunne, LLP. It's a —"

"Law firm," Ty said, finishing Derek's sentence. "I know exactly who we're dealing with."

What he didn't know was why Paul Dunne would pay Dumont a visit unless it involved Lilly's trust fund. Of course it was possible the two men were friends, but it was even more likely Dunne was filling Dumont in on his earlier meeting with Lilly.

"Good job. Keep it up."

"Will do, boss. Anything else I can do for you?"

He thought for a minute before replying. "As a matter of fact, there is. You can have Frank see what kind of connection, if any, he can dig up between Marc Dumont and Paul Dunne other than Paul being trustee of the Dumont estate."

Hell, Ty figured Hunter could ask Molly

to get some answers out of Anna Marie, as well. That is if Molly was willing. Ty had no doubt she had a thing for Hunter, but he didn't know whether she'd put her love life before her family. They didn't have much time to find out since they didn't know when her uncle would strike next.

"Consider it done," Derek said.

"Thanks." At least Ty would get information from somewhere.

Derek disconnected the line first.

Ty dialed Hunter who was working at his office and asked the other man to drop everything and meet Ty and Lilly here for a quick meeting. Then Ty headed back to the door, a part of him frustrated that he couldn't do the digging himself. He enjoyed his work and would love to be the one to find the information to nail that bastard Dumont once and for all. But keeping Lilly safe was his priority and he needed to be around to do that.

He rejoined the noisy bar and his gaze immediately zeroed in on Lilly. He immediately decided *not* to tell her about Paul Dunne's visit to her uncle just yet. She'd been so excited to join him tonight, to see how he worked, who his friends were and to just enjoy the evening. He didn't see the point in disrupting the only time she'd had to forget about her problems. She'd find out soon enough once Hunter arrived.

He wiped down the bar with a damp rag, lost in thought, his attention drifting to Lilly in between serving drinks.

Finally he heard a familiar voice. "Sea Breeze please, Bartender."

He glanced up into the eyes of Gloria, the woman he'd been dating — make that sleeping with — up until Lilly's return to his life.

Since he and Lilly had discussed Alex this morning, Gloria *had* been on Ty's mind. He'd decided to set up a time for them to meet while Lilly remained at home with his mother. He'd called her while Lilly showered, but she hadn't been home and he hadn't felt comfortable leaving a message. For one thing, he didn't want her calling him back while Lilly was around and for another, Gloria deserved better than a quick brush-off.

Sometimes, no matter how well he tried to plan, life had a way of screwing things up anyway, he thought.

"Hi, stranger." Gloria squeezed in between two people lined up at the bar and leaned closer.

"Hi, yourself." He treated her to a warm smile and mixed her drink, sliding the glass toward her. "Here you go."

"Thanks. Do you think you can take a short break so we can talk?" she asked, tucking a strand of hair behind her ear.

She'd pulled her dark hair into an updo thing he usually found sexy but now he just felt sick. Still, he hoped he had a good enough read on their no-strings relationship that she wouldn't be *needing* her drink after they spoke.

He nodded and came around to the front of the bar. On the way, his gaze strayed to Lilly but thankfully she seemed busy.

He took Gloria's elbow and led her to a private corner where they could talk without being overheard. "I've been meaning to call," he said, hearing his lame words for what they were.

"We've never played games before," she said, her voice light and chiding despite the hurt he noticed in her eyes.

He acknowledged the truth with a tilt of his head.

She let out a breath of air before continuing. "I didn't grow up in Hawken's Cove but as a waitress, I've heard the town gossip over the years. And I know Lilly Dumont's back home."

Ty opened his mouth, then shut it again. He wasn't sure where Gloria was going with the conversation, since he'd never discussed Lilly with her or with anyone for that matter. Not in years. His heart beat rapidly in his chest, not wanting to hurt this woman who'd been good to him, any more than he wanted to continue with their relationship. Since Lilly's return, he understood there wasn't room for anybody else in his life, even if she didn't stay there.

"In fact, I hear Lilly's living with you. Or she was until the fire." Gloria reached out and touched his arm. "I'm glad you're okay," she said softly. "Even if I do want to throttle you."

"Gloria, I really am sorry."

"But you never promised me anything more than what we had. I get it." But a sad smile lifted her lips. "I've been here for a while watching you."

"I didn't realize."

She shook her head. "You wouldn't have. You were too busy watching her. And I suddenly understood exactly why I could never get through to you." Looking tired, she leaned to the side, propping one shoulder against the wall. "It was because your heart belonged to someone else."

He was surprised she could see him so

clearly. "You and I had some good times." The words were lame but true. "I thought we were both looking for the same thing in a relationship." Which was why the fact that she was hurt surprised him now. He'd genuinely believed they both wanted an easygoing thing that was convenient when it happened to work out.

"That's the problem with men," Gloria said with a dull laugh. "You take words at face value. Of course I said it, because that's what you wanted. But deep down, I was hoping I'd be the one to break through those walls of yours, you know?"

"I guess that's the problem. I didn't know," he said, feeling somewhat betrayed by the lie, even as he understood the reasoning behind it. If she'd admitted what she'd really desired, he'd have walked away fast.

She shrugged. "I wish you well, Ty. I really do." She turned and walked toward the door.

He'd caught the glimmer of tears in her eyes and so he let her go. There was no reason to call her back. No way he'd give her false hope.

She was right. Lilly owned his heart.

Lacey pasted a smile on her face and tried to focus on what Molly was saying, something about the great sales at the mall next week. But Lacey couldn't think beyond today let alone seven days from now. Every time she tried to plan ahead in her mind, anxiety raced through her. Still, she knew she couldn't stay away from work much longer. She'd already been in Hawken's Cove too long.

Long enough to confirm her feelings for Ty and the direct conflict they posed to her established life at home. It wasn't that she'd denied her feelings for the last few days, but she'd refused to dissect them, wanting to live in the moment. Living for the moment was easier than making difficult choices. Choices that might rip them apart again, this time forever.

Unfortunately, this moment also included Ty deep in conversation with a woman at the far end of the room. Lacey couldn't tear her gaze away. She'd watched the pretty dark-haired woman make her way to the bar and talk to Ty. He'd mixed her a drink and a second later, he'd come around to where she stood, taken her hand and led her to a secluded corner of the room.

Nausea nearly suffocated Lilly at the sight. But as hard as she'd tried to concentrate on Molly, her gaze kept straying back to *them.*

"Now I see what has you so distracted,"

Molly said, snapping a finger in front of Lacey's eyes.

"What? Sorry. I wasn't paying attention," Lacey admitted. She refocused her attention on Molly, telling herself whatever was going on between Ty and that woman was none of her business.

It was a lie and she knew it.

"You haven't been paying attention to me for a while." Molly laughed, her good nature coming through.

"How'd you know?"

"The scowl on your face gave you away. Nobody frowns over a good clothing sale!" Molly laughed but quickly sobered, her stare traveling to the couple in the corner. "You have to realize she's no competition for you."

Heat rose to Lacey's face. "I can't believe you caught me watching them," she said, mortified.

"It's human nature to be curious." Molly snagged a peanut from a dish on the bar and popped it into her mouth. "But what I said about her not being competition is true. I've seen the way Ty looks at you and *whew!*" She fanned her face with a small napkin.

Lacey couldn't deny Ty's heated looks, but she'd noticed something disturbing — an intimacy — when she'd watched him with the other woman. "They've slept together."

"And you know this, how?" Molly leveled her with a curious stare.

"Woman's intuition." Lacey shivered and folded her arms across her chest.

"Even if you're right, it's over now," Ty said, coming up behind her.

"Caught again." She covered her face with her hands and groaned.

Molly chuckled. "I think this is where I excuse myself. I see some friends from work. It's time for me to join them." She waved and walked away, leaving Lacey to face the music.

"I'm sorry I was spying on you." She bit the inside of her cheek.

"I'm not. I'd have told you about our talk anyway." He pulled out the stool Molly had used and seated himself next to Lacey.

She swallowed hard. "But you hadn't told me yet. In fact, you never mentioned her at all while I told you all about Alex."

For all that she and Ty had been close, she realized now there were still things they didn't know about one another. There were still secrets between them.

"I didn't tell you because there was nothing for you to know. Gloria filled a need in my life just like Alex filled one in yours."

He reached out and tucked a strand of her hair behind her ear.

His hand was warm, his touch arousing. That was the problem, she thought. He could distract her easily and make her forget anything but him.

She refused to get sidetracked now. Although he'd said it was over, there was still something she needed to know. "Did you love her?"

As Lacey spoke, she suddenly understood how Ty must have felt hearing about her relationship with Alex. It hurt to ask. It would hurt even more to hear about it.

He shook his head and a weight lifted off her chest.

"There's only one thing you need to know about Gloria," Ty said in his gruff, sexy voice.

Butterflies took up residence in her belly, a warm fluttering feeling she savored. "And what's that?"

"She wasn't you."

Tears welled up in her eyes. She felt ridiculous reacting in such an emotional way but she couldn't control her relief or the overwhelming gratitude filling her. She couldn't speak but figured the wide smile on her face would be a good enough reply.

He cupped his hands around her cheeks

and tilted her head back. Slowly, without his gaze ever leaving hers, he lowered his head and let his lips touch, then seal their emotions. All the things they hadn't said, Lacey felt in the sweet, reverent way his mouth lingered on hers.

Too soon, he pulled back. "I really have to get back to work."

She nodded and gave him permission with a flirty wave of her hand.

They both knew where they'd pick up later on.

Hunter had been going over questions for a witness when Ty called. Although he'd never have said no based on the urgency in his friend's voice, he could definitely use the break. By the time he strode into Night Owl's, it was nearing eleven. Since he'd still have to finish up at the office later, he didn't glance around, not wanting to waste time on small talk with friends.

Five minutes later, he, Ty and Lilly were seated around a small table in the back. Four college students had finally stumbled out, laughing and making way too much noise. Hunter couldn't ever remember being as loose and carefree in those days — he'd been too preoccupied with "making good," as he'd come to think of his quest to achieve.

"I didn't know you'd asked Hunter to come by. What's going on?" Lilly asked.

Hunter raised an eyebrow. He'd figured Lilly was up on everything Ty knew.

"I got a call from Derek earlier and he said your uncle had an interesting visitor today," Ty said.

"Who?" Hunter and Lilly asked at the same time.

Ty leaned forward in his seat. "Not long after we left his office this morning, Paul Dunne paid Dumont a visit. Unless there's a piece of the puzzle I'm missing, I can't think of a damn reason why, unless it had something to do with Lilly's trust fund."

"Oh man." Hunter ran a hand through his hair.

Lilly, who'd grown pale on hearing Ty's rationale, remained silent.

"Do you know something I don't? Does Dumont have a relationship of some kind with Paul Dunne? Are they golfing buddies?" Ty asked. "Help me here because otherwise —"

"Let's just stop looking for excuses where there are none," Lilly said at last. "We all know Uncle Marc wanted my trust fund ten years ago and that hasn't changed. What has changed is that now he also wants me *dead*."

The word reverberated between them.

"I agree," Ty said.

"So do I. The question is what are we going to do about it?" Hunter asked.

"I'm not going to go into hiding," Lilly said before either Hunter or Ty could suggest it, although Hunter thought the idea had merit.

"Why the hell not? Would you rather make yourself a walking target? Because the next time he probably won't miss." Ty visibly shuddered at the possibility.

Lilly frowned. "Well, I'm finished hiding from the man. Wasn't that the reason I came back in the first place? To face him down? To deal with my past? Well, I'm going to deal with it."

Hunter decided it was time to step in between the two disagreeing lovers. He hated to side with Ty and piss Lilly off, but the other man had a point.

Hunter turned to Lilly who'd called him this afternoon to explain the trust agreement. "I don't know if you realize but considering the terms of the trust fund, you have three weeks to — how do I put this delicately? — you have three weeks to remain alive in order to claim your trust fund. I don't think waving a red flag in front of your uncle is going to help you do that," Hunter said.

"Exactly." Ty emphasized his point by pounding his fist against the table.

Hunter winced, sensing that his friend's take-charge manner was going to set Lilly off.

She rose to her feet but smartly kept her voice low. "I'll give you two choices. I can go home for the next three weeks and come back to claim my trust fund on my birthday."

"And make yourself an easy target in the big city where nobody knows Dumont or can keep an eye on him in any way," Ty countered.

"Or I can stay here and make myself an easy target. We'll just have to be one step ahead of Uncle Marc and be ready for him when he strikes again."

This time Ty rose to his feet, as well. "Absolutely not."

Hunter groaned. "Will you two sit down? You're calling attention to us and that's not what we're looking for."

Surprisingly they both lowered themselves back into their chairs.

"I think Lilly's right," Hunter said to Ty. "Either we draw him out by keeping her out in public or he's going to strike again when we aren't prepared."

Ty frowned.

Hunter knew Ty well. Eventually he'd come around to their way of thinking, but not because he was afraid of confrontation. He wasn't. Because Hunter was right.

"You know I'm right. Dumont is going to come after Lilly either way, so we might as well let her live her life and be ready when he does." Hunter pointedly glanced at Ty. "Well?"

"Yeah," he muttered, obviously unhappy with the situation.

Lilly put her hand over his. "I appreciate the support," she said quietly.

Ty inclined his head, saying nothing. But Lilly didn't need words nor did she need to be right for the sake of it, Hunter thought. This was why they were such a perfect fit. Lilly didn't gloat over a victory nor did she push Ty past what he could handle. She stood up for herself but also respected his views. Hopefully they'd have a chance at a future when all this was over.

Hopefully he and Molly would, as well.

Hunter stood. "I have to get back to work. I wish like hell I could help you two out but the court has me tied up with this case."

Lilly slid her chair back and rose.

Ty did the same.

"I'm just glad you're here and able to listen." Lilly walked over and gave Hunter a quick hug.

"You're doing exactly what we need," Ty said, his gratitude evident in all he didn't say.

"Listen, I'm going to go the ladies' room. I'll be right back." Lilly headed to the door a few feet away.

Ty turned back to Hunter. "One more thing. I have a favor to ask."

"Name it," Hunter said.

"See what Molly knows about Dumont's relationship with Paul Dunne. I didn't like the man at all and if they're connected in any way, it can't be good."

Hunter nodded. "I hear you."

Ty cleared his throat.

"I'm just sorry Molly's involved with that bastard at all," Hunter said. "Have the cops found anything remotely connecting Dumont to the fire?"

"No, because there's nothing to be found," Molly said as she came up behind Hunter, wearing a tight-fitting, fire-engine-red spandex top.

Hunter refrained from whistling. He was in deep enough shit already.

Ty glanced at Molly and grimaced. "I

tried to warn you," he said to Hunter.

"Well, you needn't have bothered," Molly said. "I deserve to know exactly what Hunter thinks of my soon-to-be stepfather." She folded her hands across her chest, glaring at him.

"Bye, guys," Ty said, and with a regret-filled glance, he stepped away, leaving Hunter to deal with Molly.

Ty had done the right thing. Molly's anger was directed at Hunter. He had to fix things alone. Unfortunately he didn't think anything would mend this rift.

Not anymore.

After the start they'd made the other night, this was a huge setback and a knife-like pain stabbed him in the gut. Her opinion of him mattered and he'd obviously lost both her trust and her respect.

He stepped closer, speaking quietly. "To be fair, you know I never liked the man."

Molly straightened her shoulders, her walls firmly in place. "But I didn't think you'd go so far as to accuse him of attempted murder. My mother's marrying the man. She's in love with him. And I've seen the other side of him, the one you refuse to believe exists. I'm telling you, no matter what Marc did in the past, he is not a murderer now."

Hunter merely nodded, acknowledging her words if not agreeing with them.

"You do realize that I was with Lilly at the mall. Marc wouldn't win any brownie points with my mother by running me over."

"I didn't say what we believe is flawless. But if he hired someone, that person might not know who you were."

He already knew now he and Molly would never see eye to eye on this subject. Too bad this wasn't something on which either of them would be willing to compromise.

Instead of discussing the impossible, he changed the subject. "What's Dumont's relationship with Paul Dunne, do you know?"

She cocked her head to one side. "The trustee of Lacey's parents' will? I'd think that would be obvious."

He appreciated her spunk. "Why don't you enlighten the less informed among us?" He didn't know another way to get her to open up than to frustrate her with sarcasm.

She narrowed her gaze, clearly annoyed with him. "Paul Dunne is the trustee," she said slowly, enunciating each word as if he were an idiot. "That means he dispenses the money as per Lacey's parents' wishes. Which also means he met Marc over ten years ago. So whatever plot you think you've concocted between them, give it up."

At least she was answering his questions so Hunter figured he might as well keep going. "What about Anna Marie?" he asked.

"What about her?" Molly's tone grew even more wary if such a thing were possible.

"When Anna Marie overhears things, who does she repeat them to?"

Molly rolled her eyes. "Nearly everyone. Why?"

He didn't have a direct answer he could give Molly. Not yet. "And when Anna Marie finds out things in the courthouse from her job, have you ever heard her repeat them?"

"I'm not sure. What kind of things?" She lowered herself into a chair, indicating she wasn't going anywhere for the moment.

Though he hadn't breached her barriers, at least he'd piqued her interest. It was either that or the fact that he'd turned his questions away from Marc toward Anna Marie. Either way, the sparkle had returned to her eyes and she leaned toward him, not away from him.

He considered his answer carefully. "Things like which judge is sitting on my current case."

As he spoke, he joined her at the table, careful not to sit too close and rile her up again. No matter how much he wanted to break through the distance between them, he knew better than to think she'd allow him to.

He paused before continuing and pinched the bridge of his nose, deep in thought. He could trust Molly and fill her in on his suspicions or he could walk away. For Lilly, and most of all for the sake of any relationship he might salvage with Molly, he opted to trust.

"I think Anna Marie told her brother, Paul Dunne, about my court case and he had her move it up on the docket so I'd be too busy to get involved with Lilly and her trust fund."

Molly's nose scrunched up as she considered this. "Why would Anna Marie care about the trust fund one way or another?"

"I don't think she does. You know Anna Marie. She talks for the sake of talking without considering the consequences. In this case, it would be like collateral damage from a bomb when you consider who Anna Marie's brother is and his connection to Lilly's trust fund." He picked up the pepper and shook it upside down, letting the grinds spread all over the table. "You never know what's going to get hit or who's going to get hurt."

Her chin propped in her hand, Molly

studied the pepper from his analogy, obviously mulling over the possibilities before speaking.

He enjoyed watching the wheels turn in that sexy brain of hers. And he did find her mind as intriguing as her looks.

Finally she glanced up, meeting his gaze. "Okay, so Anna Marie tells her brother about her latest case —"

"Or maybe her brother asks her what's on my plate at the moment," he said, following the theory that the older woman was merely an innocent gossip. "Either way, I'm out of the picture. That leaves Ty and Lilly."

"Why would Dunne care who inherits the trust fund? He's just the trustee. The distributor of funds."

"Now that's the question that begs to be answered." Knowing he'd captured her interest and that she had the time as well as the means to question her older landlady, Hunter made his suggestion. "Maybe you could have tea on the porch and find out?"

"I could," Molly said slowly. "But let me make something clear. I wouldn't be doing it for you. I'd be doing it to clear Marc's name."

Hunter nodded. "Fair enough."

He'd get the information Ty and Lilly needed and Molly would discover Hunter had been right. Her faith in Dumont was misplaced. As much as Hunter would hate to see her hurt, she'd be better off knowing the truth.

Without warning, Molly pushed her chair back and rose to her feet. "I have to go."

"Wait." He stood and came up beside her, grasping her hand before she could pull away. "You and I may not agree right now, but I'm on your side. I only want what's best for you and I don't want to see you hurt."

Moisture filled her eyes and she blinked back tears. "Well, I'm sorry I can't appreciate that at the moment. I was honest with you. You know how important family is to me. You know this is my first chance at even having a relationship with my mother."

Hunter tried for pragmatic logic. "Don't you want that relationship to be real and not based on a middleman who might not be what's right for her?" Hunter asked.

"I can't argue with that and I'm not as big a fool as you might think. But I just can't let myself wonder about what would happen if you're right about Marc. I don't want to imagine myself all alone in the world again." She stepped back, pulling her hand out of his. She nearly tripped on a chair, steadying herself before he could help her.

Her pain lanced through him. "Molly, I'm sorry."

She shook her head. "Maybe. But you care more about being right than you do about what I need. I'll let you know if I find out anything." Without another word, she darted past him and wove her way through the crowd until she disappeared from view.

THIRTEEN

The next morning, Lacey curled up on the bed in Ty's old room with Digger by her side. She opened her agenda and phone book and checked in with all of her clients, making sure everyone was happy with the week's service and nothing had been missed in her absence. Then she called Laura to check on how the employees were handling things. To her relief, all was well but still, a part of her missed being needed. She'd been gone for a while now and the business she'd previously thrown all of her attention and devotion into was running smoothly without her.

With a professional cleaning service airing out and cleaning Ty's apartment, she had nothing useful to do there, either, at least according to him. And he refused to let her take a walk without him. He was busy with a potential client in his mother's den while Flo had gone out for the day with Dr. San-

ford, her new *friend,* as he'd been introduced. Lacey grinned because Flo had
looked so happy it was contagious.

Antsy, she decided to do some digging on
her uncle without Ty's help. She rummaged
through her purse for the number Molly
had given her last night. But when she
dialed the other woman at work, her secretary said Molly had taken the day off. Lacey
tried her at home next.

"Hello?" Molly answered the phone.

"Hi, it's Lacey." She pushed herself up
against the pillows. "I thought you'd be at
work."

"I wasn't feeling up to it."

Lacey frowned. "Are you sick?"

"Sick of everything," Molly muttered.

"What's wrong? If it has to do with my
uncle, I promise not to pass judgment,"
Lacey said, crossing her fingers behind her
back. At the very least, she wouldn't say
anything to upset her new friend.

Molly drew a breath so deep, Lacey heard
it on the other end of the line. "Last night
Hunter accused him of being behind the attempts on your life."

"I'm sorry." Lacey shut her eyes, feeling
badly for both of them.

"Well, I went to Marc and flat-out asked
him."

Lacey practically flew into a sitting position. "You told him we thought he was after me?"

Molly paused. "If it was true, knowing you suspected him would hardly stop him. Besides, none of you thinks he's doing his own dirty work, am I right?"

"Probably," Lilly admitted. "What did he say?" She twisted the phone cord around her finger until it cut off her circulation, then released the tension before rewinding the cord again.

"He said he could understand why you'd all come to that conclusion but it's not him."

"And you believed him."

Molly could hear the question in Lacey's voice. And she couldn't blame Lacey for asking. "The thing is, I want to believe him," she said softly. "I need to believe him. My mother's been married four other times. The first time to my father and that lasted for about five years, if you include the separation period. The next time I was eight and she made me stay home with a nanny. The next two times, I was at boarding school and then college. Not once did she ever ask me to come home, let alone be a part of the ceremony. This time, she wants me to be a bridesmaid when she marries Marc." As always when she talked about her mother's neglect, a lump grew large in her throat and she couldn't have spoken more even if she'd wanted to.

Which she didn't. She'd unloaded enough on someone who was practically a stranger. Then again, Lacey didn't feel like a stranger. Hunter had been right, damn him. Molly liked Lacey after all.

"I get it." Lacey's voice traveled through the phone line. "Marc is the first person who's brought you closer to your mother instead of further away."

"Exactly," Molly said, glad the other woman had made the connection. "Hunter knows that and he tries to understand but I can't deal with him on this subject."

"But you can deal with me?" Lacey asked incredulously. "How is that when I'm the one whose very existence has everyone in turmoil?"

Molly leaned her head back and laughed, understanding Lilly's question completely. She shut the top of the washing machine and moved into the kitchen, easing into a chair. "Here's the thing. If you lived here, I think we could be friends. But I don't have an emotional connection to you. So I can talk things through and we can disagree and I don't feel betrayed or hurt. And I can't expect you to take my side and be disappointed when you don't."

Which seemed to happen more and more with Hunter when it came to Marc Dumont.

"Am I making sense or talking nonsense?" Molly asked.

"Making sense." Lacey chuckled. "I just wish things were different for both you and Hunter."

Molly smiled. "Thank you for that. So now that we've covered my problems, what can I do for you?"

Lacey paused for so long, Molly knew what the subject would be and braced herself.

"Well it's awkward," Lacey said at last, confirming Molly's hunch. "But as you said, we seem to be able to talk to each other. So here goes. I have a couple of questions on the subject of my uncle and the trust fund. I'd like answers if you're comfortable giving them."

"I'll see what I can do," Molly said despite the tension building inside her.

"You know I stand to inherit the trust fund when I turn twenty-seven, right?"

"Actually, I haven't seen the agreement. I'd only gotten as far as meeting with Marc about the possibility of him claiming the trust. You came back alive before I could look into it."

"Well, the gist of it is, I inherit on my next birthday which just happens to be in a few weeks. That's why whoever wants me dead needs to make it happen before my birthday arrives and I claim the trust. After that, it's a moot point."

Lacey had diplomatically said *whoever* wanted her dead and didn't outright name Marc. Molly appreciated her attempt at being impartial. "What can I do to help?" Molly asked.

"I'd just like to know what Uncle Marc and Paul Dunne's current relationship is. My understanding is that the two met yesterday not long after we met with Paul at his office. I need to know why. Coincidence? Or are they in cahoots somehow?"

"Hunter asked me the same thing last night and I shut him out." Molly closed her eyes tight. "I'll find out," she promised Lacey.

Because she couldn't go on hiding from the truth forever.

"You don't know how much I appreciate it," Lacey said, gratitude evident in her tone.

Molly swallowed hard. "One more thing?"

"Of course."

"Tell Hunter that Anna Marie and I had

coffee this morning and I asked her about Fred Mercer's current case and she filled me in completely. I have no connection whatsoever to Fred and no reason for asking but Anna Marie gave up all the details I wanted."

Based on Hunter's request, Molly had pumped the older woman for information about a stranger just for the hell of it.

"Tell him if Anna Marie gave up that kind of information to me, she'd have no problem revealing Hunter's information to her brother." Molly gripped the receiver hard, knowing that each step she took brought her closer to some kind of revelation that would either clear the man who'd given her the beginning of a family — or destroy her hopes of ever having one.

"Molly?" Lacey asked.

"Yes?"

"You're the best," the other woman said. "And I know Hunter feels the same way."

Molly didn't know what to say, so she merely said a soft goodbye and hung up the phone.

Her throat hurt from holding back the tears. From knowing that in promising Lacey she'd get the information she needed, Molly had given her more than she'd ever given Hunter. At this point, Molly wouldn't blame him if he gave up on her. The thought stung. She knew she wasn't helping her own cause, but right now she didn't feel as though she could.

Ty let his newest client, an older woman who wanted to find the daughter she'd given up for adoption years ago, out the door. He promised her he'd begin at least a preliminary search now and he'd be in touch as soon as he had any leads. Ty knew he'd have to turn part of the workload over to Frank Mosca until he had time to resume his normal schedule. His life, Lilly's life, were both on hold until she claimed her trust fund. After that, who knew what would happen next.

Ironically while they were in limbo, they were getting reacquainted. A part of him was overjoyed, another part cautious and wary. Because while they remained here in Hawken's Cove, they were living Ty's life. He didn't know how she felt about the future and with all the turmoil in her life at the moment, it would be unfair of him to ask.

If and when they ever had that kind of conversation, there had to be nothing pulling them together except mutual desire. No trust fund, no death threats, no Alex, he thought, wondering if the other man was really a nonissue or if Lilly's feelings for the guy would return when she did. He refused to think about that while he had her here with him.

He walked into the bedroom she was using at his mother's and found her deep in thought, papers spread out around the bed. Digger lifted her lazy head up off the mattress, eyed Ty with a bored stare and laid her head back down again. The dog no longer fawned over Ty as if he was a new and exciting treat. Apparently his newness had worn off. Ty hoped Lilly didn't get tired of him as quickly.

She wore a white robe she'd bought during their quick trip to Target for basics. In the time she'd been here, he'd learned she loved to lounge in a terry bathrobe, giving him a good view of her long legs. The tie cinched her waist and the deep V in her cleavage drove him mad. Just because he'd grown used to the sight didn't mean it had stopped affecting him.

Each time he viewed her in that fluffy robe looking soft and ready, he grew hard immediately. His desire for her never ceased to amaze him, along with the deep feelings she dredged up from places inside him he thought long shut off from the rest of the world.

"Hey there," he said, letting her know he was there.

She glanced up at him and she smiled wide, her pleasure at seeing him obvious. "Hi, yourself. Good meeting?" she asked.

He stepped inside and shut the door behind him. "Actually yes. I've got myself a new client."

She nodded. "Excellent!" Her eyes glittered with excitement, then suddenly dulled without warning. "Wait. You can't devote yourself to a new case if you're worried about me all the time. Neither of us planned such a long stay and we certainly didn't count on having your apartment destroyed all because of me." She began to gather up her papers in a frenzied state as she continued. "I'm going to go back to New York until my birthday. My uncle won't follow me there. Now that the fire department has declared the fire arson and not an accident, he must know the police are keeping an eye on him. He'd be a fool to go after me now."

Ty wasn't letting her go anywhere, but first he needed to calm her down. "Stop for a minute and listen." He sat down beside her, then placed a hand over hers, stilling her movements.

Slowly, she raised her eyes to meet his.

"First, the police have our statements but they have no proof your uncle is involved with anything. We're watching him, but they're only in the background if something happens again. It's not the same thing as round-the-clock police surveillance. Do you understand what I'm saying?"

She nodded. "That you don't think I'm safe back home alone."

"Correct. Second, we're in this together. We always have been. Have I given you any reason to think you need to go it alone now?"

"No, but —"

He silenced her by leaning over and placing his lips on hers. He lingered there, savoring the minty taste of toothpaste and Lilly, his body reacting to her nearness, the desire for her building by the minute.

"No buts," he said, as he pulled back. "Now what did I interrupt when I came in?" he asked, wanting to change the subject.

"Work. Everything's running smoothly but I was just going over some changes in scheduling for next week and making sure it clicked with the amount of girls I have on hand." She stacked the papers and put them on the nightstand. "I have other news," she said, the light returning to her eyes.

"And what would that be?" he asked, glad for any subject that didn't include her going back to New York.

"I called Molly this morning. We had a long talk and she revealed a few interesting things. First, you and Hunter were right. Anna Marie could have been feeding information to her brother Paul. Probably not as a way to intentionally derail us, though. But it is possible that her brother used her love of gossip to further his own ends. We just don't know what those are." She pounded her fist against the mattress in frustration.

Ty thought for a moment. "It could be as a favor to Dumont. There's really no other reason for Paul Dunne to want to get Hunter out of the way."

"So all roads lead to Uncle Marc." Lilly's sadness filled the room.

"Had you been holding out hope that he'd changed?" Ty asked.

Lilly shrugged, feeling like an embarrassed child caught wishing for a unicorn on her birthday. "I know it's impossible, it just hurts so much to think someone who is related to me wants me *dead*."

"I know." He held out his arms and she crawled right in, snuggling against him. She needed his understanding.

Except suddenly understanding wasn't

314

enough. Just being close wasn't enough. Lilly turned to Ty. "Move to the center of the bed."

He blinked. "Okay . . ." He pushed himself to the middle of the bed and slid back against the headboard, shoving the dog out of his spot in the process.

Digger rose, stretched, and jumped off the bed, resettling herself on the floor.

"Now what?" Ty asked. His stare bore into hers, the electricity suddenly crackling in the air around them.

She grinned, unable to help herself. "Take your clothes off."

He laughed. "We always seem to be in the position of someone wearing too many articles of clothing."

"I wouldn't think me asking you to get naked would be a hardship." She crawled over and began to unbutton the collared shirt he'd chosen for his meeting with the new client.

"It isn't." While she worked on the buttons one by one, he reached for the sash of her robe, freeing the knot.

She parted his shirt. He pushed the collar of her robe aside. She bared his sexy chest. He slid the robe down her arms and she shook it off, leaving herself completely bare to his heated gaze.

He sucked in a sharp breath and immediately unbuttoned his pants. She hooked her fingers into the waistband and slid his pants and briefs down and off his legs.

"*Now* we're even," she said.

"Not even close." He glanced down at his erection and she followed his gaze, her own desire growing at the sight of his.

Because she felt safe with Ty, she also felt daring. "So what are you going to do about it?" she asked him, her words more of a *come and get me* dare than a question.

"Lie down and I'll show you."

Her pulse raced and a heavy thick dampness grew between her thighs. She inched toward the middle of the bed and reclined on her back.

He shook his head. "Flip over." His voice held a gruff edge.

Her excitement heightened, she did as he asked, stretching out facedown on the bed, her trust in him complete.

He straddled her with his thighs, and leaned forward, then pushed her hair off her neck and kissed her tingling skin.

"Mmm." She loved the feeling of his lips on her flesh.

He continued to slide his moist mouth over her back while massaging her shoulders with his hands. She shut her eyes and allowed him to take complete control of her body and she wasn't disappointed. His tongue slid over her skin and cool air caused her to tingle with growing awareness.

As he stretched over her, his member pushed deliciously against her backside and his body pressed hers into the bed beneath her. The effect was an erotic thrust of her pelvis into the mattress, causing a sudden rush of sensation to pulse through her, a throbbing awareness and a need for so much *more.*

He must have felt the arch of her back and sensed her need because suddenly he eased downwards and slipped his hand beneath her until one finger found her slick opening. She rolled her hips into the mattress, capturing his finger just as it slipped inside of her.

A low groan escaped the back of her throat but now that she had a part of him filling her, she was beyond caring. He began a slow, steady thrust with his hand, each gentle movement bringing her higher and closer to the orgasm that was just out of reach. Finally, everything around her exploded in bright light as she went up and over, into the most spectacular climax she'd ever had — short of having Ty inside her.

As she came back to earth, she became

more aware of her surroundings. She rolled over and faced him. "Wow?"

"Was that a question?" He laughed and reached for her.

"No, that was a definite wow." She grinned and next thing she knew, he'd pulled her on top of him.

He reached for the nightstand. "I stashed a few in here the other day," he said, pulling out protection and taking care of it quickly.

"Smart thinking."

He answered with a long, deep kiss, then lifted her hips and thrust himself into her, filling her completely.

She clasped her hands around his face and lowered her lips to his. He began to move inside her, the slow thrusts timed perfectly to bring her closer and closer not just to release, but to him.

His low groan told her he felt the intensity as well and the climb toward her second climax was even stronger and more spectacular than the first. And this time when she came, she wasn't alone. Everything exploded around her and she felt the moment he joined her for the ride, clasping his arms tight around her back, his hips locked solidly with hers.

Another orgasm hit her, taking her off guard. "I love you, Ty." Unguarded, the words escaped her lips just as she came back to earth.

The realization struck her hard and she rolled off him, turning away. Beside her, she heard him take care of their protection and she intended to use the time to escape.

They'd never spoken the words, no matter how many times she'd held them deep inside her. She hadn't known if they were reciprocated, hadn't known if he missed her, or thought about her, and hadn't known whether she'd ever see him again, let alone say those words aloud. And then years passed and she'd pushed the emotions away. She'd had to in order to survive.

But she knew now she loved him still. She'd never stopped. Tears began to flow and she started to climb out of bed before he could call her on what she'd said.

Before she could rise, he grabbed her arm. "Don't."

"Don't what?"

"Don't go. Don't run away. Don't leave without acknowledging what you just said."

Lacey turned back around and forced herself to meet his gaze. He hadn't shaved today and his day's worth of razor stubble added to his sexy air.

"I love you." She swallowed hard. "You had to know that without my telling you."

He shook his head. "Some words have to be said. They have to be heard in order to be believed."

Ty Benson was insecure about how she felt about him? She couldn't imagine it was true. "You didn't know?"

"I hoped."

She blinked in even more surprise. "You did? Why?"

"I'd think that would be obvious." His heated gaze settled on hers.

Lacey ran her tongue over her dry lips. "Are you going to keep me in suspense?" she asked, her stomach tied up in knots.

"Because I love you, too." He reached out and pulled her into his arms for a kiss that was as long and hot as the first time.

After they'd made love again, her stomach rumbled, interrupting their cuddling.

"You're hungry," he said.

She laughed. "Yeah. And your mother's going to be back from lunch and the movies soon. We need to get dressed."

"We're adults," he reminded her.

"But we're in her house."

He groaned. "I know, I know."

Lacey grinned. Even when they'd been together the first time in this house, he'd been careful that his mother didn't walk in on them or find them in a position that would make the older woman uncomfortable. Lacey felt the same way.

"I should shower," Lacey said, reluctant to get up and leave the warmth and security here in this bed with Ty.

"You start. I'll fix up the bed and join you. Then we can go out and get a bite to eat."

"Ty Benson, you're going to make the bed? Hell must have frozen over," she said, mocking his messy habits with a joke and a laugh.

He nodded, a sexy grin lifting his lips. "My mother always said the right woman would have me doing backflips to make her happy."

At his words, a sense of completeness filled Lacey and she refused to let the niggling fears and doubts enter her mind completely. New York, Odd Jobs, her trust fund and her other life would have to be dealt with but she'd waited ten years to be this happy and she was going to enjoy it for the moment.

In another hour, reality could intrude. But not just yet. These last few moments were for her and Ty alone.

She nodded and forced herself to climb out of bed and hit the shower in the hall. She stood under the hot spray and waited for Ty to join her.

Love. Well, hell. It wasn't like he hadn't known he was in love with her. He'd just never let himself think the words. Did he know she'd always been in love with him? It wasn't something he'd let himself think about, either, because as he knew, love didn't solve everything. There was still long distance, the business she lived for, and the life she'd made for herself in New York. So though he floated for the minute, he also knew better than to think life was settled and perfect, either.

He straightened the bed as he imagined only a guy could, with lumps and messy pillows, and figured his mother wouldn't notice. Then he grabbed his clothes and headed for the bathroom to join Lilly but the ring of his cell phone stopped him cold. He dug into the pocket of his jeans so he could answer, then rushed to pull on his clothes as he spoke to his mother's date.

Less than a minute later, he stood in the bathroom talking to Lilly who stood naked under the stream of water, her hair soaking wet. "Mom's in the hospital," he said, breaking the idyllic afternoon they'd shared.

His heart pounded hard in his chest. Fear raced through him, as it had since he'd

hung up on his call with Dr. Andrew Sanford.

Lilly dropped the bar of soap in her hand.
"What happened?"

"Dr. Sanford said she was light-headed in
the movie theater and next thing he knew,
she'd passed out on the floor. He was following the ambulance to the hospital when
he called."

"You need to go. I'll call a cab and meet
you there," she said.

He raised an eyebrow. "Did you forget
someone is just waiting for an opportunity
to catch you alone? I called Derek. It'll take
him five minutes to get here. I'll wait for
him outside and as soon as he gets here, I'll
leave. You can finish up and he'll bring you
over."

She frowned. "Is your mother conscious?"
Lilly asked.

He shook his head, unable to answer that
one verbally.

"Then get out of here, Ty. I'll be fine in
the five minutes it takes Derek to get here.
And I promise to wait for him, okay?"

Ty was torn, but Dr. Sanford *had* said her
vitals weren't stable —

"Go," Lilly said, already shutting the water
and reaching for the towel.

He nodded, then pushed open the sliding

glass shower door and gave her a too-brief kiss before running down the hall and to his car, hoping he'd get to the hospital in time.

FOURTEEN

Ty paced the hospital emergency waiting room. Though he was immediate family, the doctors needed time with his mother, who, thanks to the paramedics, had regained consciousness on the way to the hospital. In all likelihood she'd had a heart attack, at least according to Dr. Sanford but since the man was a psychiatrist, Ty wasn't convinced. He needed to know his mother would be okay.

He rubbed his hands over his eyes and checked his watch. He figured Lilly would be here with Derek any minute, which would ease one of his concerns.

He glanced up in time to see Dr. Sanford walk out of the back room where they'd taken Ty's mother. "What's going on?"

"They've stabilized her," the other man said, placing a hand on Ty's shoulder. "She's out of the woods but she needs to be admitted so they can monitor her."

Ty nodded. "Can I see her?"

"In a little while," he promised. "They aren't letting me in, either, in case that's bothering you." The older man spoke with the understanding of someone older, someone with kids of his own.

Ty tried not to squirm or show his discomfort with the conversation. "I appreciate you saying that, but I'm glad you were with my mother when she . . . you know."

Dr. Sanford nodded. "I'll come out as soon as I have something to report."

While the other man headed back through the double doors, Ty stepped outside into the cool fall air and opened his cell phone, turning it on. He'd tried to keep it on while inside but even with vibrate mode, a nurse had caught him and made him shut off the instrument.

He glanced down at his phone and realized Derek had called him more than once. He dialed the other man's cell phone. "What's up?" he asked as soon as Derek answered.

"The cops came by to question me. Seems Dumont called them and reported a stalker outside his home." Derek paused, then said, "I think he's got a friend on the inside because this guy's stalling me."

"You're telling me you haven't left for Lilly's yet?"

"No, but I bet Dumont has."

"I'm on my way." Ty slammed the cell closed and headed inside to tell Dr. Sanford he'd be back, and to keep him informed by phone of his mother's progress.

Then he sped toward his mother's house where he'd left Lilly alone.

Lacey paced the floor, periodically looking out the window for any sign of Derek's car. Derek had promised Ty he'd be there in fifteen minutes. Almost twenty-five had passed since Ty left for the hospital which was only five minutes away. Uncle Marc's place was ten minutes by car. Derek should have been here by now. Five more minutes and she'd grab the car keys on the kitchen counter and take Flo's car to the hospital herself.

She tapped her foot against the floor, then unable to stand around and do nothing any longer, she called for Digger who hopped off the couch and ran to her, tail wagging.

"Come on, girl. You need to go into the kitchen." Lacey walked toward the room where they'd set up gates, locked the dog in for her own safety, and snagged Flo's car keys.

With a last pat on Digger's head, Lacey grabbed her purse, opened the front door and came face-to-face with her uncle Marc. Fear rose in her throat and she tried to slam the door in his face but his foot stopped her.

"Go away." She pushed the door again but he was stronger.

"Lilly, we need to talk. *I* need to talk to you. It's important."

She shook her head. "I've seen your definition of talking. Hit and run and arson. Thanks but no thanks." Her heart rate sped up and she grew nauseous just looking at him.

"It wasn't me."

"Is there anyone else who wants my trust fund badly enough to put me in foster care to scare me so I'd come begging for you to help me and sign my birthright over to you? Is there someone else who'd inherit if I were dead?" She kicked uselessly at his foot which remained wedged in the door.

Where the hell was Derek? she wondered, panic racing around inside her.

He leaned his shoulder against the door frame. "Lilly, *please,* listen. It looks like I want you dead and I understand why you think I'm behind these things, but it isn't

328

me. I can explain. Just let me inside —"

"So you can kill me in the house and not on the street?"

He shook his head. "You always were a stubborn one," he muttered. "Fine, we'll talk here."

Before he could say another word, a car screeched down the street. Her uncle turned, and a loud bang echoed around her, like the backfire of a car.

"What was —"

Her uncle jerked, falling backwards onto her, nearly knocking her over. "Uncle Marc?" she asked.

Then she saw the blood.

Lacey screamed and glanced up from her uncle's body to the sight of the car door opening. She didn't stop to see who was climbing out. Unable to shut herself safely in the house because her uncle's prone body blocked the door, she scrambled over him and ran back inside.

Digger barked from inside the kitchen and Lacey ran in her direction, nearly tripping over the gate in her rush to get to the dog. At the edge of the kitchen was a door leading to the backyard. Just as she flung the door open and let Digger run out, she heard the sound of footsteps inside the house. Outside she'd be easy target practice but inside, she realized she had a chance.

Beyond the small alcove where her old bed used to be was a pantry door that Lacey used to use as a closet. It wasn't a full walk-in, but it was large enough for her to crouch inside, and not be seen. In seconds, she was able to duck into the alcove, jump behind the couch and slip into the small closet.

Whether or not she was spotted remained to be seen.

She hated tiny, dark spaces because they reminded her of the old places she'd slept during her early days in New York City. The bugs, the rats, the awful smells. She shuddered, wrapped her arms around her knees and waited.

Loud knocks and thuds sounded outside the door. Whoever had shot her uncle was looking for her. Shaking, Lacey hugged her legs tighter. She brought her hand up to the locket around her neck, thought about the man who'd given it to her, and she prayed the guy outside wouldn't think to look for her in here.

As she sat huddled in a ball, once again she was reminded of old times. This time she recalled her first real apartment in New York. The one with the broken lock. She'd drag her dresser in front of the door to keep the drunk next door from making good on his promise to join her at night. She'd sit huddled in bed, listening to him banging around his apartment. Only when he'd pass out and it grew silent, would she catch a few hours of sleep each night.

The same fear and nausea filled her now, only worse because instead of a drunk who made rude suggestions, outside was a man with a gun who wanted her dead. And she didn't know why.

Footsteps sounded louder. He'd obviously left the kitchen and she realized he'd walked toward the couch that blocked her hiding spot.

Shaking, she held her breath as the footsteps grew closer.

Closer.

She waited for the door to creak open before she shut her eyes, kicked her feet out, hoping to come in painful contact with any part of his body, and let out a scream.

The kick to his shin took Ty off guard. He sucked in a sharp breath. "Lilly!" He called her name loudly.

She didn't acknowledge him in any way. Her eyes were wide and unfocused, and she looked ready to barrel out of the closet and tackle him to the floor. His leg throbbed where she'd nailed him with her boot and he wasn't about to take a hit to the stomach or the groin next.

"Lilly!" he said again, grabbing her shoulders and shaking her until she opened her eyes and focused. On him.

"Ty? Ty. Oh my God." She threw herself into his arms, shaking and sobbing hysterically. "I thought you were him. When you opened the door, I thought you were him."

"Shh." He ran his hand down the back of her hair, his body trembling as badly as hers.

"Uncle Marc!" She pushed herself away from him and ran for the front door.

Ty grabbed her hand, yanking her back. "He's alive. I checked him when I got here and the police and ambulance are on their way."

"What about *him?* Where'd he go? The guy who shot Uncle Marc?" She visibly gagged at the recollection before steadying herself.

Ty exhaled a long breath. "Derek pulled up at the same time I did. The guy had just run out the back door. He probably heard us pull up, panicked and ran."

"I don't understand how you knew to come back." She wiped the moisture off her face with her hands.

"Derek reached me on my cell phone at

the hospital. Dumont called the police and reported a stalker. Obviously it was a ruse to get Derek waylaid so your uncle could come here to find you."

Ty still recalled the panic he'd felt getting the call, but that was nothing compared to the gut-wrenching fear he'd experienced when he'd pulled up here and seen Dumont lying in a pool of blood, the front door wide open and Lilly nowhere to be found.

"He got away." Derek walked in from the entry off the kitchen, breathing heavily. Frustration was etched all over his face. "The bastard went through the back bushes before I even got outside."

"Where's Digger?" Lilly asked, panic-stricken. "Where's my dog?"

"Safely in the kitchen," Derek promised her.

She slumped against Ty in relief.

"Did you get a look at the guy or his car?" Ty asked her.

She shook her head. "I never saw him at all. I think the car was a tan sedan of some sort. That's all I saw before he shot Uncle Marc."

Ty nodded. "I noticed the same color car parked in front of the neighbors', but nothing more. Derek?"

"Same here."

Ty's frustration grew since they'd lost their last link to finding out who the guy was.

Lilly grabbed Ty's hand suddenly and pulled him toward the front door.

Derek followed close behind.

She bent down beside her uncle who lay facedown with a bullet in his back. He didn't move.

Ty checked the pulse in his neck once more. "Faint but he's alive."

Sirens blared, sounding closer by the second.

"Uncle Marc?" Lilly asked, leaning her face close to his.

Ty put his hand on her back which was damp from sweat and fear. "He's unconscious."

"Who shot you?" Lilly asked the old man. "Who wants you dead? Were you telling me the truth when you said you weren't behind the attempts on my life? Were you?" She couldn't help demanding answers to the questions that haunted her.

Ty lifted her away from the man just as the paramedics ran up the front lawn, cleared them away from the area and got to work.

Seconds later, the police followed. The paramedics moved Dumont into the ambulance and transported him to the same hospital where Ty's mother had been admitted. Though he was anxious to get back to her, they sat through an hour of questioning in his mother's family room. Lilly answered everything she could while Ty and Derek did their part to help. Finally, the officer ran out of things to ask, at least for the moment.

"We need to get back to the hospital," Lilly finally said, still trembling.

The cop who'd been taking notes snapped his pad shut. "I'll need you to come by and give official statements, but you can go now."

"Those statements might not have been necessary if one of your men hadn't stalled me, giving Dumont the chance to get to Lilly and get himself shot," Derek muttered. "I'm licensed and he knew it the second I showed him my badge. He should have just let me go."

The cop, a guy who knew both Ty and Derek, nodded in understanding. "We'll look into what happened. I promise. In the meantime, I suggest you stick close to Lilly until we follow up any leads that come from the investigating team." He gestured to the rest of the house, indicating the forensics team who were checking footprints, interviewing neighbors and checking on other possible leads.

Guilt rushed through Ty for leaving Lilly alone in the first place. But with his mother in the hospital and Derek on his way, the decision had seemed like a safe one at the time.

"She's not leaving my sight again," he said, reaching for her hand and pulling it tight against his side. "Right now I'm getting her out of here." She didn't need any more time in the house with the frightening memories.

"Derek, can you take the dog?" Lilly asked. "I don't want to leave her here with all these strangers coming in and out."

The house had been designated a crime scene, something that would worry his mother sick — so he didn't plan on telling her just yet. When she was stronger, he'd fill her in on everything. And she *would* get stronger. She'd be fine. He had to believe that.

"Sure. I'm not on Dumont duty anymore."

"Right. The cops have someone watching him at the hospital until whoever shot him has been caught," Ty said.

"Who would want him dead?" Lilly asked.

"And who'd come after me if not Uncle Marc?"

Ty shook his head. He'd been sorting through possibilities since hearing Lilly's version of events. "He said he wasn't behind the attempts and he knew who was?"

She nodded. "I was petrified and I wouldn't let him into the house. But after he was shot, it actually seemed like he came to warn me, not hurt me."

Ty rubbed his eyes with the back of his hands. "Let's get to the hospital and see how my mother's doing. Maybe there'll be news on your uncle by then, too."

"And don't worry about your dog," Derek said, coming back into the room with Digger on her leash, trotting happily at the other man's feet.

"Looks like you got yourself a new lady," Ty said, laughing. He knew all too well how Digger attached herself to new people.

"She stinks," Derek said with a frown. "Did you ever think of getting her breath mints? She licked my face when I was putting her leash on and I swear to God, I nearly passed out."

Lilly grinned. "It's part of her charm. Take good care of her and thanks again."

They started for the door together, when Ty turned to Derek. "She likes to sleep with

337

you," he told the other man. "And she likes to be on top."

"Swell," he muttered.

And Lilly laughed for the first time in hours.

Ty had called Hunter about the incident at his mother's. Hunter had called Molly, knowing she'd want to be there when Dumont was brought in. He'd promised to meet up with her as soon as his meeting was over. She'd told him not to rush, that she was fine.

And she was fine. At least fine as far as Molly's life was concerned. As soon as she'd hung up with Hunter, Molly had called her mother.

"I really don't do hospitals," Francie had said.

Disgusted, Molly had slammed down the phone and driven straight to the hospital by herself.

Molly heard the distance in her mother's voice. She'd sensed it for a while. Ever since the party, when Francie had discovered Lilly was alive and well and stood to inherit the trust fund that would have been Marc's and by virtue of marriage, hers, as well.

Molly had hoped things would turn out differently this time, especially since her mother hadn't yet ended things with Marc. But with her mother's refusal to come to the hospital, Molly had to face the truth. Francie was merely biding her time, waiting until she had a lead on another eligible wealthy man or at least until she had an idea about where to find one. Knowing Francie, a cruise or a trip to Europe would be her next stop as she hunted for her next victim. She wouldn't think twice about leaving Molly behind. In fact Molly would be lucky if she received a goodbye. After all, she'd been this route before.

So much for family. So much for a mother loving her daughter and realizing her past mistakes. So much for Francie having changed.

Molly stepped through the automatic hospital doors and strode up to the check-in desk. "I'm here to see Marc Dumont," Molly said to the tired-looking woman sitting in front of her.

"Are you immediate family?"

Molly swallowed hard. "No."

The woman glanced down at the papers on her desk. "Mr. Dumont is not allowed visitors just yet. Have a seat and we'll let you know when you can see him."

Molly nodded. "I see. Thank you." She turned and headed for an empty chair in which to wait.

The longer she sat, the more uncomfortable she grew and she fidgeted, unable to remain still. She didn't belong here. She wasn't related to Marc and probably never would be. But he'd been good to her in ways nobody else had been and she wanted to make certain he would be okay.

She tapped her foot. She drummed her fingers against the armrest. And she waited.

"Molly?"

She glanced up and saw Lacey and Ty standing in front of her. She rose to her feet. "I didn't see you come in."

"You were deep in thought," Lacey said.

"Yeah. Not in a pleasant place, either. Are you okay? Hunter told me what happened. I can't believe Marc was shot right in front of you. Why did he come to see you in the first place?" Molly asked, still missing major parts of the story.

Lacey shrugged. "We never got that far. Is there any news?"

"Not yet."

"I need to go inside and see my mother," Ty said.

"I'm coming." She touched Molly's shoulder. "I'm sorry."

"Don't be sorry. Go. I'll be fine."

Lacey gave Molly a quick hug and walked

off with Ty.

Molly sighed. Her gaze followed the retreating couple until they disappeared behind the emergency room doors, then she glanced around the busy room. Most people were here with someone else. A friend, a family member. Someone they loved. Not Molly.

As she waited for news on Marc, she realized something profound. She'd spent too much time defending the man and not enough time sorting through the truth, only to end up exactly where she feared she'd be when all was said and done.

Alone.

A place where she had always been and a place she knew she would be for a long time to come.

Ty held on to Lilly's hand as he walked into the room where his mother lay sleeping. Earlier today Lilly had needed him but now he needed her. As he pulled a chair up to his mother's bedside, he was reminded of the last time he saw her this frail and sick.

He'd come home from college when she'd had her first heart attack and subsequent surgery and she'd lain sleeping in a sterile room much like this one, hooked up to machines similar to these. He'd taken one look at her and realized she was all he had in the world and he stood to lose her.

He felt the same way now. Because despite the fact that Lilly had returned, despite loving each other, there were no promises exchanged, no guarantees made to each other. He knew they'd take things one day at a time until this trust fund issue was solved, but after that? Who knew.

The only constant in his life had been the woman whose frail hand he clasped in his.

"Ty?" He glanced up.

Dr. Sanford walked over to him, another man he'd never seen before by his side. "Ty, this is Dr. Miller. He's our newest cardiologist. He has some things he'd like to explain to you."

Ty listened as the young doctor who was also a surgeon explained that an angiogram showed his mother needed immediate surgery to reopen arteries that had closed off. More technical terms followed but the next thing he knew, he was signing a consent form and his mother was being wheeled out of the room.

Lilly placed her hand on Ty's shoulder. "She's going to be okay. The doctor said so himself."

He glanced up and into her comforting

eyes. "Did he? I barely remember the conversation."

She smiled. "That's why I listened carefully to every word. The surgery shouldn't take more than an hour and she'll be brought in to recovery where you can see her." Lilly wrapped her arms around his neck and pressed her cheek against his. "Then you'll see for yourself, okay?"

He covered her hand with his. "I'm glad you're here."

"I felt the same way when you opened that closet door and found me. How did you know where I'd be?"

He leaned backwards, against her. "Because I showed you that hiding space myself and I couldn't think of anyplace else you'd go that was safe." And he'd refused to believe she was anything other than okay, despite her uncle's bloody body lying at the front door.

Silence surrounded them until he couldn't stand it another minute. He needed a distraction from waiting for the surgery to begin, let alone end.

He glanced at the clock. "We have time to kill. We should check on your uncle and see what, if anything, the police have found."

Lilly straightened. "Now that sounds like a plan."

Except the guard dog nurse at the desk had no new information on Dumont. Not even the fact that Lilly was a blood relative uncovered any more news. So, along with Molly, they settled in to wait.

FIFTEEN

Twenty-four hours later, Flo was recovering from successful surgery. Lilly's uncle was still unconscious, the bullet having punctured his lung. The doctors expected him to recover, but they wouldn't allow visitors for a while.

Lilly, Ty, Hunter and Molly sat in the waiting area of the hospital, having moved out of the emergency room wing. The police were on their way to talk with them. They had new information and the hospital was as good a place as any to bring together all interested parties and fill them in.

Molly looked pale and she hadn't had much to say to Lacey or Ty since they'd met up here. Hunter had his intern doing research and he'd taken the day off to be with Molly, but she wasn't talking to him, either. Lacey didn't know if the other woman was upset over Marc's condition or the fact that Marc was obviously involved in something

bad enough to have ended up with him being shot on Ty's mother's doorstep.

Lacey was grateful when Don Otter, the
chief of police, walked in the door and broke
the silent tension.

"I'm glad you're all here," the chief said.

"Hey, Don." Ty rose to greet the man and
shake his hand.

The big man nodded.

"What brings you out so early in the
morning?" Ty asked.

Don settled his large body into a seat and
leaned forward, stretching the buttons over
his shirt. "My men have been all over the
site of the shooting. The footprints outside
definitely belonged to a man. Some matched
Marc Dumont's shoe we confiscated from
the hospital, the other prints are unknown.
No fingerprints beyond the obvious, Flo,
Lilly, Ty, etc. The bullet taken out of Dumont during surgery was sent to forensics
and we should have answers soon."

Lacey gagged.

Molly grabbed her hand.

How odd that the two women who felt so
drastically different about Marc Dumont
had formed such an unlikely bond, Lacey
thought.

"Then we started interviewing the neighbors," the chief said.

"Did anyone give you anything more on the car or the shooter beyond what we saw?" Ty asked.

"Which amounted to nothing useful," Lacey said in frustration.

"You were running for your life. Nobody's holding lack of detail against you," Hunter said. "Besides, we have a car color. I wouldn't call that nothing." Hunter shifted his gaze to the chief of police.

The man nodded his agreement. "And one of the neighbors reported the same car color you did, along with some new information."

"What did they see?" everyone asked at the same time.

The chief chuckled. "Ty, your mother's best friend and the neighbor across the street —"

"Mrs. Donelly?" Ty asked.

The other man nodded.

"Viola Donelly said she was sitting in her study that overlooks the street reading the latest John Grisham novel when a tan car pulled up in front of her house."

"Did she see the man get out of the car? Did she see who shot Marc?" Molly asked.

"Unfortunately no," the chief said. "But Viola managed to catch the first few numbers of the license plate," he said, obviously pleased. "We traced it back to Anna Marie Costanza, of all people."

Molly's gaze jerked toward Hunter.

Lacey knew what the other woman was thinking. Hunter believed Anna Marie had told her brother about Hunter's court case, and her brother, the trustee, had talked the judge into moving the date, keeping Hunter too busy to get involved with Lacey. Then her brother, the trustee, had paid Dumont a visit soon after he'd met with Lilly. And not long after that, Marc Dumont was shot while paying Lacey an unwelcome house call.

Lacey doubted she could explain it all to the police, but somehow, Ty summed it up for the chief in a clear, concise manner.

The big man scratched his head. "You're saying you think Paul Dunne's involved in the shooting?" the chief asked, surprised.

"And the attempts on Lilly's life," Ty said.

Molly jumped up from her seat, more animated than she'd been all morning. "Did Anna Marie ever say she lent her car to her brother, Paul?"

The chief shoved his hands into his front pants pocket. "Why?"

"Because she does that often. Anna Marie doesn't drive the car much except to work. She says she likes to keep the engine running smoothly, so she has Paul drive it about once a week."

Which meant Paul could have followed Uncle Marc to Lacey's. But why would the trustee want Uncle Marc dead, Lacey wondered.

The chief shook his head. "She said her car was stolen."

Hunter narrowed his gaze. "Had she reported it?"

"No."

"And didn't you find that suspicious?" Ty pushed the subject.

"We did, yes. But we don't have the car, so we can't dust it for prints. And even if we could, we now know finding Paul's fingerprints wouldn't amount to squat. There's a good reason for them to be there." Chief Otter shrugged. "Listen, guys, I see you have your theories and Ty, I trust your judgment, I really do. But in this case, you're accusing an upstanding citizen of our town without a shred of proof. And that means we have to be careful."

"Then search his house or his office. I'm sure you'll find *something*." Lacey pounded her fist against her thigh. "I don't know what the link is between Uncle Marc and Paul Dunne but there is one. I'm sure of it." Her voice cracked and she turned her head away in embarrassment.

Ty came up behind her chair and wrapped his arm around her shoulders.

"I'm sorry, but there's no probable cause for a warrant. We'll keep looking into it and when Marc Dumont regains consciousness, the hospital knows to call me immediately. Maybe he'll reveal something of interest."

"I'm not holding my breath," Lacey muttered.

Ty squeezed her tight. He must have known a search warrant was asking for the impossible.

The chief apologized and went to check on her uncle's status, leaving the four of them alone.

Lacey rose and started to walk away, unable to speak without screaming in frustration. She just couldn't believe they'd hit a brick wall. Again. Three incidents and they were no closer to finding out who wanted her, and now her uncle, dead.

"I have an idea," Molly said, stopping Lacey in her tracks.

Lacey pivoted. "I'm listening."

"Anna Marie wouldn't talk to the police but maybe she'll talk to us." Molly gestured between herself and Lacey. "She's a good woman. She might be protecting her brother but there's no way she knows she's hurting people in the process. I really believe if we talk to her, she might break down and give us something to go on."

Lacey nodded, slowly warming to the idea. "I like how you think."

"I don't," Ty said. "I don't want either of you going to question Anna Marie. If her brother *is* involved you're putting yourselves in the direct line of fire."

"Then come with us if you want to. But Molly's idea is a good one and we're going to talk to Anna Marie," Lacey said, her tone leaving no room for argument.

She couldn't allow Ty's fear, or even her own, to sway her. They had to end this thing once and for all.

Before the meeting with Anna Marie, Ty wanted to spend some time with his mother. Since Anna Marie wouldn't be home from work until later, he had the afternoon to spend at the hospital. Hunter had gone back to work, though he'd promised he'd meet Molly for dinner later. Molly had tried to avoid seeing Hunter again today but Hunter had insisted. Things didn't look good for the couple if Molly's withdrawn attitude was anything to go by. Ty felt awful for his friend. And he hoped he wouldn't find himself in a similar situation not too far in the future.

Ty had talked the chief into posting a plainclothes person in the hospital to keep an eye on Lilly, who very well could have been the target today, too. At the very least, the shooter might think Lilly could ID him and come after her to protect himself. Ty wasn't taking any chances with her safety. While the women went to the cafeteria for a cup of coffee, they had an escort.

Meanwhile, Ty waylaid the food service cart in the hallway and picked up his mother's tray. He knocked once and let himself in.

To his relief, Flo sat up against her pillows. Although she had an IV attached to her arm, the color had returned to her cheeks and she had a smile on her lips. A quick glance at the visitor's chair revealed the reason.

"Hello, Dr. Sanford," Ty said, setting the tray down on the mobile cart by the bed.

"Call me Andrew, please." The other man rose and extended his hand.

Ty shook it, pleased his mother wasn't alone and had someone in her life that obviously made her happy. She'd lived on her own for too long, Ty thought.

"Andrew, I'd like to have a word alone

with my son," his mother said.

The doctor strode to the bed, leaned down and kissed her on the cheek. "I'm going to visit some patients and I'll be back soon."

Ty waited until they were alone before pulling a chair up beside her. "You scared me," he admitted.

"I scared myself." She leaned back into the pillows. "The doctors say I can go about my normal routine though. There will be no repercussions."

He nodded, then paused in thought. They had to talk about her relationship with Dr. Sanford, among other things lingering between them, Ty thought.

"I like him," Ty said at last.

"Andrew?"

Ty nodded. "I like him because he seems to have your best interests at heart." And he'd shown that by being respectful to the mother/son bond.

Flo smiled again, the one that left her face beaming. She deserved that kind of happiness.

"There's something else I need to say." Ty rose and walked to the window overlooking the parking lot. "Nice view," he muttered.

His mother laughed. "It costs me extra."

He grinned. Her sense of humor had

returned, another good sign. "Mom . . ."

"The thing about loving someone is that you don't need to rehash things," his mother said, letting him off the hook.

He didn't deserve it. "That might apply had we hashed things out to begin with. We didn't. I didn't let you. Oh, you explained taking Marc Dumont's money and you said you'd done it for me, but my anger got in the way of hearing anything else."

He ran a hand through his hair, the memory of the day he'd discovered his mother had taken money in exchange for giving Lilly room and board, vivid in his mind.

"All kids think their parents are saints. It hurts to find out we're human," Flo said.

Ty stared out the window. "The thing is, it wasn't you I was angry at so much as myself." The admission wasn't an easy one for him to make.

"Why in the world would you be angry at yourself?" his mother asked.

Ty didn't turn around. He couldn't face his mother while confronting issues that had haunted him for years. But while she'd been in surgery, Ty had done a lot of thinking. With Lilly's head resting on his shoulder, he'd contemplated losing the mother he loved, and he forced himself to deal with what had *really* bothered him about learning she'd taken the money.

In reality, Flo's taking the cash had probably saved Lilly's life. To be mad at his mother for giving Lilly a good home in exchange for cash was ridiculous. It had just been easier to be upset with his mother than to face his anger at himself.

"It's complicated," he said. "All the while I was upset with you for not telling me Lilly wasn't really a foster kid, that I was angry at you for keeping the money a secret, I'd been keeping a huge secret of my own." He breathed in deep. "For years, I let you grieve, knowing Lilly was really alive." His pulse pounded in his temple as he spoke.

"We both made mistakes," his mother said. "Or should I say we both made choices that we felt were necessary at the time. Who knows? Maybe they were necessary," she said, once again letting him off the hook.

He wasn't ready to do the same thing for himself, at least not yet. Hopefully he'd reach that point, but first, he needed to say all that was on his mind.

"What else is bothering you, Tyler? What are you still holding inside of you?" his mother asked.

"Besides letting you suffer for ten years?" This time he turned, determined to face his mother while he admitted his mistakes.

His flaws.

His faults.

"What did I do? I sent Lilly off to New York alone. She was all of seventeen years old and I didn't go after her. Hell, I didn't even check on her for five goddamn years," Ty said in disgust.

And he'd used a ridiculous promise never to talk about that night again as an excuse for staying away. Then when he had discovered she was alive and living in Manhattan, he hadn't gone to find her. Instead he'd blamed *her* for not coming back to him. Talk about the height of arrogance. But it had taken Lilly's return, her nearly being killed and his mother's heart attack to open his eyes.

He'd been a coward, Ty thought.

"How old were *you* when we concocted that scheme to stage my death?"

Ty jerked away from his mother's bedside toward the unexpected sound of Lilly's voice. She stood in the doorway, tapping her foot and staring at him in disbelief.

"I believe she asked you a question, son," Flo said, a smile pulling at her mouth.

Ty cleared his throat. "I was eighteen."

"And you think that made you so much

older and wiser than me? You think that you should have known better?" Lilly asked, stepping into the room. "I'm sorry for interrupting, but I'm glad I did."

"So am I." Flo gestured for her to come in and stay. "She's got a point, you know."

Ty scowled. "Don't you two gang up on me," he muttered.

"Well, who appointed you everyone's guardian and savior?" Lilly asked. "Don't get me wrong. I've always been grateful that you looked out for me. Who knows what would have happened if I'd been forced to go back to Uncle Marc instead of staying in foster care with you? But nobody placed you in charge and certainly nobody designated you as the one who always had to get everything right. Cut yourself a break, Ty. I'm sorry to be the one to break it to you, but you just aren't perfect." She threw her hands in the air in disgust.

He let out a long puff of air. She didn't know it but she'd answered one important question. She hadn't heard them talking about his mother taking the money from her uncle. *That* secret, like the others, had to come out. Something else he'd realized while his mother had been under the knife.

"What do you mean I'm not perfect?" Ty asked, focusing on the lightest part of her monologue. "How could you say such a thing in front of my mother?" he asked in a joking tone.

Lilly frowned, obviously not finding him the least bit amusing.

"Well, this has been exhausting," Flo said. "I need to rest but Ty, you need to listen to Lilly. She's got more knowledge in her pretty head than the two of us combined." She leaned back against the pillows, her skin paler than when he'd entered the room.

Which meant his mother's secret would wait for another day, Ty thought. With any luck, so would the continuation of this conversation with Lilly.

They started for the door. His mother fell asleep almost before they left the room. Ty stopped by the nurses' station and asked them to make sure she ate when she woke up, then steered Lilly toward an empty alcove near the waiting room.

He pulled her into his arms and lowered his mouth to hers. Her lips softened and she wrapped her arms around his neck, letting out a soft little moan before kissing him back.

"Mmm." He threaded his hands through her hair and pulled her closer.

"Mmm is right," she said as she tipped her head back, breaking the kiss. "Unfortunately, we can't continue this now. We have to go talk to Anna Marie."

Ty groaned. "We do?"

"We do." Molly laughed, answering from behind them. "Besides, this isn't the place to play around. Someone might catch you."

"Someone did." Ty shifted on his feet, hoping his arousal would fade quickly. "Did I mention that I think you two talking to Anna Marie is a bad idea?"

"You're just worried about me," Lilly said. "But if we get her to cooperate, you'll think it's a great idea."

Before he could argue some more, Lilly leaned over and kissed his cheek. "Now let's go talk to your neighbor," she said to Molly.

Ty knew when he was outnumbered, especially by two determined women. He had no choice but to go along and keep them safe.

Lacey knew better than to hold out hope that Anna Marie Costanza would provide the key to solving all of her problems. Still, she couldn't stop the little voice chanting *please, please talk to us,* in her head.

The first fifteen minutes in the older woman's home were torture for Lilly. The house smelled of mothballs and Anna Marie took her time steeping tea for her guests regardless of their insistence that they didn't want or expect her to entertain them in any way.

"I sent flowers to your mother, Tyler," Anna Marie said as she placed delicate-looking flowered teacups on the table.

"That was sweet of you and I'm sure she'll appreciate them," he said.

Lacey noted he was kind enough not to tell her they didn't allow flowers in Flo's area of the hospital. The arrangement would probably be diverted to the children's wing, which would also be a nice gesture.

Molly took her time adding milk and sugar cubes to her tea, slowly stirring. She met Lacey's gaze, imploring her to do the same. Obviously Molly had been this route before and if they wanted to talk to Anna Marie, they had to drink and make idle chitchat before getting to anything serious.

Lacey was just so nervous, she was surprised she hadn't jumped up from her seat, grabbed the older woman by her frilly collar and shaken her for information.

Ty leaned back in his seat and waited. Obviously he'd decided he was exempt from tea drinking because he hadn't touched his fragile-looking cup. Probably from fear of breaking it, she thought.

"I sent flowers to your uncle, as well,

Lacey. Molly, dear, your mother must be devastated," Anna Marie said.

Molly murmured something unintelligible.

"Biscotti?" Anna Marie asked, gesturing toward a plate of almond cookies, quickly changing the subject.

"Don't mind if I do." Ty plucked one from the plate, took a bite, and grinned. "Delicious."

"I made them myself," Anna Marie said, pleased. "My mother taught me way back when. Being the only girl, we had lots of time together while my brothers were out doing things with my father."

"About your brothers," Lilly said, but Ty placed a warning hand on her thigh. They'd discussed taking things slow and leading into conversation. "It must have been interesting growing up with so many boys," Lacey said, instead of the accusations she wanted to make about Anna Marie's brother Paul.

Anna Marie launched into childhood stories, growing up in their hometown. "And that is how my father knew your father," the woman said to Lacey. "Like yours, my father loved antique cars. Actually he just loved cars. He taught me to take care of an automobile, which is why I am able to hang on to a car for so many years. Love it and keep it driven, my father used to say."

"So you must have been devastated when your car was stolen," Molly said, finally easing into the reason for their visit.

Lacey had to admit Molly had chosen the most benign way of doing it. She would have just barreled in.

"Yes, yes, I was quite upset." Anna Marie rose and carried her cup and saucer to the sink.

An obvious escape from having to look anyone in the eye, Lilly believed, and she didn't think she was looking for clues that didn't exist. The woman was nervous. And when her teacup toppled from the saucer into the sink, Lilly grew even more certain the other woman was uptight about something. But she wasn't mean or evil.

Watching her, something inside of Lilly softened. There was no way this gentle, kind woman had deliberately done anything to hurt anyone. At least, not knowingly.

Although Molly had broached the subject of the stolen car, Lacey suddenly thought of another way to reach Anna Marie and her conscience. "Your brothers must have been very protective of you. When we were younger, I know Ty and Hunter looked out for me just like I imagined real brothers would have."

Anna Marie turned away from the sink. "Oh yes. Would you believe I've had to do the same for them over the years? You wouldn't believe the things those boys got themselves into. I had to regularly come to their rescue with Mother and Dad," she said, remembering with a laugh.

Molly rose and walked over to the older woman. "I'm sure you still find yourself in the position of having to protect them, even now that they're grown men."

"No, they don't need me anymore. They humor me and listen to my stories from work, but they take good care of themselves now. And they have wives to look out for them, too."

"But blood is thicker than water, as one of my stepfathers used to say. I'm sure if, say Paul, needed a favor, he'd come to you first." Molly placed a comforting arm around the woman's shoulder. "Come sit," Molly urged, walking Anna Marie to a chair by the table. "Did the police tell you who-ever was driving your car also shot Marc Dumont?" Molly asked softly.

Anna Marie twisted her gnarled hands in her lap and didn't look up. "They came in here and asked all sorts of questions about my car. I told them it had been stolen." Her voice shook as she spoke. "They didn't tell me why they were asking until after I told them it had been stolen."

Molly knelt down beside her. "Except by then, you'd already lied to them to cover for your brother, Paul, right? Because he borrowed your car like he does sometimes? To love it and keep it running like your father said?"

Ty and Lacey remained silent, letting Molly, who had the relationship with Anna Marie, talk to her and draw her out.

Anna Marie nodded. "Paul never had it easy. He was the oldest and the burden of perfection and expectation always fell on him. He needed an escape and since we live so close to Saratoga, the horses provided one for him. He'd go to the track to place bets during the season. And soon the horses weren't enough."

"Paul has a gambling problem?" Ty asked.

"I don't know if it's a problem, but sometimes on the days he drives my car for me, he'll take it over to the track or to that offtrack betting place in the next town over." Anna Marie sighed. "I used to have to beg him to take my car. These days, he asks to borrow it. That's where I thought he was going. And when he asked me to say it had been stolen, I thought maybe someone had seen the car at the track. If it was stolen, nobody would link it to me or to him."

"So you agreed to cover for him and say it was stolen," Molly said.

Anna Marie pulled her sweater tighter around her. "Paul always has answers and takes care of things. I thought he'd handle it like he always did."

"Except the police came by and told you about the shooting," Molly said. "And you panicked."

"You bet I did. I haven't been able to eat or sleep since. I couldn't admit I'd lied or I'd be an accessory," she said, her history in the courthouse showing through. "And if I'd told them Paul had taken the car, they'd arrest him for shooting Marc Dumont, and I don't really know if he did it or not!"

Molly patted the older woman's hand in sympathy. "But you knew he asked you to lie, so he had to have been up to something that involved the shooting, right?"

The other woman bobbed her head up and down. "And he involved me. His only sister. His baby sister! But it was too late for me to tell the truth or so I thought. I wanted to talk to Paul first, then I was going to call the police myself."

"Have you spoken to Paul since?" Ty asked.

She shook her head. "Not since he called and asked me to say the car was stolen."

"Where is the car?" Lilly asked.

Anna Marie shrugged. "I don't know. And I don't know where Paul is. He left me here with all these unanswered questions and lies." The woman broke down, her shoulders shaking as she put her head in her hands.

While Molly consoled her, Ty pulled Lacey aside and spoke quietly. "We now know Anna Marie gave her car to her brother. That means the police have probable cause to search his garage for the car."

Lilly nodded. Her head was swimming with facts and disjointed pieces of information. She wanted to talk it through with Ty and make the connections. "What else have you put together?"

He rubbed his hand over his unshaven face. He had to be exhausted from sitting up all night with his mother at the hospital and she felt awful he had to deal with her problems, too. But she knew better than to suggest he leave and get some rest.

"I can't say I'm one hundred percent sure of anything at this point. But gamblers have to get their money from somewhere," Ty said.

"Maybe Paul had enough money to cover his gambling debts," Lacey said.

"He didn't." Anna Marie rose from her chair. "He's been broke for years, spending everything he has. I don't make enough to help him and my brothers even cut him off last year. But he always said he had a safety net."

Ty narrowed his gaze. "Do you know what that safety net was? Where he got the money to pay for his habit?"

Anna Marie shook her head.

"I bet I do," Ty said, suddenly. "For the last ten years, the man has had access to a trust fund that nobody could check on or look into until Lilly Dumont was declared legally dead or Marc Dumont claimed the money instead."

"But I'm alive," Lacey said.

"And Paul Dunne wanted to make sure you didn't stay that way long enough to claim the money and find out he'd been stealing from it," Ty said, his eyes blazing with certainty.

"No! Paul wouldn't kill anyone. He wouldn't hurt anyone," Anna Marie insisted, her voice rising.

Molly held on to the woman's hand. "Addiction does strange things to people," she said softly.

Lacey's head buzzed as she tried to process this theory. "If he'd succeeded in killing me, Uncle Marc would have inherited the money and *he'd* be the one to find out about the embezzlement."

Ty nodded. "Exactly."

"So maybe it *never* was Uncle Marc who was behind the attempts on my life." Lacey couldn't believe the relief she felt on voicing the possibility aloud.

Molly stepped forward. "Maybe Paul wanted you both dead," she suggested.

"But Derek and I showed up in time to stop him," Ty said.

Lacey felt light-headed and dizzy. "That still doesn't explain why Uncle Marc would come to see me that day."

Ty shrugged. "Some things we need him to answer for us, but in the meantime . . ." He flipped open his cell phone and dialed. "Chief?" He spoke into his cell phone. "It's Ty Benson."

Ten minutes later, the chief of police showed up at Anna Marie's house, the district attorney along with him. They listened as a crying but now calmer Anna Marie told the truth about her brother borrowing the car which they'd ID'd at the site of the shooting.

The police and the D.A. agreed they had enough proof to arrest Paul Dunne for a host of things, including the attempted murder of Marc Dumont and obstruction of justice in asking his sister to lie to the police about her car. They put out an APB on Paul Dunne.

In addition, the D.A. headed to court to obtain a search warrant for the man's garage to search for Anna Marie's car; and another warrant for his house and office to look at the trust fund files and documents. If Dunne had been embezzling from Lacey's trust in order to pay off his gambling debts, his motive for the shooting and even the arson at Ty's would be clear.

As for Anna Marie, no charges were filed against her because she'd come forward of her own free will. Knowing how much she loved her brother, turning him in was punishment enough. Like her gossip, this lie had been told with no ill intentions.

But until Paul Dunne had been arrested, and he and Uncle Marc revealed their motivations and roles in each event, Lacey remained in the dark and confused.

Much like she was about her life and her future.

SIXTEEN

Marc finished giving his statement to the police. He'd left nothing out. He had nothing left to hide.

With a stenographer present in his hospital room, he'd admitted everything leading up to the moment of his shooting, from the day he'd fallen in love with Rhona, lost her to his golden-boy brother, Eric, and become guardian to their daughter Lilly.

He'd included his foster care scheme in the story along with his hope that by scaring Lilly, she'd return pliant and willing to sign her trust fund over to him. Of course in his recent sobriety, he'd realized that she probably couldn't legally sign over anything until after she'd inherited at the age of twenty-seven, but alcohol had dulled his wits, and he'd believed in dreams of money coming his way. He explained how he knew Paul Dunne had embezzled, although not to the extent that he had.

And he admitted to getting trust money from Dunne to pay Flo Benson to take Lilly into her home and claim it was foster care. That one had elicited a shocked gasp from Lilly and a groan from Tyler Benson. Of course Tyler and his friend Hunter had been more than happy to hear him admit to using influence to have Hunter pulled from the Benson home after Lilly's 'death'. He'd neglected to go into detail about their role in faking Lilly's death — information he'd learned from Molly — because Marc had caused enough pain over the years. Everyone assumed she'd run away and as far as he was now concerned, that is what she'd done. Bravo for her.

Part of Marc's AA program was about apologizing and taking responsibility. It looked as if he was doing it big-time today. He told the police about how Paul Dunne had been behind the near hit-and-run on Lilly as well as the fire at Ty's apartment. He described the other man's plan to have Marc do his dirty work and included Dunne's threat to frame Marc either way. He'd refused, calling the other man on his cell phone the day of the shooting.

Marc's solution instead had been to go to Lilly and tell her the truth. Unfortunately Dunne had been scared to death that Marc would reveal all of his transgressions. His fear of losing his status as a respected attorney had overwhelmed him. While Marc had been worrying about waylaying Tyler Benson's watchdog P.I., Dunne had followed him to see Lilly. Marc had been so preoccupied, he'd never seen the man until he felt the burning, searing pain in his back.

Though he'd turned his life around and was actually helping the police capture the guilty party, the woman he was supposed to marry wasn't impressed with him. Francie's scowl and cool attitude froze the room. Marc sensed it without looking her way. Their confrontation would come next, he was sure. After which, she would stomp out in her Jimmy Choos that were probably on his current credit card statement. Next time around, he needed to find a poor woman with few needs except love, he thought wryly.

Then there was Molly. She stood behind her mother's chair. A good woman, she'd taken this hard because in Marc, she'd seen a chance at family. The poor girl had made the mistake of putting her hopes in him. He'd disappointed everyone in his life. The bright-eyed lawyer would be no different. But he'd have been proud to call her his daughter and he needed to tell her so. For all the good it would do.

What a goddamn mess.

The police finally took off, as did Ty, Hunter and Lilly, all without a word. They knew better than to stick around for the show. But he and Lilly had unfinished business to discuss, assuming he was still conscious when Francie was finished with him. Marc didn't wonder where his sense of humor was coming from. It was all he had left, all he owned, all he could proudly claim.

Francie strode to his bedside, a place she hadn't visited since his admission. "This isn't going to work," she said.

He leaned his head back against the pillows, exhaustion overwhelming him. "What, no how are you feeling? No I'm sorry I haven't visited?"

"Oh please don't tell me *you're* the wounded party," Francie said.

He raised an eyebrow — the one part of his body that would work right now. "The only part of you that's been wounded is your wallet, Francie. The sad part is, I truly loved you. Which shows you how little I think of myself and what I deserve out of life."

She walked over and braced her hands on the bed. Her position gave him an ample look down her white fitted jacket, into her ample cleavage. Which, he proudly noted, he hadn't paid for.

"Is that your pathetic way of saying you're sorry?" Francie asked.

"It's my way of saying we want different things in a relationship."

Molly coughed and turned away.

Francie rose and squared her shoulders. "I never lied to you about enjoying money and now that you have none —"

"Please don't concern yourself," he told her. Surprisingly, he meant it. He'd been preparing himself for this day since he'd learned Lilly was still alive. "I wish you well."

She inclined her head. "The same here. I have an eight o'clock flight tonight for London."

Molly sucked in a sharp breath. For the first time, Marc felt a real pang of regret. Not for himself, but for Molly.

"I'm assuming you charged it?" he asked wryly.

She had the good grace to flush.

He shook his head. "Find yourself a rich one, Francine. You need it."

She kissed his cheek and sashayed out of the room. Marc's gaze never strayed from Molly's pale face.

Francie paused in the doorway. "Molly?"

Marc held his breath.

"Yes?" She held on to the back of the chair with a death grip, her knuckles white.

In her eyes, he saw pure hope and knew the disappointment to come would hurt her worse than anything else today.

"I left a box of things at Marc's. When I'm settled, I'll call with an address. Please ship them to me, will you, dear?"

"I'll see to it," Marc said, before Molly was forced to answer and probably burst into tears.

She blew a kiss that could have been directed at him or at her daughter before walking out the door without looking back. She didn't care which of them she'd hurt. Which made him wonder why he'd loved her at all, but he knew. He'd been taken in by his good fortune — he'd had so little in his life.

Marc held out his arms and Molly crawled right in, careful not to jostle or hurt him in any way. After the brief hug, she stepped back.

"I wish you were my daughter," he told her, knowing somebody had to love this girl.

She smiled, a sad one that broke his heart. "For what it's worth, I believed in you. You know, about not being behind the attempts on Lilly's life. You didn't disappoint me." She stepped back to the foot of the bed.

"That means a lot." His eyelids grew heavy, complete exhaustion setting in. "When I'm out of here, what do you say we order in pizza and just talk?"

Molly leaned against the end of the bed frame. "I would love to but I'm not going to stay around. I care about you but now that I know you're going to be okay, I need to go."

"Where?" he asked, understanding even if it hurt.

She shrugged. "Anywhere far away."

"You don't have a license to practice law *anywhere*," he reminded her.

"I know. I haven't figured out what I'm going to do yet. But I just can't stay here with all the memories and could-have-beens surrounding me."

"What about Hunter?" Marc asked. He'd noticed the chemistry between them. He knew the man cared for Molly. He'd seen it in Hunter's eyes when he looked at her. And as hard as it was for Marc to admit, he knew Hunter would take care of her the way she deserved to be cared for.

"Hunter deserves a woman who has her shit together. I'm a mess," Molly said bluntly.

Marc nodded. He didn't blame her for feeling that way. "Give it time. You never know what the future holds. Keep in touch?" he asked hopefully.

She nodded. "I'll stop by before I leave for good."

But in Marc's mind, she was already gone. He'd lost the one person who believed in him. That was okay though. He needed to learn to rely on himself. One of the doctors who'd come to see him had suggested he enroll in private therapy as well as AA. He would, if he could afford it. Once Lilly inherited and threw him out of the house, he'd have to cough up rent, homeowners insurance, all things that had come under the umbrella that was Lilly's trust fund.

He'd have to live like a grown man. What a concept. And he'd thought he had his hands full fighting the need for a drink. Still, he realized that with his confessions to the police and the people he'd hurt in his life, he wasn't feeling sorry for himself. Instead he was looking ahead.

And that, Marc thought, was progress.

Though Hunter had listened to Dumont's statement this morning, he'd been more affected by Molly's blank expression than he was by the man's admissions. In Hunter's mind, Marc Dumont was already a part of his past. But Molly was his future, or so he hoped and despite her withdrawal, he didn't want her to find it easy to relegate him to *her* past.

He knew how badly Marc's description of his actions had hurt her. On the other hand, she'd been right about the man now. He hadn't been behind the attempts on Lilly's life. Her faith in him had been rewarded. Hunter hoped that counted for something in Molly's mind.

He needed to know how she was holding up. He had to know where they stood. And he wanted to see her . . . just because. He shoved his work aside, rose and grabbed his jacket.

Half an hour later, he pulled up to Molly's house. He wasn't surprised Anna Marie was nowhere to be seen. From what Ty had said, the older woman had a rough day and she was probably hiding inside.

As Hunter stepped onto the porch and rang Molly's doorbell, Hunter was grateful for the privacy. He heard the sound of footsteps on the stairs and Molly opened the door.

She greeted him wearing gray sweats and a white T-shirt with smudges on the front. She looked as if she'd been cleaning.

"Hi," he said, suddenly incapable of anything clever or smart to say. He was just glad to see her.

She inclined her head. "Hi."

"Rough morning," he said.

She shrugged. "Actually, it got even rougher. Listen, I'm kind of busy —"

"I'd still like to talk. I won't keep you long."

She paused, then taking him by surprise, she pushed the door open wide. "Come on in."

He'd expected more of an argument. He followed her up the flight of stairs, wondering if maybe he'd get through to her after all. Then he stepped into her den and saw the suitcases spread out all over the room, the sight hitting him like a kick in the stomach.

He glanced around. There weren't just clothes in the suitcases — her personal things were packed into boxes. "This looks like a lot more than packing for a vacation."

She reluctantly met his gaze. "It is."

Her words confirmed his greatest fear. "Then there are some things I want to say to you before you go."

She nodded. "Go ahead," she said softly.

"You were right about Dumont. I'm sorry I couldn't believe you."

Molly looked into his handsome face and saw the truth in his eyes. Hunter's choice of words had been deliberate. It wasn't that he hadn't believed her, he couldn't. Because Marc had done too much damage. She'd heard it all firsthand today.

But Hunter had been there and supported *Molly* even if he couldn't agree with her belief in Marc. She appreciated his integrity more than he knew.

"Don't apologize. I understand."

He walked around, stepping over the suitcases and boxes she'd managed to pack in a short amount of time.

Without warning, he turned. "Damn it, Molly, don't do this."

She swallowed over the lump in her throat. "I have to."

"You do know that you're leaving without giving us a chance?" he asked, his tone imploring.

Molly closed her eyes. She hadn't wanted to hurt Hunter. She'd avoided him for years to prevent doing just that, yet here they were anyway. "I need to find out who I am and what I want out of life. I can't do that here, in a place where all I see are my childhood wishes for the family I never had."

"I never had family, either. I understand what you're going through. Why not work through it together? Unless of course, I'm mistaken in thinking you care about me, too." A flush rose high on his cheekbones and he shoved his hands into his front pants pockets.

Molly knew how difficult it had been for Hunter to lay his heart on the line and it hurt her to have to reject him. But one day he'd thank her for doing it.

"It's because I care about you that I'm leaving." She met his gaze, silently begging him to understand her reasons. "I need to grow up." And to do so, she needed time alone.

Time to heal and put her mother in her past. She absolutely had to learn to stand on her own two feet without old hopes and expectations weighing her down.

He stepped closer. She inhaled and smelled his sexy cologne. Wherever she ended up, she'd miss his wit and his persistence. But until she could look in the mirror and like who she saw, Molly had no choice but to leave.

"I have no ties here, nothing to keep me from leaving. Let me go with you and we can start over someplace new."

It was so tempting. *He* was so tempting.

She clasped her hands around his face. "You're such a good man and I wish I could say yes. But finding myself has to be my priority."

A muscle ticked in his jaw. "Everyone has baggage," he told her.

"Mine's just heavier than most. Or at least too heavy for me at the moment."

"And there's nothing I can do to stop you?"

She shook her head. "Just don't think this is easy for me." Her voice caught in her throat.

And her lips, mere inches from his, were so close to kissing him and letting him change her mind. Which was why she leaned forward and brushed her mouth over his quickly. Then she stepped back before he could react.

He ran a thumb over his bottom lip. "Good luck, Molly. I hope you find whatever it is you're looking for."

So did she, because she couldn't feel any worse than she did right now.

Lacey left Ty visiting with his mother who was due to be released in another day or so. Because Lacey had a guard following her, Ty hadn't questioned her when she'd gone for a walk. She just hadn't mentioned that her goal was a heart-to-heart with her uncle Marc.

Lacey found him sitting in a wheelchair in the solarium, an all-glass room donated to the hospital by a wealthy patron.

"Are you feeling up to a talk?" she asked, waiting in the doorway. Although she knew he wasn't the one who'd tried to kill her, she still wasn't comfortable being alone with him.

He glanced up, obviously surprised to see her. "I'm fine and until the nurses decide to take me back to my room, I'm enjoying the view. Please come join me."

She stepped inside, careful to sit in a chair by the door. Silly, since she was in an open room with a view. He couldn't hurt her, not that he'd want to. She just had a difficult time believing it.

"What did you want to talk about?" he asked.

She shook her head. "I'm not really sure. I guess I needed to say thank you for trying to warn me about Paul Dunne."

Uncle Marc shook his head. "If it weren't for me, none of this would have been set in motion in the first place. Paul has a gambling problem. I have a drinking problem." Uncle Marc adjusted the blanket on his lap as he spoke. "I did things that if not illegal, were unethical and immoral to say the least. He'd rather I inherit than you because he thought he could blackmail me and keep me from informing the police about the embezzlement. You, on the other hand, would have turned him in. He wanted you dead and he wanted me to kill you."

He repeated the same things he'd said to the police, but Lilly had been so over-whelmed at the time, she hadn't processed it all. She appreciated hearing it again.

"So he shot you because you refused to kill me." She nearly choked over the word.

"And because he believed I was about to warn you. He was right."

She glanced down at her trembling hands. "When will they let you go home?"

"Possibly tomorrow but don't worry. Once I have the strength to pack, I'll move out of your house. I called my brother and asked if I could move in with him for a while."

Lacey opened her mouth, then closed it again. Somewhere in the back of her mind, she knew she'd be inheriting not just the money but her childhood home. Paul Dunne had told her as much during their meeting. She'd just never let herself think about the fact.

Now that she was forced to face the truth, she realized something important. "I don't want the house," she said, the words com-ing out before she could stop them.

"Your parents would want you to have it."

"I want you to stay there. It's your home, not mine."

He wheeled his chair closer to her. "That's awfully generous."

Lacey wasn't sure she'd call it an act of generosity. It was more like one of necessity. When she'd attended his engagement party, she'd shut the door on that part of her life.

"It's not part of who I am anymore and you've lived there for so long, I can't see any reason for you to move."

"Well, I have one. I can't afford the house anymore."

"Uncle Marc . . ."

"Please. I'm not trying to make you feel bad. It's just a fact. And you know for the first time I do believe I'll survive." He shook his head and laughed, then winced in pain.

"This isn't a pity party, you know. It's called moving on in life."

Lacey rose from her seat. "I don't know what's left of the trust fund but doesn't it cover the house?"

"If you're living in it, then yes. It's your money, Lacey. Starting soon."

She rubbed her hands up and down her arms. She didn't know what the future held, but she did know she had very little left in the way of family beyond Uncle Marc. Although the man had been the cause of her childhood trauma, he may well have just saved her life. She didn't know if they could ever have a relationship, but as gestures went, he'd made a start.

She raised her gaze to meet his. "You can stay in the house," she said. "As I said, it's your home, not mine. Whatever basics the trust has always covered, well that can continue as far as I'm concerned. I'm sure my parents would want it that way."

"I doubt it after all I've done to you." His gaze shifted out the window, his embarrassment and humiliation clear.

"Actually I think my father would be grateful you saved my life, so let's just start from here, okay? From where I stand, you don't have any more family than I do."

He blinked. "Your parents would be proud of the woman you've become," he said. "Through none of my actions, that much is for sure."

She thought his eyes were moist but she couldn't be sure. Before she could reply, a knock at the door startled her. She turned to see Ty and the chief of police standing in the entry to the solarium.

"We didn't want to interrupt, but I'm glad you're both here," the chief said.

Beside him, Ty scowled but said nothing.

Lacey felt sure he'd overheard at least part of her conversation with her uncle and didn't approve, but the money was hers to spend as she wanted. Or it would be soon.

"What's going on?" Marc asked.

"Paul Dunne was arrested at the airport before he could board a flight to South America." Don's grin told a story of his own. The man was obviously pleased they had caught their suspect. "You're now both safe. You can relax and things can go back to normal," he said.

"Whatever that is," Ty said as he shook the man's hand and thanked him for his hard work.

Lacey studied the man she knew she loved. However would she handle what had to come next? She could no longer avoid returning home to New York, but was that what she really wanted?

They walked out of the hospital and headed for Ty's car. A cool breeze blew around them and the sun shone bright in the sky.

Avoidance and procrastination. Two things Lacey had never considered herself an expert in before now. She had a business waiting for her in New York but she couldn't bring herself to bring up the subject and tell Ty she had to leave.

He knew, of course. Her leaving was like the pink elephant trailing behind them. The more they avoided talking about it, the larger it loomed. But now that the reasons for her return had been resolved, she couldn't avoid her responsibilities back home any longer.

He paused by the car, leaning against the passenger side door. He studied her with those intense eyes and she couldn't tell what he was really thinking.

"My apartment's been cleaned. I can move back in anytime," he said, obviously choosing a safe topic of conversation.

"Why do I hear a 'but' there?" she asked.

He laughed. "You know me so well. *But* I thought I'd stay at Mom's for a while at least until she's back on her feet."

"I think that's a really good idea." Not only for his mother, Lacey thought. Now that she had her opening, she drew a deep breath and dove right in. "It'll be easier for you when I —"

"Leave?" he asked.

She exhaled hard. "Yes. With things here resolved . . ." she trailed off, knowing she and Ty were anything but *resolved.* "What I meant was with my uncle no longer an issue, I can return to New York."

"I notice you didn't say return *home*." He folded his arms across his chest, looking smug even for Ty.

She stepped closer. "It's where I live. It's where my business is." The problem for Lacey remained though. Ty was where her heart was.

"Okay then." He nodded, his easy agreement taking her off guard.

She blinked. "Just like that? You're going to wave goodbye and say have a nice life?"

"It sounded to me like that's what you wanted." Already, he'd erected an invisible wall of self-protection.

"I don't know what I want," she said, not bothering to disguise her frustration. "Maybe you could split me in two. That would be a nice easy resolution." She could run her business and live life in New York while a part of her remained here with Ty. Upset and confused, she ran a hand through her hair, tugging at the windblown strands.

Ty grabbed her hand and lowered it to her side, never letting go. "You need to go back to New York. You need to live your life and with distance, maybe then you can decide what you want. I can't do that for you," he said in a gruff voice.

He was right, something she'd sensed deep down in her heart. She forced a smile and squeezed his hand tighter. "I lived for ten years on my own. I defined myself by my business. After a short time back here, I barely gave my old life a thought. I don't understand how that could have happened."

And it scared her, especially since most of what remained in Hawken's Cove was a host of bad memories. Not that she could discount the good ones, but the past still held on tight, choking her.

"Which is exactly why you should go back. It's what you planned to do. It's what you need to do."

Lacey swallowed hard. "You're right. I do need to go home."

Everything that had happened since Ty had shown up on her doorstep had occurred too fast for her to process. She needed time away from here so she could think clearly. She just wished she didn't have to leave Ty to do it.

"I can drive you back after my mother is released from the hospital," he offered.

She shook her head. "Thanks, but I can rent a car and drive home myself."

"You've obviously thought this through," he said, his words sounding like an accusation.

"Not really. I just don't want to be a burden and driving three hours back and forth to Manhattan is a hassle you don't need right now." She turned away so he wouldn't see the tears forming in her eyes.

She might have to leave, she might understand her reasons for doing so, but that didn't make it any easier to do. "It's still early in the day. I can take care of the car and still spend some time with your mother before I leave. I want to see Hunter and Molly, too."

"Actually Molly's gone."

His words took her by surprise.

"Hunter called earlier to tell me she packed up and left." Ty unlocked the car doors and held hers open for her.

"Just like that?" Lilly asked. Stunned, she turned back around. "Didn't Molly have her law practice here? Her mother? Her life?"

Ty shrugged. "It seems her mother took off, as well. There's a lot of leaving going on," he said, wryly.

Lacey knew he wasn't as cavalier about the subject as he sounded. "Poor Hunter," she murmured and climbed into the car.

Ty shut her door without responding. He'd had to bite his tongue not to remind Lilly that Hunter would have Ty to keep him company soon. He didn't want to come off sounding pathetic in any way.

He'd held on to his sanity by a thread as he and Lilly walked out of the solarium, her words to her uncle ringing in his ear. Giving her parents' home to her only relative didn't bode well for Ty's hopes that she'd developed ties to her hometown. Ties to him.

Although he'd only heard part of the conversation and he knew nothing she'd said to Dumont took her feelings for Ty into account, his gut had been churning ever since. He'd promised himself he wouldn't push her for answers until the threat to her life was over.

Now that the time had come, he couldn't bring himself to push her at all. Once before, Lilly had chosen not to come back and he couldn't just forget how easily she'd put him in the past and left him there. If he hadn't shown up and begged her to reclaim her trust fund, she'd still be living her life in New York, without him.

So if Lilly wanted to leave again now, far be it from him to stand in her way. No promises had been exchanged and he was glad he'd reminded himself of this possibility all along.

Not that knowing made the inevitable any

easier to handle, he thought. But he'd survive without Lilly. Just as he'd done once before.

SEVENTEEN

Flo Benson had been home from the hospital for a week. The doctors assured her that her heart would perform like it always had. She'd be fine. Unfortunately she couldn't say the same for her son. Since her release, Ty had stayed with her in the house. After the first two days, he'd gone back to work. During the day he'd be at the office and most evenings he was doing surveillance, which freed up Flo to be with Andrew.

Still, she knew Ty was merely keeping busy to avoid thinking about Lilly and how he'd let her go. Again. Damn stubborn man, Flo thought. Not only was he torturing himself, he was driving her crazy, hovering whenever he was around.

"Mom? I made you a cup of green tea. It's supposed to be full of antioxidants and good for your heart." Ty stepped into her bedroom where she relaxed watching the late news.

"You aren't working tonight?" she asked.

He shook his head. "Derek's got things covered." He placed the cup and saucer on her nightstand.

"Ty, I need to ask you something and please don't take this the wrong way. When in the hell are you leaving?" she asked her son.

He cocked his head to the side. "I can be out of here now if that's what you mean. My apartment's been ready for a while. I just thought you'd appreciate having some company when you came home."

She shook her head. Sometimes men, including the doctor that she adored, could be so thickheaded. "I meant when are you leaving Hawken's Cove and going after Lilly?"

He lowered himself onto her bed with a heavy thud, but remained silent in the face of her blunt question.

"It's not that I don't love you and appreciate you taking care of me, but I don't need it. I'm fine. The doctors told you so. The fact that you're still here at all is more for your benefit than for mine. I'm thinking you don't want to go back to your small lonely apartment and think about what an ass you've been letting her leave you again." She folded her arms across her chest, defying her son to argue.

He scowled as he replied, "I am not going to discuss my love life with my mother."

"What love life? As far as I can see, you don't have one and you never will. Give me one good reason why you didn't ask her to stay?"

"Why am I the one getting flack when she's the one who packed up and left?" he asked.

"Because you're the one who's miserable and I'm the unfortunate one who has to watch you suffer."

Flo pushed herself up against the pillows, getting more comfortable. She winced at the slight pulling in her chest, a normal reaction, the doctor had assured her.

"But that's what is bothering you, isn't it? The fact that she left you. A part of you can't get beyond the fact that she never came back the first time and you wanted her to be the one to step up now. Am I right?"

Ty squirmed, uncomfortable in the glare of his mother's questions and accurate guesses. "Do you want to know what life has taught me?" he asked her.

She raised her eyebrows. "Do tell."

"People leave. Dad left. Lilly left. Hunter went next. Lilly has a life in New York. Why the hell should I expect her not to want to return to it?" He wasn't one for spilling his guts but his mother knew how to push all the right buttons and make him angry enough to talk about things he'd normally leave bottled up inside.

Flo shook her head. "I hate to say this to you, but it's time for you to grow up. Your father was a no-good drunk and a gambler. His leaving was the best thing that could have ever happened to us. As for the rest, well pardon my French, but shit happens."

Ty stared at his mother. He'd never heard such frank talk from her before.

"You need to get over the past. Lilly has. I heard she had no real reaction to Marc Dumont's confession that he paid me to take her in. That she was never really in foster care. Did you notice?"

He rubbed the back of his neck with his hand, his muscles tense. "Yeah, I noticed." He'd been shocked that she hadn't been more hurt by the news or angry at her uncle for placing her in a home he knew nothing about. Or felt betrayed by his mother for conspiring with Dumont and taking such an excessive amount of cash.

"She shocked you, didn't she? You've been protecting her from a secret that she didn't need protecting from. And you've also eaten yourself alive with guilt because you had nice things and she struggled to survive. But she's over it, Tyler. You're the only one still suffering."

He rose to his feet and walked to the window. The shade was drawn, blocking out the dark night sky. He turned back to his mother, glancing at her from across the room. "You're very perceptive all of a sudden."

"A brush with death will do that to a person. I love you and I don't want to see you end up alone because you're scared to let yourself feel too much. You're afraid of being hurt but guess what? You can't feel any worse than you do right now."

He shook his head and laughed. "Leave it to my mother to tell it like it is."

"I figured if I wasn't honest, you'd never leave."

"Don't tell me I'm cramping your social life?" he asked jokingly. Then he caught his mother's blush. "I *am* cramping your social life," he said, shocked he'd never realized it before. "You could have just asked me to move out already."

"I believe I just did." Flo grinned, the flush in her cheeks brighter than before.

His mother wanted him to move out so

she'd have time with her boyfriend. "I'll be gone first thing in the morning," he muttered, shaking his head at the ironic turn of events.

"Are you going to talk to Lilly?" she asked hopefully.

Ty grinned. "I thought I told you I wasn't going to discuss my love life with my mother?" He walked over and kissed her cheek. "Thank you for caring enough to toss me out on my ass," he said, chuckling. "As for the rest, I promise to think about everything you said."

He'd think. And then, maybe, he'd find the courage to go after what he wanted.

Back for a week, Lacey now remembered why she loved her business. The girls who worked for her were so happy she'd returned, they had shown up at her apartment with a welcome-back cake. As a special surprise, one of them had looked Marina up and brought her along with them. Whenever Lacey talked to one of her employees, she remembered her early days in New York and how grateful she'd been when Marina had given her a chance and a job. She loved doing the same.

As for the people who employed her company, some were a pain in the rear end, complaining endlessly about towels not folded right, dogs who'd pooped in the house, which must be the dog walker's fault, and grocery lists filled wrong. Then there were those who just appreciated having someone other than themselves do their odd jobs while they put in a long day at the office. Either way, Lacey found herself back to multi-tasking all day and loving every minute.

She also missed Ty. Constantly, desperately and always. Still, she'd done the right thing by going home and remembering what it was that she loved about her life. A life she could duplicate in Hawken's Cove if that was the only way to be with Ty.

Because another thing she'd realized by coming back was that home wasn't a place. Home was a feeling. Home was where her heart beat a little faster and a place she could come to at the end of a satisfying or frustrating day and know he was there waiting. At this point she didn't care if her parents' old house and her uncle were there to remind her of all she'd lost. She'd gained so much more by reconnecting with Ty.

She had a few days left until her birthday, the day when she'd go back to Hawken's Cove and claim her trust fund. A day when she'd sign the house over to her uncle for good. She wanted nothing to do with that part of her life.

As for the money, the court-appointed trustee who'd taken over for the now jailed Paul Dunne had informed her that Paul had embezzled hundreds of thousands of dollars over the years. The estate itself now consisted of one point seven million dollars, excluding the house and real estate. An amount she could barely comprehend.

Despite the loss, more than enough remained for her to cover her uncle's cost of living in the house, and for her to start up an Odd Jobs in Hawken's Cove. Marina was retired, but Lacey had asked and the older woman had agreed, to oversee the business in New York. Over time, Lilly could either sell it to her or one of her employees. Time would tell.

Of course all of her plans hinged on the assumption that Ty wanted her to come back. That he wanted to spend the rest of his life with her and make babies together when they were ready, and let his mother shower their children with love and affection.

She just didn't know what he wanted and the few times she'd called, she'd gotten his answering machine. She assumed he was out working, either the night shift at the bar or on a case. Because she didn't know how to broach her feelings on the phone, she hadn't left a message. And he hadn't called her, either. Or like her, he hadn't left a message.

She fingered the locket around her neck. She still couldn't bring herself to part with the sentimental piece of jewelry and she wouldn't. Not unless Ty told her to get lost for good. She swallowed over the lump in her throat and continued to think positive thoughts.

Like what would she do with the rest of the money in the trust fund. It seemed a waste to let the money sit and just accumulate doing nothing. She had some thoughts but she hadn't come to any firm decisions yet.

A loud knock startled her and Digger began her obsessive barking, jumping up and down at the door without even knowing who was behind it.

Lacey glanced in the peephole and nearly passed out. She flung the door open wide. "Ty? What are you doing here?" she asked, excited, hopeful and also scared something had happened to his mother. "Is Flo okay?" she asked.

"Depends on your definition of okay. She threw me out, if you can believe that." He set down his oversized duffle bag which Lacey eyed warily.

"What do you mean she threw you out?"

He grinned, that cocky, sexy grin she loved. "She said I was getting on her nerves and cramping her style. Then she told me to get the hell out."

"She did not!"

He laughed. "Not in so many words, no. But her point was clear."

She looked from his bag up into his eyes. Eyes that now looked light and free of excess baggage. She didn't understand what was going on but she had a hunch she was going to like it. A lot.

She rolled forward onto the balls of her feet, then back again. "So did you move back into your apartment?" Lilly asked.

"Nope. I told Hunter to camp out there for a while."

"Doesn't he have his place in Albany?"

"It'll be a long trip for him late at night when he fills in for me at Night Owl's. Besides, he really hates that stuffy apartment he's leasing. He only did it to make his point that he's *arrived* and he's past caring what people think anymore."

"He's hurting, isn't he?" Lacey asked.

Ty nodded. "Molly did a real number on him. Did you know he offered to go with her wherever she was going?"

Although Lacey had been in touch with Hunter and she knew he'd withdrawn, he'd left out key parts of the story. "I had no idea," she murmured. "She turned him down?"

"Flat." Ty crossed his arms over his chest.

She winced. "Poor Hunter. But at least he had the courage to offer to go with her," she said pointedly. She wasn't only referring to the fact that Ty hadn't offered the same, but neither had she.

"It didn't get him very far, unfortunately."

"But at least now he knows where he stands."

Ty nodded. "Good point."

They remained that way for a while, at a standstill, neither one of them knowing what to say next.

Lacey took the opportunity to look him over for the first time. He hadn't shaved in a few days, his hair was as long as it'd been before, and his leather jacket appeared well-worn. He was her sexy rebel and she was so glad he was here.

"So your mother threw you out and you gave up not just your apartment but your part-time job at Night Owl's," she said, spelling things out when she couldn't stand the tension any longer. "What about your

P.I. business?"

"Handed that over to Derek." He shrugged off his jacket, hanging it on a hook in her front hall. "Seeing as I'm licensed in New York State, it didn't seem like a big deal to start over."

Her mouth grew dry. "Start over where?"

"Here." He ran his hand through his hair. "In New York, the city that doesn't sleep. Seems like a good place for an out-of-work P.I. to start over."

When she glanced at him this time, she didn't see the cocky kid she'd fallen in love with at seventeen nor did she see the man with walls a mile high. Instead she saw a vulnerable guy who'd come here with his heart on his sleeve and no idea what kind of reception he'd receive.

She had just one question. "Why? Why leave your home and everything you love behind?"

"Because a smart, beautiful woman once told me home is about the people you're with, not the place you choose to live. Besides," he said, his eyes gleaming. "I wouldn't say I left everything I love behind. I came to find the person I love most in the world and that's you."

"That's all I needed to hear." With a huge smile on her face, Lacey stepped forward and jumped into his arms, wrapping her legs around his waist and kissing him like there was no tomorrow.

"God, I missed you." He ran his hand down the back of her head, sifting his fingers through her hair.

"Then what took you so long?" She peppered his cheek with kisses as she asked.

Ty let her slide down the length of his body, but kept her close as they headed for the couch in the other room. "I had some things to sort through," he admitted.

"I thought I was the one who needed to come home, get some distance and think," she said, teasing him.

He shrugged. "Turns out we both did. All the years you were gone, I held it against you that you didn't come back. It wasn't something I verbalized or even realized I thought about until I saw you again. But once I knew, it wasn't something I could let go that quickly."

"Because you were afraid I'd leave you again," she said, catching on quickly and understanding him as she always did. "And what did I do? I turned around and came back home just like you thought I would." She lifted their tightly held hands and placed them close to her heart. "I'm sorry."

"Don't be. You had to be independent to

have survived at all. I needed to get over my hang-ups." He nearly choked on the word. "And I have. Because I love you too much not to be with you."

"I love you, too. So much that I was making plans to leave New York and come back anyway." She kissed his cheek, letting him know he didn't have to worry that she'd ever let him go again. "One way or another, we were going to be together. I'm not going to leave you again. Cross my heart," she said, her words a solemn vow.

As his gaze fell to the locket she'd never taken off, Ty knew for certain. When Lacey made a promise, she knew for sure never to break it.

"I'm never going to leave you, either," he said. "Cross my heart," he said and sealed their vow with a long, long, long kiss.

EPILOGUE

"What do you think about expanding Odd Jobs?" Lacey asked Ty. "The suburbs have an equal need for people to do things they can't possibly fit into their day. Beyond housekeeping and dog walking, there's food shopping and cooking . . ."

Her husband glanced at her over his morning newspaper.

They'd married soon after she claimed her trust fund in a small, private ceremony in his mother's house, with just Flo and Dr. Andrew Sanford, Hunter and Lacey's uncle Marc present. The unique group could have made for an awkward family unit but everyone had been on their best behavior. Only Molly had been missing. Though Lacey had received a postcard from California and knew the other woman was traveling — make that running — she hadn't put down roots anywhere.

Poor Hunter had thrown himself into his

work and women — too many women — to the exclusion of everything and everyone else.

"Are you suggesting we move out of the city?" Ty asked, bringing her focus back to him, not that it had strayed far.

She still loved looking at him every morning. His sexy razor stubble and sleepy-eyed grin never failed to stir her desire. Fate had brought them together again and she didn't plan to take their second chance for granted.

"Wouldn't you like more space and fresh air, not to mention room for another dog," she said, teasing him and gauging his reaction at the same time.

"Somehow I don't think Miss Smelly Breath would appreciate the competition." He petted Digger's head. The dog lay on his lap where she always happily perched herself, choosing Ty over Lacey given the choice.

Lacey laughed. "What about you? You could do detective work in Westchester County or you could keep this apartment as your base and use it as an office and still work in the city. It's an easy commute by train or by car."

He laid the paper down on the table. "You've looked into this already, haven't you?"

She grinned. "I thought it would make sense to have all the facts before I presented my case. I checked out all the possibilities and the fact is the traffic on Long Island is horrendous and would drive you insane. Of course you could take the train from there, too. In either case there are good schools and different cities we can look into. Of course if you'd rather —"

"Why now? All of a sudden you want to move? I thought you loved the city and this neighborhood. You thought this apartment cozy and perfect."

"I do think it's cozy and perfect for the two of us and the dog." Lilly rose and walked over to his chair, giving Digger a gentle shove. The dog was forced to hop onto the floor so Lilly could settle into Ty's lap and wind her arms around his neck. "But if we were to expand this family then this place is too small, don't you think?" she asked.

Hint hint, she thought, snuggling in closer to his warmth.

"Hey, are you trying to tell me you're pregnant?" he asked, clearly surprised and a little nervous if his roughened voice was any indication.

She shook her head. "I'm trying to tell

you I want to be. That is if you're game, too."

He wrapped his hands around her waist. "Oh, I'm game." He shifted his thighs beneath her, letting her feel exactly how ready he was to make her dreams come true.

She laughed. "What about in here?" she asked, lightly tapping his chest. "Is a family something you've thought about?"

He nodded. "I just knew we'd been using protection and so . . ."

"No surprises," she assured him, understanding now what had caused his nervous reaction.

Ty liked things planned and thought out, as she'd been learning about him the longer they were together. It was what made him such a great P.I., that he could pull the strands of different things together and figure out possibilities other people might otherwise miss.

"Not to worry, you'll be in on this project from the very beginning." She wiggled her bottom against his erection and let the waves of desire wash over her.

Not just desire, she corrected herself, but love. She loved him with all her heart and soul.

"We can start looking at houses anytime you want." He planted a kiss on her lips.

"Happy?" he asked.

She nodded. "Very. It's just that I feel guilty being so blissful when Hunter is so miserable."

Ty tipped his head back and met her gaze, understanding in his eyes. "There's not much we can do for him until he gets his act together and gets over Molly."

Lacey raised her eyebrows. "Would you get over me so easily?"

His lips turned downwards in a frown. "It's not the same thing."

"You don't know that. I saw how they were together. He loves her."

"And she betrayed him. He put his heart on the line and she stomped all over it," Ty said in true defense of his best friend. "People get involved with the wrong person and they move on. Look at you and Alex."

Lacey's ex had called her not long after Ty's arrival. Ty had answered the phone and passed it to her with a growl, but at least he hadn't hung up on the man. They'd had a brief talk and to her surprise, Alex had apologized for his behavior when she'd broken up with him. He'd nursed his wounded pride just long enough to get over the idea of *them,* he'd said. And though they both knew they'd never be friends, at least their relationship hadn't ended on a sour note, for which Lacey was grateful. Alex played a defining role in her life and she believed he'd allowed her to realize how much she missed and loved Ty.

Lacey sighed. "Alex and I had a meaningful relationship," she said carefully. "But I never loved him and he admitted he'd been in love with the idea of marrying more than he'd been in love with *me*."

"That makes him an idiot and me a lucky man," Ty said. "As for Hunter, let the man find his own solution. You can't fix this for him."

She pursed her lips in a pout. "But —"

"But nothing. You've already done all you can for Hunter, starting by paying off his student loans."

Lacey winced, recalling Hunter's angry tirade, but underneath his pride, she knew he appreciated the gesture. It was the least she could do for the man who'd done so much for her. "He's still working too hard, going from woman to woman, it's —"

"None of your business," Ty insisted. As he spoke, his hands found their way beneath her T-shirt.

His palms were hot against her skin and his desire for her was very evident, pressing against her thigh, distracting her. Which she knew was his intent. She did her best not to moan aloud and send Digger running to interrupt.

"Hunter will fix his own future," Ty said in a determined tone that instructed her not to meddle in their friend's life. "In the meantime, let's get started working on ours."

And how could Lacey argue with that?

ABOUT THE AUTHOR

Carly Phillips started her writing career with Harlequin Temptation in 1999 with *Brazen,* and she's never strayed far from home! Carly has since published sixteen books, including the *New York Times* bestsellers *Summer Lovin'* and *Hot Stuff.* Carly lives in Purchase, New York, with her husband, two daughters and a frisky soft-coated wheaten terrier who acts like their third child. When she's not spending time with her family, Carly is busy writing, promoting and playing online! To learn more about this quickly rising star of romance, you can visit Carly on the Web at www.carlyphillips.com or write her at P.O. Box 483, Purchase, NY 10577.